THE FORTUNE BROTHERS

TWO COMPLETE NOVELS

DARA GIRARD

ILORI PRESS BOOKS, LLC

P.O. Box 10332

Silver Spring, MD 20914

www.iloripressbooks.com

Table for Two

Gaining Interest

Careless Rapture

Dangerous Curves

Familiar Stranger

It Happened One Wedding

Unexpected Pleasure

Midnight Promise

Sweet Temptation

Always and Forever

Clifton Sisters

The Sapphire Pendant

The Amber Stone

Fortune Brothers

A Tempting Proposal

A Seductive Arrangement

Novels

Honest Betrayal

The Daughters of Winston Barnett

Remember My Name

Illusive Flame

Winterwood Lane

Collections

DARA GIRARD

A Tempting Proposal

CHAPTER 1

A wife.

He was not supposed to end up with a wife. At least not yet. He had plans, dreams and goals. This was not one of them. James Fortune gritted his teeth as he listened to the melodious soft voice of Pastor Valentine, her pink reading glasses hanging precariously low on her nose, inches away from falling. Much like the present state of his life.

He'd managed to achieve most of his goals. He'd gotten degrees in both Biology and Mechanical Engineering and become head of Research and Development at BioMed Solutions. Yes, it was his stepfather's company, and at thirty-four he was the youngest division manager in the company, but no one could deny that under James's watch and careful leadership more innovative projects had been developed and funded. Morale was up and the people liked him, unlike his predecessor, a charismatic man who wasted money on pet projects that only highlighted his interests instead of others or furthering the success of the company.

James knew he wouldn't stay in management for long, he wanted to launch his own ventures, but he'd given himself two more years before he would embark on his next career goal. He believed in taking calculated risks.

Not insane ones.

James glanced at Pastor Valentine's reading glasses again, noticing that they'd fallen down a little further. He flexed his fingers resisting the urge to say something. Couldn't she feel them moving? Would she let them fall off her face?

He inwardly groaned, knowing his attention and annoyance were misplaced. It wasn't the pastor's glasses that really bothered him, or even the sound of her voice, which always reminded him of someone in a musical about to burst into song (he half expected her to snap the bible shut, rip off her glasses and start singing), it was the entire ceremony.

He knew that what he was doing was not only reckless and insane, but criminal. He'd never done anything illegal in his life. Okay, so maybe he had done some speeding, and once— just once—when he was under charged for an item at the grocery store, he didn't report it. But he was a law abiding citizen. A good man. Now he was a fraud. He'd put his reputation and future on the line all because of Jackson.

His twin brother was supposed to be standing at the altar, inside this elegant stone cathedral, bearing the scrutiny of hundreds of guests from the Americas and the Caribbean, marrying the beautiful, brilliant and influential Ava Simone Hughes.

James made sure to keep his gaze on the pastor, instead of her. He knew Ava's brilliance by her reputation. She'd won an international science prize at sixteen and her research in the field of biodegradable implants preceded her. Her findings were almost legendary in the industry; her influence was also unavoidable from her innovative lab work to her connection with top universities. But her beauty.

That was his weak point.

He feared his heart would stop when the cathedral's double doors opened and she walked down the red carpeted, flower adorned aisle towards him. Damn, why did it have to be *him*? He'd always found her attractive, even in the dark suits she liked to wear—sometimes with trousers other times with a skirt, always black or dark blue—but at this moment she was breathtaking in a floor-length tulle lace gown with beaded sequins. The ivory colored fabric, accented with a translucent hint of sky blue, complimented her exquisite dark skin.

She looked like a princess, her carriage regal, her fine high cheekbones striking, but he knew she was no innocent, blushing bride. She had dangerous brown eyes and without the benefit of a veil to shield him from her gaze, he had to face them head on and make sure she didn't suspect a thing. She was the kind of woman who could kiss a man tenderly on the lips and drive a steak knife through his heart at the same time. He knew his deception would come at a price if she ever found out.

He couldn't let that happen. He had to be careful.

He'd discovered that the first time Jackson formerly introduced her to him. Her keen, steely gaze hit him like a brick. With one look he'd seen her power and vulnerability and that combination had floored him. He knew a woman like her could be trouble, but his brother liked courting trouble so James had dismissed the feeling. He couldn't dismiss it now.

James briefly looked at the ceiling. He was doing the right thing. Jilting a woman like Ava would have far reaching consequences and too much was at stake. He was doing this because his brother was too weak to accept his duty to his family and the business.

James took a deep breath, wishing he would wake up from this nightmare, but when he touched Ava's hand and slid a white gold band of hand selected diamonds on one of her long, slender fingers he knew it was all too real.

At least his hands didn't tremble and he didn't drop the ring as he feared, trying his best to ignore the reality that every action he made was being watched. Unlike his brother who welcomed it like a parched horse at a watering hole, he didn't like being in the spotlight. James inwardly groaned. He could use a drink right now. Something cold and biting. He stood stock still as he felt a trail of sweat slide down his back. He remembered saying "With this ring..." but the rest was a blur as he fought to imitate his brother's casual flair in every word and gesture.

He'd never switched places with Jackson before, despite all his brother's urgings when they were younger, trying to convince him that it would be fun. James never thought it would be either fun or practical. Definitely not practical. Even as a child he knew a day in the life of his brother would be exhausting.

Instead of being alone in the library, with his science club, discussing a new discovery with a teacher or training with the track team, he'd be charming the students (especially the girls, but guys liked him too) and teachers of both genders, and partying. There would be too many names to remember, too many places to be. He liked to live a regimented, quiet life and said he'd never switch places. Ever.

He'd been wrong.

But he didn't have a choice.

James had sensed there was a problem last night at the rehearsal dinner when he'd found his brother in the dark tiled restaurant men's room. Jackson stood in front of one of the sinks, wiping water from his face with a paper towel.

"You've been gone nearly fifteen minutes," James said exasperated, looking at his brother in the mirror reflection. "What's wrong?" The dinner was a chance for the two families to get to know each other before the big event. James had been paired with Ava's Uncle, a boisterous man who liked to brag that the only exercise he did was work on his Molson muscle as he proudly patted his beer belly. Since he was the man giving Ava away tomorrow, she had told them she was not close to her father so he wouldn't be attending, James tried his best to laugh at all her uncle's jokes. But after his brother's disappearance he was starting to feel the strain of pretending.

Jackson threw away the paper towel then tugged on the collar of his purple shirt. "I can't do this."

"Do what?"

He stretched out his arms. "This. Everything. It's all a mistake."

"What are you talking about?"

Jackson looked at him with a flat expression. "You know what I'm talking about. I can't—"

James swore and shook his head. He usually knew what his brother was thinking, but this time he didn't want to believe it. He couldn't believe it. His brother's wedding mattered too much. "Shut up."

"Don't worry, no one else is in here."

James checked the stalls just to make sure before he looked at his brother again. "I don't care. Shut up and come back to the table."

"I have to say it."

James rested his hands on his hips and shook his head again. "No, you don't."

"I can't marry her. There's something about her. Something that's just not right. She scares me."

James playfully patted his brother on the side of his face and said with a grin, "She was always scary." He turned to the door. "Now come on."

"You noticed that too?"

James paused then slowly turned back to him. "It's hard to miss."

"It's those eyes, right? I didn't notice them before."

"She's not scarier than some of the other women you've been with."

Jackson waved his finger at him. "No, there's something different about her." He turned back to the mirror and gazed at his reflection. "I can't go through with it. I thought I could, but I was wrong."

James rested a hand on his brother's shoulder. "It's nerves. You're not scared of her, it's the thought of marriage that frightens you. You're worried about how marriage will change your life, and it will, for the better."

Jackson shook his head. "It's not that," he said in a grim tone. "There's just something I didn't notice before. I can't put my finger on it." He shifted his gaze to James's face. "You know I'm good at reading people when it's important."

James swept his hand past the faucet sensor, letting the hot water hit his palm and slide through his fingers. He cupped some water in his hand and threw it at his brother.

Jackson jumped back and scowled. "Watch the shirt."

James placed his wet palm on the dark marble counter. "Watch your mouth."

"I told you I had to say it," Jackson said, checking to see what possible damage the water had done to his shirt.

"It's arranged. It's planned."

Jackson smoothed down the front buttons of his shirt. "I know."

"Mom needs this."

Jackson looked up, met James's gaze and softly swore.

James nodded. He now had his brother's full attention and also had him where he wanted him—feeling guilty. Their mother was thrilled about the upcoming wedding and the chance to see one of her sons getting married. She had been like a little girl during the holidays taking care of all the preparations, which Ava had graciously allowed their mother to be a part of. James remembered when his mother had shyly hinted that since she'd had no daughters she'd been disappointed that she never would have the opportunity. When James had mentioned it to Ava, she'd expertly invited her to participate fully in all the wedding plans, he'd always be grateful for that.

Jackson sighed and nodded looking defeated. "You're right. You're right. Maybe it's just the thought of the ceremony. You know I hate things like that."

"No, you don't. You like being the center of attention."

"Just go along with me, okay?"

James grabbed a paper towel and dried his hands. "You'll be fine."

"What if I forget the words?"

"Just repeat what the pastor says."

Jackson nodded again and rubbed the back of his neck, looking just as miserable as he had before. "Right, right."

James patted him on the back. "You like her. She likes you. You work well together. A lot is riding on this and—"

Jackson tugged on his collar again. "I feel like I can't breathe." He sent a wary glance at the exit. "I can't go back in there. There's so much expectation from..."

"Edgar," James said when his brother didn't finish.

Their stepfather, Edgar Fortune, was founder of BioMed Solutions, a company that manufactured joint replacements, and with a growing aging population living longer with more active lives, business was booming. Edgar lived and breathed the business and loomed large in their lives. They both had vague memories of their father, an economics professor originally from Grenada, who'd disappeared a year after their younger brother Rudy was born.

Their mother had met Edgar through a mutual acquaintance at a cocktail party. Edgar swept into their lives when they were both six years old and captured their attention, if not their affection. He was a hard man to get close to. Jamaican born-US raised, in the state of Virginia, with a taste for Cuban cigars, boxing and fast horses. Driven, ruthless, with more women than most, many wondered why he'd decided to settle down with a woman with three children. A woman who, at the time, worked as a secretary for a speech pathologist. Almost thirty years later, people still wondered how the marriage had lasted.

Although Florence "Flo" Fortune had turned herself into the perfect corporate wife, her sweet manner was in direct contrast to her husband's. Soon after the marriage, Edgar adopted them and they lost their last name 'Brownson' and became Fortunes, and Edgar liked to constantly remind them of the same thing he'd told them the day of their adoption, "I gave you my name for a reason. It means your fortunes have changed. So you owe everything to me." And they believed him and worked hard to please him.

There was no fear, just expected loyalty and they were both eager to give it. When Edgar announced that it was time one of them got married it surprised everyone when Jackson said he'd met someone. They were even more surprised when he told them who she was—Ava Hughes. A woman whose small company had developed an injectable agent that could be used in various replacement joints. Most of the replacement joints their firm created had to be replaced over time due to erosion, slippage and/or growth, especially in children, but the agent Ava's company had developed was a biodegradable solution that allowed the joints to be able to stay in place longer and to eventually be replaced by the patient's own cells within two or three years.

Ava's arrival in their lives had come at an opportune time. Edgar had suffered a heart attack last year, making shareholders nervous. And there was the competition. While Ava's research and development was way ahead, attempts to steal and duplicate her success was a constant threat.

Edgar made it clear that it would be in Ava's best interest to join forces, both personally and professionally, offering her a handsome deal. It included a generous amount of shares; full access to the inner workings of the company; guaranteed bonus package and use of a state of the art research lab and funding to develop other ideas if she agreed to marry into the family. He didn't want any major position outside of his control. To James's surprise, Ava agreed to the deal and Jackson, in his carefree way, went along with it.

And now, eight weeks later, his brother was having second thoughts.

"Yes, I mean Edgar," Jackson said with a sigh. "What if I screw this up?"

"There's nothing to screw up."

"I just feel the pressure. It's happening too fast. I'm not good under pressure." He took off his jacket then unbuttoned his shirt.

James watched him in alarm. "What are you doing?"

"Just for tonight."

James shook his head, reading his brother's thoughts. He wanted to switch places. That wasn't going to happen. He held up his hands, warding him off. "Oh no." Although they were identical twins they both dressed very different and tonight was no exception.

"Just for a couple of hours."

James waved his hands. "No. Absolutely not."

Jackson took off his shirt. "Dinner's almost over anyway."

"No."

He held the shirt out to him. "Otherwise I'm walking out of here. I mean it," he added when James didn't move.

James swore. He knew his brother would. When he felt trapped, Jackson's first instinct was to run. "All right," James said, unbuttoning his own shirt, "but this is the first and last time I'll ever do this for you."

Jackson smiled. "Thanks."

James glared at him. "Save your thanks for later, I haven't pulled it off yet."

CHAPTER 3

The other one.

Ava knew the moment the vacant seat beside her was taken that its new occupant was 'the other one'. That's how she'd gotten used to thinking of James Fortune. While Jackson radiated light and energy, James radiated a more subtle heat.

She didn't know why he always made her feel too warm and uneasy. She never felt comfortable around him. She rarely felt comfortable around anyone, preferring the sight of a computer screen, microscopic organisms or a book to people, but he put her on edge in a way no one had before. He made her nervous. She couldn't understand why. She wasn't afraid, few things frightened her, and if she planned to marry into the Fortune family she'd have to be strong, but he still put her off-guard.

Jackson was easy to play with, fun, simple to read. She'd navigated their relationship by approaching Edgar first and getting into his good graces *before* she orchestrated her meeting with Jackson. She'd even made sure that Edgar thought the marriage arrangement had been his idea.

Such a strategy would be harder to pull off with James, but not impossible. He was just more...something she couldn't fathom and had no interest in figuring out. She had to marry Jackson for her plan to work. So she would wait and see what their next move would be.

As identical twins there was nothing about him that should have bothered her. He and Jackson shared the same tall, powerful physique reminiscent of the ancient Douglas fir tree she'd seen as a child growing up in Vancouver, British Columbia. She'd been amazed by their size and history and since then had been drawn to trees, hiding in them when she wanted to get away from her lonely days at home and school. James, however, would be no sanctuary. He was like a tree occupied by a black bear.

He and Jackson both had elegant, clean shaven features and even white teeth that contrasted with their smooth brown skin in an attractive way.

But that's where the similarities ended. In appearance they were identical, in personality and style they couldn't be more different. Jackson preferred loud, bold colors like the purple shirt he wore under his dark blue jacket with matching purple lapels, cotton slacks and shoes; James, in contrast, wore grey trousers matching his jacket and a simple white shirt. Of course now he didn't, since he was wearing his brother's clothes.

Ava had to tap down a wave of anger. What game were they playing? James had slipped into his brother's role well, returning to the table with a wide smile and making the guests laugh at a joke she'd heard Jackson make many times before, but she couldn't be fooled because James had given himself away. It was a small simple act no one else would easily notice, but it was something she'd used to distinguish them.

When James and Jackson had returned from the washroom to take a seat at the table, Ava watched as James noticed his younger brother. Their younger brother Randolph, who everyone called Rudy, had Down syndrome and although he had a mild form, earning a university degree and running his own business, he still had triggers that could upset him and James was fiercely protective.

That evening, Rudy had noticed his brothers' long absence from the table and that had upset him. Although his mother and stepfather tried to assure him, his mood grew more anxious and he wouldn't eat.

When they returned to the table that's when she saw it—Jackson took his seat (as James) without looking at anyone else, while James (as Jackson) quickly surveyed the mood of the table, saw Rudy's expression and paused. He took a moment and bent down next to his brother, said something that made his brother smile before he gently rubbed Rudy's cheek with his knuckles. It was a tender action she'd seen James do before and always seemed to have a calming affect on Rudy. His smile widened and James looked at his mother sending her a silent message before he took the seat next to Ava.

In those few seconds, he'd given himself away by doing something Jackson never did—comfort his brother and assuring his mother. Ava took a sip of her white wine, resisting the urge to dump it over his head and demand to know what he was up to. Were they trying to humiliate her? Did they think this upcoming wedding was a joke?

He nudged her with his elbow and said something that

Jackson would say, in the cocky, funny way Jackson would say it. Ava didn't really pay attention because she knew it didn't matter. She did what was expected and smiled at him; he smiled in return. She held his gaze a lot longer than she should have but was unable, or unwilling, to look away, wondering if he could bear the full force of her gaze.

For a moment, a vulnerable hesitancy entered his brown gaze, and her grin widened a fraction in triumph. *You idiot. Your eyes aren't right. What are you trying to pull?*

Jackson's gaze was more carefree, more inviting, James's were too serious. He couldn't smile enough to take that sheen away.

But before she could bask in her small victory his eyes darkened with a glint of interest that made her grin fade as a wave of heat swept through her body. At first it felt faint then grew more intense. It was a feeling she never felt with Jackson and she wondered if his heated gaze reflected James's true interest or if it was part of the role he was playing.

If he thought this was how Jackson felt, he was doing it wrong, because Jackson never looked at her like that. He never made her feel as if he was marrying her for any other reason than to make his stepfather happy and for the company. Ava pulled her gaze away from his and silently seethed, hating her physical response to him. She'd wanted him to be the first to look away, but she'd get him back another way. She wouldn't let the Fortune brothers make a fool of her.

CHAPTER 4

"Is something the matter?" Flo asked her husband as she softly closed the door to their master bedroom. She was tired but happy after a long day and still full from the food she'd eaten at the rehearsal dinner.

She'd finished checking to make sure Rudy was safely tucked in bed and now found Edgar sitting on the side of their large platform bed with an unlit cigar in his hand. He usually did so when he was worried about something. Even in repose he looked ready to fight. He was a man of average height with a thick, muscular build, belying his advanced years, and skin the color of roasted almonds.

"Did Jackson seem different to you?" he asked in a low voice.

"Different how?"

He shrugged. "I don't know. At the wedding rehearsal he flubbed a few lines and at the rehearsal dinner... At first he seemed like he didn't want to be there and then he did."

"And why is that a problem?" Flo asked with a soft smile. "I think the reality of what he's doing is settling in."

Edgar's voice remained grim. "As long as that's all it is."

She sat down beside him but not close enough to touch. "He will not disappoint us."

Edgar sent her a dismissive glance before looking away. "You sound certain."

"I am. There will be a wedding tomorrow. I know my boys."

She tenderly touched his hand and he felt a moment of guilt, remembering the real reason why he'd married her. It wasn't for her soft, pretty features that age had been kind to, or her pleasing manner, which still gave him comfort in a way that surprised him. Few people could ease his bad mood the way she could.

At times he wondered if he'd made up for the selfish reason he'd asked her to be his wife. He'd had so much to prove and gain back then and now, so much to lose. That was the problem with years, intangible things like respect, dignity, and ones reputation, mattered more.

He'd raised his stepsons by instilling a tradition of loyalty that he never had. His father had been a useless plumber who'd managed to sleep with half of the housewives in the neighborhood, and rumored to have knocked up two before he was killed in a hit-and-run on his way home from a church bible study. But his father had left him with a love of boxing, which he'd instilled in him after starting him in the sport at the age of five, and a hunger to be somebody, because his father showed him that being a nobody was for punks.

His mother's brother, Uncle Frank, a barrel-chested man with an ability to inhale a cigarette and turn it into ash within minutes, had taken pity on them and given them a place to stay, begrudgingly, reminding them every moment he could that Edgar and his sister, and their father, had ruined their mother's life. How she'd been the smartest in the family and would have been the first to graduate from college if their father hadn't entered her life and sweet talked her into running off with him.

While he berated their very existence he also used them to his benefit, catching the eye of a wealthy woman at church who thought his care for his widowed sister and her children meant that he was a good man. He milked her sympathy into marriage, moving their entire family into her house, where he managed to work as little as possible, pretending he was helping his sister doing charity work while he lived off his wife's sense of obligation and Christian duty until she died.

From his uncle he learned the power of appearance and promised himself that he wouldn't be anybody's burden.

Edgar worked to prove his uncle wrong. He wasn't his father. He wasn't like any of them. He got his degree, in a field of study his uncle couldn't understand, bought his mother a house and even paid for his uncle's care until his death. Not that the bastard ever thanked him for it. He learned, on his own, what being a man was. What it took to survive in this world and gain respect.

And he'd passed that knowledge down. Now, more than ever, he needed to see it come to fruition. BioMed Solutions, despite their global market and consistent business, had nearly run out of money twice due to overexpansion and costly, futile research that went nowhere. With Jackson's help he had been able to restructure the company and James had tightened the spending in R&D and their profits had grown again. He'd made a good investment in them.

He'd seen their potential early but never thought they would be this useful to him. Now the next piece was taking BioMed Solutions to the next level. Ava Hughes's new product could take them beyond their competitors in a way that would last for generations. He needed this wedding to go without a hitch. He stared at the ground, thinking of his uncle. He wanted to achieve a level of success that would continue to make the old bastard turn in his grave.

CHAPTER 5

This was not what he'd expected.

James ran a hand down his face, wondering how he'd ended up in Ava's apartment. No, he knew how he'd gotten there he just couldn't believe he hadn't managed to come up with an excuse to get out of it. He'd played Jackson long enough and now had entered dangerous territory.

He closed his eyes and reimagined the scene in the men's room in the restaurant. He should have taken Jackson's shirt and thrown it back at him. He should have forced him to get through the evening and said they'd talk about it later. Maybe he should have bribed him. His brother loved classic cars. He could have said he'd buy him one. Instead, he'd listen to him and now he was sitting on a couch that felt as comfortable as a cement block. Or maybe that was just how he was feeling, he couldn't seem to get comfortable.

He pounded his fist on the cushion and swore when pain shot through his hand. No, it was the couch. It was hard as stone. He lifted the fitted sofa cover to see what it was made out of and paused when he saw stacks of hardcover books—some textbooks, some coffee table books. What the heck?

James crouched down and lifted the cover higher just to make sure. They were books alright, but were they real? He poked a spine with his forefinger surprised when it shifted. They were actually real books not fakes fused together. Who makes furniture out of books? Did his brother know about this?

"Do you want anything to eat?" Ava called out to him from the kitchen where the smell of coffee was filling the air.

James gently tried to put the book back in place, but failed. "No, I'm fine." He let the sofa cover fall and sat back on the couch, wincing when he sat down too hard. At least he knew one thing; Ava didn't expect him to get comfortable.

Ava hummed with malicious pleasure as she prepared coffee. She knew James was sweating in the other room and she planned to enjoy every second of it. She'd almost laughed at the expression of shock on his face when she'd told him to drive her home after dinner had ended and people started to leave.

"I said I would what?" he said, while helping her put on her coat.

"Drive me home." She smiled up at him over her shoulder. "Don't you remember?"

"Yes, of course." He looked towards Jackson who was talking to Flo. "Let me just—"

Ava looped her arm through his, trapping him. She wouldn't let him get away and switch places again. She'd make him pay a little for his deception. "They'll be fine."

"I know but—"

She led him towards the exit before he could catch his brother's attention. "We've already said our goodbyes."

"But Rudy—"

"Is with James. It's not like you to worry. You know that James takes care of everything."

His jaw twitched. She hid a grin knowing she'd struck a nerve. He nodded and held the door open for her. "Right."

She paused. "You don't sound happy. I thought you looked forward to spending some time alone with me."

He nodded again, his expression briefly becoming more resolute before it softened into a smile. "I did—uh do." He winked. "I was just building up for tomorrow night."

She returned his smile then walked past him and let it fall as she headed out into the parking lot. The warm spring evening breeze brushed her skin and the scent of roses from the bushes lining the restaurant greeted her. She would have enjoyed the aroma if she hadn't been annoyed. Her heels clicked along the gravel path, her black skirt whispering against her legs. It took her a moment to realize hers was the only footsteps she heard. Had he abandoned her? Had he taken this chance to run back inside? She stopped and spun around, gasping in shock when he loomed over her.

James stopped short and stared at her with a frown. "What's wrong with you?"

"I didn't expect you to be so close."

"If you hadn't stopped, I wouldn't have ended up so close."

"I was just checking to see that you were still there."

"Why wouldn't I be here?"

It was a good question, but she'd gotten suspicious because she'd barely been able to hear his footsteps. How could a man of his size walk so softly? She was certain Jackson made his every step known. "I thought you may have changed your mind about seeing my place. You'd said you wanted to."

His voice cracked. "I did?"

Ava had to stop a smile. "Yes, you wanted to see what it was like."

"But—but I thought I was just supposed to drive you home."

"To see my place. Don't you remember?" She frowned. "How much have you had to drink?"

James snapped his fingers clearly finding a way out of having to take her home. "That's right. I shouldn't drive." He pulled out his cell phone. "I'll get you a—"

She pushed the cell phone away. "You hardly drank anything, which isn't like you. Stop stalling. I'm ready to go." She walked to Jackson's car then slowed her gait when an unsettling thought hit her. What if James didn't have his brother's car keys? What if James said he'd left them inside and the brothers switched on her again? Did she really care?

To her relief the sound of Jackson's red Porsche unlocking answered her question. At least he was thorough. James opened the passenger door for her.

"It's going to be a long day tomorrow," he said.

Ava slid into the passenger seat then looked up at him. "I'm not asking you to spend the night." She crossed her legs and noticed his gaze looking at her skirt. "Unless..."

He looked away. "I think I see James—"

"No, you don't," she said impatient. If he did stall long enough, his brother would come out and ruin her plans. "Come on, you know I don't like to be kept waiting."

He hesitated then got in the car.

Ava remembered the silent car ride as she poured the coffee. Now she had him exactly where she wanted him, sitting on her couch, not knowing what to do.

His discomfort in the car had been delicious. It was even more so when he entered her apartment. Watching James playacting the role of the sexy Jackson was a study in contrasts. Although Jackson had never been to her apartment, Ava knew the first thing he would do was ask for a drink, as he checked his reflection in a glass clock she had near the door; he'd send a cursory glance at the large window, noticing the window trim and light fixtures, he liked to pay attention to details like that, before taking a seat, complaining that it was too hard, and teasing her to not take too long.

James, on the other hand, didn't notice the clock or the window, but instead noticed the hand woven rug in the middle of her living room, picked up a magazine she'd absently thrown on the floor and set it on her coffee table. He didn't take a seat until she refused his offer to help her in the kitchen and when he did, he pretended the couch was comfortable, even though it wasn't. He did it all with Jackson's flair but without his carelessness.

However, the biggest difference between the two was that James took up too much space. Jackson would have entered her apartment like a cool breeze, swift and light; James was like a humid summer, making everything feel close and tight, making her want to open a window and strip down. Punishing him came at a price because the same feeling had followed her in the car, making Jackson's Porsche feel like a Mini Cooper.

But she'd get rid of James soon. Unfortunately, not the memory of him making her two bedroom apartment feel as large as a tiny closet, so that was fine. She returned to the living room and a soft smile touched her lips when she saw him sitting with his hands gripped on his knees and head lowered like a condemned man. He obviously didn't like doing this deception. That was good, he had a conscience. But then why do it? What was Jackson up to?

Ava set the tray down on the coffee table. "Having second thoughts?"

James's head shot up and he stared at her alarmed. "No, no."

"You don't look happy."

He looked at her for a long moment. "What's with you and me being happy?"

She bit her lip, he was right. That was out of character for her. She had to be more careful and not try to push this too far.

"I guess I'm a little nervous about tomorrow."

"Tomorrow will be fine. Thank you," he said when she handed him the coffee. He moved over giving her more room on the couch. Another small slip. Whenever they went out, whether to a movie or formal event, Jackson always stayed in place. James was too considerate for his own good.

"I don't believe you."

He sipped the coffee. "Why not?"

"Because you haven't touched me all evening."

Ava inwardly smiled, biting the inside of her cheek. She could picture his mind racing for a response. *What do you say to that James?*

At first he didn't move and she wondered if he'd heard her. He stared at his coffee, he was so still she wondered if he was even still breathing. She was about to say something else when he set the cup down on the coffee table with a soft click. He turned to her and said, "I wanted to wait for us to be alone."

And although that was exactly something Jackson would say the look in his eyes was pure James. Pure, unadulterated James and it was a heady sensation to be captured under that serious, penetrating gaze that dared her to look away while a hypnotic heat that seemed to fill the air around him, drew her close.

Her heart responded. She knew she should stop him now. Call him out. Throw him out. Get him out of her apartment—now. But she didn't. She didn't move, waiting to see what he would do next. She'd given him enough time alone to text his brother and get instructions on how to proceed. She expected another smooth line and then he'd leave.

"I see," she said, crossing her legs, but this time his heated gaze didn't leave her face.

He kissed her.

With no hesitation. Like a eagle swooping down to capture its prey. She'd never seen James as a predator before, but now she did. She felt it the moment his lips touched hers. A shiver of fear coursed through her as she realized she'd fallen in his trap. She'd underestimated him.

It had been a dangerous mistake to believe that his concern for his mother and brother, his soft footsteps and considerate acts were the actions of a weak man.

He was more controlled and calculating than that. His every gesture and move was not by accident, but design. She hadn't realized he'd kept her off-balance all evening until this moment when he'd been prepared to strike, giving her no recourse to deny him, claiming her as if she were his woman.

He pulled away, his voice a velvet whisper against her lips. "That's just a taste of things to come."

Another smooth Jackson line that sounded completely different coming from James. It felt like a promise. A promise she wanted him to keep. She stared at him wanting to be afraid, wanting to hate him but instead feeling aroused, excited.

She covered her mouth with a trembling hand and rose to her feet putting much needed distance between them. Rage and desire warring within her. How could he treat her like this? How could he make her feel this way?

"What's wrong?" James rose to his feet and looked at her alarmed, that same expression he'd had when she'd told him to drive her home. How could a man be deceitful and innocent at the same time?

She pounded him in the chest with her fist, not enough to hurt him but enough to release some of her frustration. He didn't flinch or even blink, he continued to look at her in a way that made her want to shake him and kiss him at the same time. "You should go."

He rested his hands on his hips and sighed. "Ava—"

"Just go."

"It will be better tomorrow. I promise." He flashed a Jackson grin. "I'm not on my A game tonight. Don't worry, I'll—"

"I'm not worried," she said in a flat tone.

"Good."

"Are you?"

He shook his head. "No. I want this."

She looked into his eyes wishing she could read his mind, but unable to hold his gaze long she looked away. "Good."

He walked to the door. "Tomorrow will be better."

She opened the door for him. "Because we'll be husband and wife."

He walked through then turned to her. "Right."

"And you'd better show up. I won't take being the jilted bride well."

"I'll be there."

"Good." She waved goodbye then closed the dcor. "Or there will be hell to pay."

He'd briefly lost his mind. That was the only way to explain it. Between the hard couch and her soft mouth he'd gone insane and crossed the line.

James rested his head on the steering wheel. He'd made an ass of himself. He'd almost blown his cover too all because...all because he wanted to. He could lie to himself and say that he hadn't wanted her to feel unsure, especially when she mentioned him not touching her, he wanted her to feel good, but that wasn't the reason. He'd worked hard to keep her a little unsure all evening so that she wouldn't notice any differences between him and Jackson.

He'd kissed her for purely selfish reasons. He'd wanted to. He'd always wondered what her raspberry lips would taste like, the sensation of feeling the soft give of her breasts against his chest. But he'd forgotten one thing—she didn't like him.

He'd noticed the subtle signs from the beginning, how she kept her distance from him, how she gravitated towards his brother, instead of him. But if he'd been given the choice he would have offered to marry her instead.

Tonight he'd pretended she was his and he'd felt her respond to him in a way that made him crave more, then she pulled away and stared at him with a look he'd never seen before. Was it horror?

It was something that struck him to the core and for a wild moment he feared he'd exposed himself. Jackson was always free with the ladies, hadn't he kissed her like that?

He felt like a guilty fool. Indulging in a fantasy that would never be his. A woman like Ava was out of his reach, no matter how much he could pretend to be Jackson, he never would be that charming nor have the charisma. Could she tell the difference? He felt sick and humiliated that a woman would respond to him that way. Not any woman—Ava Hughes.

He still remembered the blue dress she'd worn the first time he'd met her, the way she'd quickly pulled her hand from his as if he'd burned her. He was keenly aware of her wary gaze, wondering if his initial attraction to her had been evident. He was careful, few people could tell what he was thinking, but something about him seemed to put her on edge no matter how much he tried.

But never again. He'd learned his lesson.

He'd done his brother a favor and now everything was back in place. Lusting after his future sister-in-law wasn't in the cards. She'd never know what he'd done, but it was something he'd never forget.

His cell phone rang. "Where's my car?"

James sighed, that was typical Jackson. Not, How are things? Is she okay? But, Where's my car?

He was tempted to say that he demolished it, instead he

disconnected and turned the ringer off, knowing he'd have a series of messages and texts when he finally looked again.

THE SMELL of ginger bread greeted him when he entered the family house. He had an apartment in town, but presently lived in the European style mansion. He headed for his bedroom but stopped when he noticed a light on in the library. He walked inside and saw his mother asleep on the tan leather couch, wrapped in a pink robe, her matching fuzzy slippers on the hardwood floor. James glanced at his watch, it was past eleven she should be in bed.

He grabbed a throw from the back of the chair and gently placed it over her.

"It's about time you came home," she mumbled. She sat up, running a hand through her short, silver afro.

"What are you doing up?"

She slipped her feet inside her slippers and stood. "Waiting for you to tell me what's going on."

James glanced towards the stairs.

"Don't worry, Edgar doesn't know, but he was a little suspicious."

James sighed and let his shoulders droop. "I—"

"Tell me in the kitchen."

Moments later they sat in the breakfast nook with ginger bread and a plate of sliced bananas and oranges.

"You were out late," Flo said. "Where have you been? What have you been up to?"

Kissing my brother's fiancée. "There's nothing for you to worry about."

"I will anyway. Why did you pretend to be Jackson at the rehearsal dinner?"

Damned if I know. "Jackson had a case of cold feet, but he'll be ready tomorrow."

"Poor James," Flo said, stroking his cheek. "You had to come to the rescue as always."

"Not always."

"Remember when you had to convince Jackson to finish his degree? Dump that piano teacher who was only after his money?"

"No, that was the swimsuit model."

"I thought the swimsuit model was the one with the husband."

"No, that was the lawyer."

Flo shook her head. "Your brother has terrible taste in women."

"Which is why he was panicking tonight, he thinks Ava may be one of his mistakes."

Flo looked at him for a long moment. "And what do you think?"

"I don't know." He shook his head. "I don't think so. Edgar vetted her."

"But we both know sometimes Edgar cares more about the business than the person."

"I don't think there are any skeletons in the closet. Besides, it's too late now."

"Do you think she suspected anything?"

Almost. "No." He set down his fork. "Thanks for that."

She took the plate away. "Do you want anything else?"

James sat back in his chair and watched her place the dish in the sink, a wave of sadness crushing his heart and briefly touching his eyes with tears. *Yes, please don't die. Don't be sick anymore. Give me a couple more years with you.* But he knew that was a request she couldn't grant him. The bone cancer was aggressive, the doctors—she'd visited three just to make sure—had given her six more months.

It had started as a swelling in her arm last year, followed by unexpected weight loss and fatigue before Edgar convinced her to see a doctor.

The stage III diagnosis was something none of them wanted to hear for a woman in her mid-fifties with hopes for the future.

Before Jackson's engagement, his mother had fought depression along with suffering the pain of her disease, her energy had gotten weaker, as if the cancer was taking hold at a faster pace than expected, but after his announcement she'd gotten brighter, her energy more vibrant. She'd blossomed under the thrill of working with Ava to arrange and plan everything, which was why this wedding had to take place. It was her final wish to see one of her sons married. James half wondered if Edgar had made the arrangement with Ava with that thought in mind, but doubted it. His stepfather wasn't a man known for sentiment. However, James would make that wish come true if he had to drag his brother down the aisle himself.

Unfortunately, he didn't get the chance.

He found his brother looking resolute and defiant as he sat on the edge of his bed. Jackson rarely stayed at the family house, but had agreed to do so, so that he and James could arrive at the wedding together. James looked at the cell phone in his brother's hand.

"What are you doing?" James asked, coming into the room. "We have to leave." His mother, Edgar and Rudy had already gone ahead of them.

"I need to call Ava first."

"Why?"

He shook his head. "I'm sorry. There's something about her—"

"Just go through the ceremony. We can figure the rest out later."

"I'm sorry."

"Stop saying that."

He lifted his phone ready to call her. "I can't marry her."

James grabbed the phone before he could. "You have to."

"No, I don't."

James silently swore. "It's too late. Do you know what day it is today? It's your *wedding* day. Not a rehearsal, not an engagement. It's the main event."

"I know that."

"You have to show up."

"No, I don't."

"You can't jilt her."

"It's better than making a mistake."

"The wedding is in less than an hour," James said through gritted teeth. "And you're just figuring this out now?"

"I told you how I felt last night." He held out his hand. "Give me my phone."

"No, I won't let you do this."

Jackson stood and walked past him, heading to the door. "I'll go to her instead."

James grabbed his arm and spun him back around. "Stay away from her," he warned in a low voice. "The only moment you'll see her is when you're prepared to say 'I do'."

Jackson yanked his arm away. "That's the point. I'm not." He walked out the door and headed down the stairs. "I have to stop this."

James followed close behind. "You can't. Edgar depends on you and Mom needs this."

Jackson paused, gripping the railing. He closed his eyes. "I just feel like..." He let his voice fall away then folded his arms. "We're doing this for Mom."

"Yes," James said, pleased his brother was starting to understand the magnitude.

"Mom wants a wedding."

"Yes." He slapped him on the back. "Now come on."

Jackson didn't move, a cunning expression crossed his face. "I've got an idea."

James read the expression and frowned. "No."

Jackson held up his hand. "Just listen. It will work. You do the ceremony."

"No."

"And then we'll switch places at the reception. I'll handle everything from there." He playfully punched James in the side. "Race you to the car." He dashed down the rest of the stairs.

James ran after him. "You're crazy."

Jackson grabbed his car keys from the table in the foyer and tossed them in James's direction. "So are you."

James caught the keys then followed him outside. "No, I'm not." He pointed the keys at the Porsche and unlocked it. "I'm not doing this again."

Jackson smiled at him over the hood of the car. "Yes, you are."

"Why would I marry Ava in your place?"

"Because then the marriage would be invalid." He sat inside the passenger seat.

James got in the driver's seat and started the ignition. "And why do you want the marriage to be invalid?"

"Because I don't trust her."

"I don't care." James turned and backed the car out of the driveway. "I'm still not doing it."

"Either you do this or I tell Ava the truth." Jackson took off the yellow flower on his tuxedo, the color was the only thing that distinguished him from his groomsmen. "Either way I'm not getting married today." He reached over and pinned it on his brother's tux then patted it in place. "Just say the vows and give Mom the wedding she wants then at the reception I'll take over. Do we have deal?"

James shifted gears with force, realizing he didn't have a choice. "I'll get you for this."

James still remembered his brother's smug grin as James stood beside Ava in the church, although, to his relief, he hadn't stumbled over his vows as Jackson had during the wedding rehearsal. But his cover had nearly been blown early in the ceremony as the wedding march played and Ava walked towards him when Rudy said in a loud whisper, "But Mom, I thought Jackson was supposed to marry Ava."

His mother quietly told him to hush, but his anxious glance darted between his two brothers.

"But Mom," Rudy said, growing more agitated, "but Mom, why is James up there? Jackson's in the wrong place. We practiced this and they forgot—"

"Quiet," Flo warned in a low voice, "or I'm taking you outside and you'll miss everything. Do you want that?"

He bit his lip and shook his head but looked at James confused. James forced himself to look away feeling guilty for the look of misery on his brother's face. He glanced at Jackson who was instead ogling one of the bridesmaids in a way James never would.

Ava appeared at his side and didn't seem to have heard or noticed his brothers. He was sure if she suspected something she would stop the wedding, but she didn't, so he felt his secret was safe.

"I now pronounce you husband and wife."

James swallowed, not daring to look at Jackson as he gave her a quick kiss, knowing he had nothing to prove—everyone knew this wasn't a love match—and he didn't want to give himself away. But even the light touch of her lips against his seemed to send an electric charge through him. He made the mistake of meeting her gaze and saw them narrow a little. He smiled in a way he knew his brother would and quickly looked away. He then took her hand and led her down the aisle to the sound of joyous applause.

He smiled his way through the endless array of poses the photographer took of them, but the worse was when the photographer said she needed a picture of the couple signing the license."

"Do you really need to see that?"

"It's a very important moment," she said.

"But—"

"What's the big deal?" Ava asked. "We have to do it anyway and it won't take long."

He was going to get his fraud photographed and set in time forever. *It's okay, no one will know. No one can ever know.* He returned to where Pastor Valentine stood, the marriage license laid out on a polished wooden table. "Ladies first," he said when the pastor held out the pen to him. Ava signed with an artistic flourish, that surprised him. The constant click from the photographer's camera memorializing the moment. He would have expected a more subtle businesslike signature.

"Now it's your turn," Ava said, holding the pen out to him while the sound of the clicking camera continued. How many damn pictures did the photographer need?

He took the pen, flashing a classic Jackson smile at the camera, before he signed his brother's name.

"Perfect," the photographer said pleased. "Now we can—"

"I think that's enough for now," Ava said. "There are plenty more pictures we can take at the reception."

The photographer nodded then left. Moments later, James stared out the tinted limousine windows as they drove to the hotel for the reception. Just a couple more minutes and it would be all over. He could escape this madness.

After he and Jackson switched places at the reception he'd keep his distance from Ava and try to forget this nightmare had ever happened. Maybe one day, years from now, he'd be able to laugh about it all. When the limousine pulled up to the hotel, James stepped out releasing a sigh of relief as he gallantly assisted Ava to do the same. Escape was in sight. Soon Jackson would take over, when he showed up.

Except Jackson never did.

CHAPTER 8

Another damn restroom.

James paced, his polished black shoes pounding against the white floor of the empty hotel restroom.

He didn't know how much more he could take. He'd survived the thunderous applause of guests when he and Ava entered the reception hall; listened to Jackson's friend's raunchy and funny toast as people joked that James should have been giving it but had likely skipped out because he hated public speaking. Someone suggested that he'd likely be found at work instead.

James forced laughter he didn't feel. As the reception progressed he felt even less like laughing. He didn't remember what he ate, only that one plate replaced another as the various courses made their appearance then disappeared. He nursed his champagne until it was flat, his gaze scanning the crowd, looking around the room, at the entrances, waiting for his brother to make an appearance. He briefly noticed Ava's friend, Camy Hakata, was missing and remembered that

Jackson had been eying her at the wedding. A thought of dread crossed his mind. Was his brother having a quickie somewhere?

Before James could give his fear credence, Camy appeared dashing that possibility.

After more than an hour James excused himself and disappeared into the restroom, just to have time alone to think and plan what his next move should be. He called his brother, but it went straight to voice mail. He texted him but received no reply.

James removed his ring, the flower on his tux and paced, pretending to go into a stall or washing his hands when someone else came in. After several minutes passed, he peeked his head out of the restroom but saw the hallway was empty. Where the hell was he? The church wasn't that far from the hotel. James swore and was about to dart back inside the restroom when something grabbed a hold of his ear.

"Ow!"

"What is going on?" Flo demanded, pulling him into the room.

"This is the men's room, Mom."

"I can see that. Now tell me what you and your brother are up to." She yanked hard.

James gritted his teeth. "That hurts."

"I know. I'm glad." She yanked again. "I expected more from you."

"I don't know what you're talking about."

She squeezed some more.

"Okay, okay," James said quickly. "Let go of my ear and I'll explain everything."

She released him and folded her arms, flaring out the sleeves of her pale pink dress. "I'm listening."

James rubbed his throbbing ear. "I don't know what you want me to say."

"You took your brother's place at his wedding!" She grabbed his collar. "Do you know how serious this is?"

"Mom, calm down," James said worried about her health. "I really don't know what you're talking about." He tapped his chest. "It's me. James. I was his best man."

Flo released her grip on his shirt and looked at him hesitant. "If you're James then why didn't you do your speech at the reception?"

"Nerves. I just arrived. I wanted to miss it."

She narrowed her eyes, biting her lip. "But I thought—"

"That I took his place?" James finished with an indulgent smile. "No, why would I do something like that?"

She frowned. "You did it last night."

He turned to the mirror and straightened his jacket, no longer able to face her. "That was different."

A man entered the restroom, saw the two of them then turned back around and left.

"Mom we should go."

She didn't move. "But Jackson just left the reception. Have you seen him?"

"No, like I said. I just arrived a couple minutes ago."

"Rudy thought—"

"My flower was a little yellowed, that's all. He got confused."

She looked up at him unsure. "You're really James?"

He turned to her and smiled. "Of course I'm James." At

least that wasn't a lie. He held up his hands. "See? No ring. I'm still a single man."

"I could have sworn...I guess I was wrong." She placed a hand on her chest. "That's a relief."

"I'm glad."

She looked in one of the stalls. "Then where's Jackson?" She bent down to look for feet. "You're positive he isn't in here?"

James took her arm. "Mom, don't do that."

She straightened. "But if he's not in here where could he be?"

James took her arm and led her out of the restroom. "I think you should sit down. There's no need to worry. He could have briefly gone outside. I don't know, but I'm sure he's around here somewhere," he said. He kept his voice light in order to reassure her. "How's Rudy?"

"Ready to go home. You know how he doesn't like crowds."

"I think you and Edgar should take him home. You're looking a little flush."

"I'll admit that I was worried."

He kissed her lightly on the cheek. "There's nothing to worry about, Mom. You got the wedding you wanted."

Her eyes shone. "Wasn't it beautiful?" She clasped her hands together. "And oh, James, you looked so handsome and dignified up there. I wasn't sure she was the right one for you until I saw you two up there together."

"You mean Jackson. Jackson married Ava."

She frowned. "Yes, that's right, Jackson." She touched her forehead. "I don't know why I keep imagining you standing up there with her. You made such a handsome pair."

"Hmm."

She flashed a watery smile. "I guess I'm being a little greedy wanting you to find happiness."

He saw the anxiety on her face and softened his tone. "I'm happy. Now don't worry about the reception, Jackson will show up somewhere."

"Okay," She turned.

James watched her go back into the ballroom then looked around before he slid Jackson's wedding ring back on his finger. He hated lying to his mother but he knew he'd have to keep up the charade a little while longer.

James paused at the entrance watching Ava dance with the man who'd caught her garter. The man held her too close, taking advantage of the moment. He could understand the temptation, he'd done the same when he'd danced with her, liking how well their bodies moved together, noticing the delicate curve of her mouth, the sweep of her neck, the solid curve of her hips. James gripped his hand into a fist, he may not be the real groom, but he would keep an eye on Ava until his brother showed up.

He took a step forward, ready to reenter and make his presence known, but was stopped when a woman grabbed him and kissed him on the mouth. She then pulled away and winked. "Wow, you're right. Married men do taste different."

James could only make a noise low in his throat not trusting himself to speak. He remembered her face, she was easy to remember with dark lashes, short brown hair and a feline smile, but couldn't remember her name.

"I didn't really think you'd go through with it," she said,

resting a hand on her hips, reminding him of handcuffs for some unknown reason. "You were so nervous the last time we talked."

"I'm fine now."

She let her gaze travel the length of him. "Yes, fine as always and no longer on the market."

"That's right. I'd better get back to the party."

She frowned. "Aren't you even curious what I found out?"

Found out? Jackson had her looking into something? James snapped his fingers finally placing her. Sylvia Prentiss, the cop. That's why he'd thought of the handcuffs. He remembered his brother once saying she could frisk him and lock him up any day.

Sylvia sent him an odd look. "Are you alright?"

"Yes, I'm fine. I do want to hear what you have to say, but not now."

"It's not much yet anyway. You didn't answer all my questions."

James glanced towards the ballroom eager to leave. It was either pretend to be Jackson surrounded by a crowd, or alone with a woman who was used to spotting liars. "I've got to go. People are waiting."

Sylvia smirked. "Your new bride already has you on a short lead, huh?"

His tone hardened. "No." He knew he'd said the wrong thing when he saw her face change. She looked wary. "I just need to stay away from temptation."

Her smile returned. "I know that's right."

"Send me what you have and uh...thanks for coming." He slipped out of her grasp and entered the ballroom scanning the crowd in hopes he'd see his brother.

He couldn't have left him like this. Jackson could be reckless, impulsive but not this inconsiderate. What had happened between here and the church? Had his brother gotten into an accident? Should he call hospitals?

He pulled out his cell phone to try and reach him again when it alerted him to a text.

Don't worry. I'm fine. Don't ask.

What did he mean "Don't ask?" He called him back surprised and relieved when he picked up. "I can't make it back," Jackson said before James could speak. "You're going to have to carry this out for me. Do whatever you need to." The line disconnected. He swore. His brother wasn't hurt, he wasn't dead, which was a relief, but he felt like killing him.

"I was looking all over for you," Ava said, snaking her arm around his. "I thought you were trying to make your escape."

I wish I could. "No, just catching up with people I haven't seen in a while."

"You seem to know a lot of people."

Yes, too many. "Hmm."

"I thought you could introduce me to some of them."

"Not yet."

"Why not?"

Because I don't really know most of them. "I'd rather dance," he said, pulling her into a dancer's embrace. But he made the mistake of pulling her too close, pressing her body intimately against his. He spun her away. "Better yet, let's get something to drink."

"Jackson, my man," a lanky, tall man said with a grin. "What are you two still doing here?"

He frowned.

The other man beside him sent Ava a slightly drunken leer. "Do we really need to spell it out?"

One of Ava's bridesmaid and Camy playfully pushed Ava towards him. "Yes, it's time for you two to go."

Panic gripped him. No. No, he couldn't leave yet!

Ava smiled up at him. "That's a good idea."

Nooooo!

She took his hand and said with a sly grin. "Let's say goodbye to everyone first."

His ears rang. He didn't remember his mouth moving, or his body either as she led him around the room and they thanked their guests and said their goodbyes. He felt like he was saying a different kind of goodbye—goodbye to his freedom, to his plans, to life as he knew it. There was no turning back now.

As the elevator doors closed and slowly ascended to the top floor, he felt Ava's tight grip on his hand and silently said goodbye to any chance of escaping.

CHAPTER 10

The woman was a witch.

He'd sensed there was something dangerous about her and now there was nothing he could do about it. Jackson pounded his fist into the flat of his hand.

He didn't want to think about how Ava was torturing his poor brother right now. He still remembered the mistake he'd made. He shouldn't have responded to the sweet come-hither smile of Ava's friend Camy, looking alluring with her dark red lips and ink black hair with purple highlights piled high on her head. If he hadn't met her at the back of the church after his brother and Ava had driven away, he wouldn't have found himself being detained in a storage room by two guys who looked like they were straight out of a yakuza gangster film.

Camy introduced them as her brothers before they covered his face, shoved him into a waiting van and drove him to a place he still didn't know. At least they'd removed the hood.

Jackson rested his head on the locked door then turned to look at one of the large men who watched him. One of Camy's brothers. He doubted they were truly related. But the man had a hell of right hook. He found out when he tried to outwit him. They guy had actually apologized before knocking him out.

Jackson tenderly touched his cheek. Damn, what did they feed these guys in Canada?

"I don't like to miss a party so I don't have a lot of time," Camy had told him once they'd removed his hood. She sat across from him on a grey metal chair. When he opened his mouth to respond she shook her head, stopping him. "If you do what Ava wants, nothing will happen."

His eyes widened. "Ava's behind all this?"

"Of course."

"What does she want?"

"A lot of things, but first she doesn't want you to make it to the reception."

"Why not? I have to see my brother Jackson."

Camy held out her cell phone and played a recording of Ava's voice. "We know who you are," she said. "We know what you're doing and if you don't want me to destroy this precious day that means so much to your mother you will do exactly what I say."

Jackson clenched his fist. "My mother will recover."

Camy played the recording some more. "Will she recover from seeing your father's company tank? A man with a weak heart shouldn't run a business that's so unstable."

Jackson frowned annoyed that he was so predictable. "What do you want?"

Camy hit the recording again. "I want you to disappear for two days."

"No."

"Otherwise I will charge your brother with fraud right now in front of everyone. How would you like that?"

Jackson pointed at the phone. "Can't you turn that thing off and talk to me?"

Camy shook her head. "No," the recording said. "And don't get mad at her. This is your fault for trying to mess with me."

"You can't prove anything."

"All I need to do is sow a seed of doubt."

Jackson rested his hands on his hips and briefly stared at the ceiling—a dirty brown color with a single light blub. "Where is this place?"

When Camy didn't reply, he tried another question. "How much money do you want?"

"I don't need money," the recording said.

"Revenge?"

"In time."

"For what? For this?" He threw out his hands, amazed. "The truth is I didn't want to marry you, but my brother wanted to help you save face. He's more of a gentleman than I am."

"We had an agreement."

"You're right and since he went through with it, I'll do my part. Just let me talk to—"

"It's too late for that."

He swore. "I can't believe I'm talking to a stupid recording."

"Don't try to ask for any favors. Do you think I'd let you two get together to change places again?"

"This is my mistake."

"No, you didn't do it alone. You will have to suffer equally."

Then the recording went dead.

And there was no way for him to warn his brother.

Jackson sat on the cold metal chair, imagining Camy and Ava partying like nothing had happened. He should have gone through with his initial plan and jilted her. He knew there was something strange about her. But he still couldn't put his finger on it. She didn't want money. What kind of revenge did she have in store? His mother and stepfather didn't need the stress she could cause. He'd bide his time until he could figure out what she truly wanted.

Ava opened the door to the honeymoon suite then looked up at James with an expectant look. "Well?"

"Well what?"

"Aren't you going to carry me over the threshold?" She tilted her head. "Unless you want me to carry you."

"Oh." He swept her into his arms, trying not to be entranced by the scent of her lotion, the heat of her body. He walked forward a few feet, closing the door with his foot and scanned the room with a small sense of relief. The elegant room didn't look like a bordello—his brother would have liked that—or a romantic getaway with red rose petals, but instead it was just an impressive hotel room with soft carpeting and a bouquet of red, white and pink flowers on the wooden dining table.

The lights of the darkened city of Kirkland glittered outside the large window. He walked over to it. His brother was out there somewhere, he still couldn't understand his strange message. His voice sounded strange too. More serious than usual. Was he in trouble?

"You can put me down now," Ava said.

James glanced down, startled. He'd forgotten he was still holding her, and now he was aware of nothing else. Her face was so close to his. "Sorry," he said slowly letting her down. He had to come clean. He had to tell her the truth. He had to...

"Don't be," Ava said then kissed him.

He promised himself he wouldn't go too far as his mouth pressed against hers. Just some kissing, a little foreplay then... then he'd take a shower. Or find some way to ruin the mood. No, there was no way he could ruin this mood. Could a broke man turn away from a million dollars? A hungry man from a buffet? He wanted to push her away but couldn't.

She drew away from him with a sexy, alluring smile of invitation before she slowly turned her back to him. She slipped off her shoes then reached for the zipper at her neck. He bit his lip, eager to watch her undress, hoping she'd take her time. One part of his mind telling him to stop it, stop her, another part saying, That's right, baby. Keeping going.

If he didn't touch her he'd be safe. Look but don't touch. He was a disciplined man. A principled one and sleeping with his brother's bride wasn't the way to go. Although technically she wasn't.

She sent him a look over her shoulder. "Aren't you going to help me?"

Okay, so he had to touch her, but he'd just unzip her dress. That was all then he'd walk away. He slowly pulled the zipper down watching as her creamy dark brown skin slowly revealed itself.

"You're not saying much," Ava said.

"What do you want me to say?" James replied, his voice deeper than usual.

"I don't know."

He'd just kiss her shoulder. That's all. Then he'd stop. James pressed his lips against her skin, feeling the warmth of it and inhaling the scent of her lotion. Was it roses? Cherry blossoms?

She turned to him before he could pull away and kissed him again. He swore as her hands quickly unbuttoned his shirt.

"Did I scare you?" she said with an impish grin.

"No."

"I can feel your heart racing."

"Yes, well—"

"I like it." She kissed him again, trapping his words in his throat. She pushed him towards the bed. "You know I'm a woman who likes to take charge."

James was tempted to let himself stumble back and fall on the bed, she wasn't strong enough to force him no matter how powerful she thought she was, but he was tempted to pretend. He was tempted to let her think anything she wanted if he could feel the weight of her body against his.

However, when the back of his legs hit the bed frame, he stopped himself. If he went that far there was no turning back. He held out his hands. "Ava—"

Ava pushed his shirt off his shoulders, baring his chest, and grabbed one of his nipples between her teeth, before teasing it with her tongue. She looked up at him. "Yes?"

James briefly closed his eyes and swallowed, she was playing dirty and he liked it. He quickly moved away and turned so that he stood facing the bed while she stood with her back to it. "I need to take a shower first."

"We can take a shower later." She took off his shirt then wrapped her arms around his neck and fell back on the bed taking him with her, wrapping her legs around him. "I know you want this."

James hid a grin; she was really upping the stakes. Part of him wondered why, but another part didn't care. He did want it— her. Now. Naked in his arms, warm, wet and willing. From the first moment she came into his life he'd wanted this. He'd think about the consequences later. She'd never need to know. He'd give her a night she'd never forget. He bent down to kiss her again.

She stopped him, pressing the flat of her palm against his chest. She gazed up at him and said in a soft whisper, "I just have one question."

"What?"

Her tone turned flat and cold as did the expression in her eyes. "How far are you willing to take this James?"

CHAPTER 12

He didn't know whether he should lie or run, so he waited.

Ava shoved him away from her. "You bastard."

Yes, that was true. He blinked and sat on the side of the bed as she adjusted her dress. His heart cracked a little with disappointment at a lost opportunity, his body going from hot to cold in seconds.

"You think I wouldn't find out?" When he didn't respond she released an angry sound of frustration. "You're a fraud and a liar."

That was true too. He rubbed his forehead, shocked by how far he'd been willing to go. For a moment he didn't know himself. But he had to take control. She was upset and he had to tell her the right story to give himself some time. "Jackson was delayed. He wanted to be here and I didn't want—" He shook his head, knowing no reason made sense. "I'm sorry."

Ava jumped to her feet and glared at him. "That's it? That's all you have to say?"

"Jackson should be here any minute."

A cold smile touched her mouth. "Don't you wish."

James rubbed his fingers together. She looked mean and he liked it. "He will. My brother may come off shallow but family means a lot to him. This switch was just supposed to be for a couple hours."

"Why?"

He picked up his shirt from off the ground and dusted it off. He didn't remember tossing it there. It wasn't like him to throw things on the floor. "Cold feet, but it was nothing. I was filling in and—"

"What about last night?"

He put on his shirt, hiding a smile as he remembered Ava had been the one to put his shirt there. "What about last night?"

"Why did you switch then?"

James paused and chewed the inside of his cheek. He should be paying more attention to her. She was smart. He'd forgotten how smart she was. Somehow he'd blown his cover last night. "You knew," James said in a flat voice.

"Of course I knew."

"How? Was it the kiss?"

Ava rested a hand on her hip. "Why would I tell you that? You'd just make it harder for me to distinguish between you next time."

"There won't be a next time."

"You're right. How are you going to fix this? Our marriage isn't legal. You married me under a false name." She narrowed her eyes. "Or was that part of the plan?"

Yes. "No."

"Jackson and I had a marriage agreement. The deal was that I marry into the family. For *real*."

"No one needs to know."

"I'm so angry I'm ready to tell the world how humiliated I am. How two brothers used me like a toy. Were you *really* going to sleep with me as Jackson?"

He thought for a moment. "I-I...probably." Definitely yes.

Her mouth fell open and she stared at him for a moment, amazed. "Really?"

He shrugged and sat down on the bed. "You asked."

"And I thought you were different." She turned to the door.

James leaned back against the headboard and watched her. "Where are you going?"

"To tell your stepfather that the deal is off."

"No need to do that." He clasped his hands behind his head. "I have a new proposal for you."

She looked at him uncertain but curious. "What?"

"I'll accept my punishment. You can do whatever you want. Just wait six months."

She folded her arms. "Six months? Why six months?"

He hesitated then let his hands fall to his sides. "This day meant a lot to my mother. She wanted to see one of her sons married and I was able to make that happen. I can't see that taken away from her. I'll pay you whatever you want and after..." He hesitated, determined not to stumble over what he had to say, "after she's gone you can do what you want. Reveal everything." When he'd asked Ava if his mother could be part of the wedding preparations, he'd briefly told her about his mother's prognosis and current state of health.

Ava tilted her head to the side, studying him. "Six months you say?"

He nodded.

"That's not much of a proposal."

"Why not?"

She held up her forefinger. "Because you're forgetting one thing."

He leaned forward. "Enlighten me."

"What do I get out of this? After six months I'd still be a phony bride. I don't know if your brother will show up to even pretend that he's my husband, so why should I keep quiet?" She held up her hand before James could speak. "I'll tell you why, because I'll have what I wanted." She pointed at him. "Fortunately, you're taking me to Vegas."

He blinked, looking bored. "I am?"

"Yes, we're going to elope."

Ava reread Camy's initial text of Jackson's kidnapping with a smile as she sat in the plush first class airplane seat. She'd changed out of her wedding dress and wore a comfortable black pant suit with a grey colored blouse. Back to business as usual.

She remembered her friend's apprehension when she was able to slip away from the reception, into a quiet alcove to find out how her plan had worked. "Are you sure you have to go this far?" Camy asked her via video chat.

"My father depends on me. You know what the Fortunes did to him." It was also why her father was conspicuously absent. They'd decided that he couldn't attend the wedding and give her away because Edgar or Flo might remember him.

Camy's boyfriend, Tommy Park, stuck his head in the frame. "You've got to give me some love too, eh? It's not every day a Korean guy pretends to be a yakuza thug so convincingly."

Ava grinned, she'd always liked the man Camy had met in the theater department at the university. "Was he scared?"

"Tried not to show it."

She blew him a kiss. "Thank you."

"What if he goes to the police?" Camy asked.

"He's not going to report this," Ava said, certain. "I know Jackson, he'll do what I asked and you just confirmed it."

"I just think this may have gone a little too far."

"He made the move first, I'm just finishing the game."

"I hope your father will appreciate this."

I hope so too. "He will," she said used to defending her father against Camy's doubts. Camy thought Ava's father, Walter Hughes, could be overly critical and harsh, but Ava understood the reason why.

They had met through one of Ava's father's girlfriends, a distant relative of Camy. The girlfriend didn't last but a long standing friendship with Camy's family and her aunt, a Japanese woman who lived in the neighborhood and had a sort of finishing school for young Japanese adults, did. Every summer she and Camy would help entertain a group of students when she brought them to Vancouver.

Camy was more outgoing and friendly than Ava and was a successful makeup artist. Their friendship had managed to stay strong in spite of Ava's constant moving and her father's melancholy moods. Camy never seemed to be put off when Ava's father glowered in front of the TV and told them about how much the Fortunes had ruined his life.

Ava had grown up knowing that Edgar Fortune was a thief and a liar. He'd stolen her father's work, taking whatever joy he'd once had in life, and turned him into a bitter man. While her father's life crumbled, Edgar Fortune built a multi-million dollar business, leaving her father to struggle.

He'd told her how in the early days he had tried to use lawyers to get his fair share, but Edgar had defeated him before the case even went to court. No matter what battle he tried, Edgar always came out on top and untouched.

"You're the only way I can get back at him," he'd told her when she was seven. "When the law doesn't work, you've got to work outside of the law." And for the next twenty-four years he prepared her for this moment. For the moment he would finally get his revenge.

She now had the two brothers right where she wanted them. Jackson thought he was so smart, he should have known better. She wouldn't let the Fortune brothers get the best of her.

She glanced over at James as he sat looking out the airplane window. Her mind roiled with anger while her body still remembered his touch.

She still didn't know why she'd allowed her pretence to go that far. She told herself it didn't matter which brother she married. Either one would work to put her plan into action. But she knew marrying James was a gamble as bright as the lights of a Las Vegas casino. This was not what she had in mind, but it was the only option. She needed to return home with the guarantee and status that marriage into the Fortune family would give her.

Six and a half hours later she was officially his wife. They'd married in a simple and elegant wedding chapel she'd chosen. She found it embarrassing enough to have to go through an elopement with a man she hardly knew than to add insult to injury by having a gaudy décor and an Elvis impersonator, so she'd made sure to select the venue.

As she sat in the hotel room, which was decidedly, to her annoyance, even more impressive than the honeymoon suite in Kirkland, boasting floor to ceiling windows with a view of the Las Vegas Strip (she vaguely remembered James asking her on the plane whether she wanted to wake up to the sight of the strip or the mountains), and three flower vases—one on a side table in the entry way, another on the small dining table and one on the dresser. She still wondered why she was going through this.

It was a risk, but she felt that a contract would make it easier to control him. Now that she knew how deceitful he could be she couldn't be too cautious.

It was official now. The prenuptials signed (once they divorced after six months she'd be left with nothing, but she didn't care since she didn't expect to be around long), the license real. Now she could work on slowly destroying Edgar Fortune and taking control of BioMed Solutions.

Ava drummed her fingers on the dining table where she now sat, she heard James moving around in the washroom taking the shower he'd talked about before. She groaned. James. She'd married James. Unfortunately, James came with baggage that would complicate her mission a little. A dying mother and a brother with special needs, she could handle, but the fact that he lived in the family house was why she'd targeted Jackson instead. His mother wouldn't be around long enough to see the devastating impact of her plan and Rudy wouldn't understand enough to be personally hurt.

She planned to make sure he'd be provided for so she wouldn't feel too guilty about what needed to be done. The

Fortunes had lived charmed lives long enough. But living in the family house with Edgar? That was never her plan and soured her thoughts.

"It's not too late to get it annulled," James said behind her.

Ava looked up, a cutting remark on her lips, then stopped when she saw him. James stood over her wrapped only in a white towel from the waist down, his well made body still damp from the shower.

She jumped to her feet. "What are you doing?"

He paused. "Talking to you."

She gestured to his towel. "I mean what are you doing like this?"

He frowned.

"Wet and half naked," she clarified, wondering if he was being dense on purpose.

James narrowed his eyes. "I bet if you think *really* hard, you'd come up with the solution yourself."

Ava folded her arms. "I know you took a shower. What I mean is shouldn't you be dressed? Don't you feel...uncomfortable?"

He pulled out a chair and sat. "Why would I feel uncomfortable?"

She pointed at him. "You're trying to seduce me."

He shook his head with a slight smile. "No, I'm not. I felt dirty and wanted to get clean."

"Oh, so marrying me made you feel dirty?"

His smile disappeared, his eyes grew dark. "Don't put words in my mouth."

"I didn't force you to do this. Jackson did and I hope you're not expecting me to—"

James rested his elbow on the table, held his chin in his

hand and watched her. "You've never been seduced before, have you?"

"Of course I have," she said embarrassed he could guess she hadn't.

"Clearly by someone young, clumsy or both." His eyes captured hers, his silken tone deep with meaning. "When I seduce a woman she doesn't know it."

She believed him, that's what made her nervous. She swallowed hard determined not to show how much he affected her. She knew she would always have to be on guard with him.

"Ava, relax," he said. He freed her from his gaze by looking towards the window. "I know how you feel about me. Why do you think I reserved a room like this? I knew I would be sleeping on the couch." He returned his gaze to hers. "Feel better now?"

No. She felt too hot when he was fully clothed, now she felt like she'd jumped into an inferno. She glanced at his chest, her face burning as she remembered the feel of his hard nipple against her tongue. She shouldn't have done that. She'd hoped to frighten him a little, she'd frightened herself instead. She'd been stunned by how good it felt. "Do you sleep in the nude?"

James leaned back and casually crossed his legs. "Don't worry, I won't tonight."

Ava briefly closed her eyes not wanting to imagine him completely naked. She failed. "I mean do you normally?"

"Does it matter?"

"I need to understand your habits if we're going to live together."

"We may live in the same house, but we won't be sleeping together. Unless..." He lifted a questioning eyebrow.

"Absolutely not."

He shrugged nonchalant. "Then we'll have separate bedrooms."

"However, I still want to know if—"

"The answer is no. Do you?"

"No."

"Any more questions?"

"No."

He stared at her for a long moment then moved towards her, grabbed her by the shoulders and lifted her to her feet.

"What are you doing?" she asked as he moved over to the bed.

He forced her to sit down then stood in front of her. "Let's get a few things clear."

She smoothed down the bedspread with trembling fingers hoping he didn't notice. "I think you've made everything clear," she said in a steady tone.

"Not clear enough."

She glanced down unable to meet his gaze and noticed a droplet of water slide down his calf. "Go on."

"I'm sorry I scared you."

Her head snapped up. "What?"

He sighed. "I know I shouldn't have taken advantage of the situation in Kirkland."

"Situation?"

"The hotel."

"You call nearly sleeping with me while pretending to be your brother a 'situation'?"

"I'm trying to apologize and explain that I won't ever touch you again."

"That's not—"

He rubbed his chin, pensive. "No, that's wrong. I'll try, but you'll have to promise me not to do three things. One, don't kiss me on the mouth."

She stared at him outraged. "Why would I kiss you on the mouth?"

"Two," he continued, ignoring her question. "Don't grab my hand."

"If I—"

"And three. Don't pretend to like me. If you do, I will use it to my advantage." A glint of mischief entered his eyes. "That much I can promise you." Before she could reply he said, "Follow those rules and you're safe with me. So you can stop being jumpy."

Ava rubbed her hands together annoyed. "I haven't been jumpy."

James folded his arms and looked at her with pity.

She hated that look. She couldn't let him think she was afraid. She was the one in control now. No one told her what to do. She reached out and grabbed his hand then looked at him defiant. "I broke your rule, what will you do now?"

He pulled her roughly to him, his cold brown eyes bore into hers. She felt his wet chest dampening the front of her blouse. "Don't toy with me, Ava. I'm attracted to you, but that's not one of my weaknesses. You need me as much as I need you, but I can be scary when I want to be. I don't think you're ready for that yet." He released her.

She pulled her damp blouse from her chest, feeling hot and cold at the same time. "Was that a warning?"

"You're a smart woman stop asking dumb questions."

She didn't trust him. He could lie easily and it annoyed her that his words gave her a little thrill. The attraction was mutual, but then she remembered how he'd been able to keep her off-balance while pretending to be Jackson. He was a calculating man; he didn't say or do anything without a hidden agenda. Did it matter whether he was really attracted to her or not? She had to be careful not to underestimate him again. His attraction may not be a weakness, but if she was not careful it could be hers. "I'm still angry with you. Both of you."

James nodded. "Fair enough. But you can relax. For the next six months you'll be safe from me as long as you abide by my rules."

"Don't worry I'll follow your silly rules."

He sent her a long look. "Good and I'll do my best not to make you want to break them."

"That won't happen."

He only smiled then disappeared back inside the washroom.

CHAPTER 14

"This isn't what we agreed."

Ava closed her eyes at her father's biting tone on the other end of the phone. She'd received his call on her cell phone while James was in the washroom and quickly dashed out into the hall so that he wouldn't be able to overhear her. "I know, Dad, but I had to make a quick decision."

"Without consulting me. If you ruin all the years of planning I have put into this—"

"I won't. I know how important this is to you. Nothing will go wrong."

"It already has. You married the wrong brother."

"No, I can use this switch to our advantage. I now have the Fortunes exactly where I want them. This will not ruin our plans in the least, it will make it easier."

"How can it be easier with Edgar breathing down your neck? You'll be living in his house!"

Ava leaned against the wall. "I'm sure the house is large

enough that we'll rarely see each other, besides, isn't it good to get close to the enemy?"

He paused. "That is a good point."

Ava pushed herself from the wall with renewed confidence. "I'm glad you think so."

"But James still concerns me. Jackson had been our target for a reason."

"But James has more loyalty to his family than Jackson. Manipulating him will be a weapon we hadn't thought of."

"Another good point. Where are you now?"

"Still in Las Vegas. We'll be flying out early tomorrow morning and then let the fun begin."

"Be careful."

Ava smiled. "Always am."

CHAPTER 15

The housekeeper, Abigail Todd, a sturdy looking woman from Jamaica with braided black hair, stared at James and Ava in confusion when she met them in the large, angular foyer of the family house. "But why didn't you call first?" she asked, taking Ava's bags from James. "I don't understand. I thought...I thought...didn't Master Jackson get married yesterday?" She touched her chest a little embarrassed. "I admit I might have enjoyed myself a little too much at the reception."

"A change of plans," James said in no mood to elaborate. "Ava's my bride now."

Abigail's face fell in dismay. "I don't have a room made up yet and have you eaten? I have to consult with the chef—"

"Don't worry," Ava said, sensing the woman's discomfort, although James didn't seem to mind, "I'm sure any room will do and I can eat anything."

Abigail looked at James sending him a silent question. He nodded in response. "Yes, you can use that room."

She smiled then nodded and took Ava's bags.

"That sounded mysterious," Ava said, following him down the hallway. "Is it a locked room?"

"It was. Clearly it won't be anymore."

"What was in there?"

He walked into the great room, a high ceiling structure that seamlessly combined the features of a traditional living and family room, and gestured to a large couch. "Would you like anything to drink?"

"No, but a tour of the house would be nice."

"Yes, I'm sure the housekeeper will show you around later. I have some work to do. I'll see you at dinner."

"But it's barely past noon."

"Let's just say I want to make myself scarce before—"

"Do you mind telling me what the hell is going on?" a voice bellowed.

James briefly shut his eyes. "But that's not going to happen," he said with a sigh. He spun around and faced his stepfather. "Let me just—"

Edgar pointed at him. "Who are you?"

James gestured to his subdued blue shirt and light grey trousers, which was in direct contrast to what his brother would wear, and said incredulous, "You can't be serious."

Edgar frowned and his tone hardened. "I'm very serious."

"I'm James."

"Where's Jackson?"

He shrugged.

Edgar looked at Ava who also shrugged.

"Why are you coming home with James when you just married Jackson yesterday?" he demanded.

Ava twisted the ring on her finger. "Actually I didn't really marry Jackson."

"What do you mean?" Edgar said, his voice rising. "We all saw you."

James cleared his throat. "Actually that was me."

Edgar fell down into a chair. "This doesn't make any sense."

"All you need to know is that Ava is now married to me."

"How?"

"We eloped."

"In Las Vegas," Ava explained.

Edgar frowned and narrowed his eyes. "Are you sure you're James? This isn't a joke?"

James nodded.

"It just doesn't sound like something James would do," he muttered to himself.

"It's all my fault," Ava said, taking James's hand. But when he gave her a low growl of warning, reminding her that she was breaking one of his rules, she quickly switched and looped her arm through his. "It happened suddenly. I told Jackson how I really felt and he helped me capture the one I wanted." She looked up at James with feigned adoration.

Edgar's keen gaze darted between them. "I see."

"I'm legally a Fortune and there's nothing to worry the stockholders and interfere with our business plans. Actually, I have a few things I want to discuss with you tomorrow."

Concern swiftly left Edgar's face. The mention of business always put him in high spirits. "Good." He stood appearing more relaxed. "I'm still confused, but as long as things are still going in the right direction I suppose it doesn't matter." He shook her hand. "Welcome to the family...again."

She smiled. "Thank you."

He left.

Ava looked up at James with a smug expression. "How did I do?"

"You almost had me fooled," James said impressed. He looked around. "Now let me see if I can escape before—"

"James, Ava, what a surprise!"

They turned and saw Flo with her arms outstretched in greeting. "Abigail just told me."

James hugged her and placed a kiss on the cheek. "It's good to see you, but I have to—"

"I knew you were up to something since the night before last." She took a seat and patted one of the cushions. "Sit down and tell me everything."

James reluctantly did, sending Ava a look that she could release his arm, but she ignored him, so they ended up sitting side by side on the loveseat. "There's not much to say."

Flo frowned in disappointment.

"I have plenty to say," Ava said.

Flo smiled, eagerly leaning forward. "I knew you would."

"The truth is, although I'd agreed to marry Jackson, I secretly fell for James. At the last minute we realized we couldn't pretend how we felt about each other so we had James and Jackson switch places."

Flo furrowed her brows. "But why did you go through the ceremony? You could have announced the change."

"Yes, I could have," James said, turning to Ava to see how she'd lie her way out of it.

"We didn't want to disappoint you," she said smoothly. "We weren't sure how you'd feel about us. So we did it for show."

James nodded. "Knowing that the marriage wouldn't be valid..."

"Allowing us to legally elope," Ava added.

"Which we did."

Flo covered her eyes.

"Mom," James said worried.

She looked at him with tears. "You're even finishing each other's sentences. I'm so happy I can't put how I feel into words." She wiped away tears. "I got to see a love match. I was so worried that Jackson was making a mistake."

James stiffened. "But you never said so. You said you wanted to see us married before..." He let his words fade away.

"I wanted to see you happy. That matters more to me than anything."

James briefly closed his eyes feeling a little sick. "But if Jackson had cancelled the wedding you would have been devastated, right?"

"I would have been disappointed, but I would have understood." She motioned to them. "Instead I got this. This is better than I could have imagined. I knew it was you standing up there. It wasn't my imagination."

"No," Ava said with a light laugh, nudging James to remove his frown and pretend to be happy.

He plastered on a smile.

Flo sat back with a happy sigh. "Thank you for loving my son. I was so worried he'd never find someone who would truly understand him."

"Yes, well..."

"You'll have to tell me more about this secret romance between you two."

"Yes."

"Later," James said. "I have things to do. As you know the housekeeper is getting Ava's room ready so—"

Flo frowned. "Separate bedrooms already?"

"Just for convenience. You know I work a crazy schedule."

"You don't have to pretend on account of us."

"I snore," Ava said.

"Make him too tired to care."

"Mom," James said embarrassed.

She stood up and winked. "You didn't invent sex, you know."

ABIGAIL LOOKED at Ava anxiously as Ava looked over the futuristic décor of her new bedroom, which was down the hall from James's. "It's a bit unusual, but it's one of the best rooms in the house," she said.

"It's beautiful," Ava said, although she wasn't sure that was the word to use. "If I need anything I'll let you know." Abigail nodded and left. Ava walked further into the bedroom not sure what to make of it. It was like something she'd never seen before—both beautiful and strange. The room was completely white with a touch of red accents in the pillows and curved lamp. The bed's glass backrest had a crocheted backdrop that cascaded from the ceiling like a white waterfall adding beauty and calm, the wispy bed seemed weightless as it floated near a large window. Angel soft fabric covered the bed as if the room was supposed to be a heavenly paradise.

Ava turned when someone knocked on the door. "Come in."

"Suitable?" James asked, coming into the room.

"Yes, who used to stay here?"

"Edgar's first wife."

Ava widened her eyes. "He was married before?"

James nodded. "No one knew about her. He kept her locked up in this room for years. One day she disappeared. I'm hoping the same fate won't happen to you." He shoved his hands in his pockets. "We Fortune men have our secrets."

She sent him a baleful look. "You have a very imaginative mind for an engineer."

His mouth kicked up in a grin. "I had you worried there for a minute."

"Not even."

"A couple seconds then." He sat on the side of the bed.

"But what was the room before?"

"You're really curious?"

"Yes."

"Ask the housekeeper."

"Stop calling her 'the housekeeper'. Her name is Abigail."

"Is it?" he said with little interest.

"You should at least know the name of your staff."

"Really?"

Ava opened her mouth to respond then stopped when he sent her a look and she realized her was teasing her. He had a playful side she hadn't expected.

"Why won't you just tell me?" she said.

"You won't believe me."

"Yes, I will."

"It's a guest room."

Ava shook her head. "No, it's not."

"See? I told you you wouldn't believe me."

Ava gestured to the hallway. "She—"

"Who?"

"Abigail."

He frowned. "Who?"

"The housekeeper, the one—" Ava paused when she realized he was teasing her again. "She wouldn't have given you that secret look if it was just a guest room."

"It's not just a guest room. It's a special guest room."

"Special?"

"Yes, when I want to entertain."

"I don't understand."

"That's okay." He stood. "See you later."

Unable to hide her curiosity, Ava promptly searched and found Abigail in the chef sized kitchen. "What's the story behind my room?"

"Story?"

"Yes, why is James being mysterious about it?"

"I wouldn't know. Is there something wrong with it?"

"No, thank you," she said not wanting to stress the poor woman more than she needed to. She'd figure out the true history of her bedroom eventually.

She'd been left alone the remainder of the day, getting a tour of the house and meeting the staff before changing for dinner, choosing a simple blue satin dress, although James had assured her they weren't that formal.

"What am I supposed to tell her about our secret romance?" Ava asked as she and James headed down the curved staircase to the dining room for dinner.

"I don't know what you can say about our secret romance," James said. "You're the one who came up with the idea."

"You're the one who wanted to have a wedding she didn't even really need."

"She needed something," James countered, unperturbed. "You saw how happy she is about this."

"The only one."

"Relax, six months won't be that long."

"And what if she stays so happy that she lives longer than six months?"

James sent her a sharp look and Ava felt her breath catch as she realized how cruel she sounded. "I didn't mean it like that. I meant—"

He stopped at the bottom of the stairs. "You don't have to worry. She's really dying. There won't be any miraculous cure so you'll be free in six months."

She felt wretched. She didn't like the Fortunes, but she'd gone too far. "James, listen I didn't—"

He continued down the hall. "Let's not keep them waiting."

Ava softly swore and followed him. She didn't mean to sound so callous. She liked Flo, she'd gotten to know her more working on the wedding preparations, and was a little sad that she was ill, but she had bigger things to think about.

James's love for his mother bothered her. She didn't want to care. The Fortunes had never cared about anyone. Did they care about building their wealth by stealing from others? They were users and James was only using her to please his mother. It was only fair that she'd use him in return.

CHAPTER 16

"And that's when we knew."

Flo clasped her hands together with a happy sigh at the end of Ava's tale. "What a wonderful love story." She looked at Edgar. "Don't you think?"

He sipped his wine. "Almost sounds unbelievable."

Flo dismissed him with a wave of her hand. "He's not a romantic."

"Wonder when we'll see Jackson."

"He's probably out somewhere celebrating his freedom," James said.

"I wouldn't say that." A familiar voice said from the entryway.

Flo turned with delight. "Jackson!"

Ava stared at him. He was back earlier than expected. He had reneged on his promise to stay away for two full days. She'd hoped to have a meal with his parents without him present.

Jackson entered the room pointedly ignoring her as if the scent of the coconut rice and spiced grilled chicken set on the table had captured his attention. "Have I missed anything interesting?"

"Ava and James were just filling us in on how they fell in love," Flo said.

Jackson took a seat across from Ava as Abigail quickly set a place for him at the table. "I'd love to hear it sometime."

Flo frowned. "But I thought you already heard it since you agreed to this charade."

"Right," Jackson said quickly. "I meant I'd love to hear it again. Ava's good with stories."

"I was right," Rudy said with pride. "I knew I was right. It wasn't you up there next to her."

Jackson patted his brother affectionately on the head. "Yes, buddy."

"So where did you disappear to?" Edgar asked.

Jackson fixed Ava with a look. "You wouldn't believe me if I told you."

"Bet it included a woman," Edgar said.

Jackson nodded, filling his plate. "Oh yes. A dangerous woman. I just don't know how to pick them."

Flo nodded in agreement. "Perhaps your brother could give you some tips."

He sent his brother a secret look. "I'm all ears."

"ALL SETTLED IN?" Jackson asked Ava as they and James sat in the great room after dinner.

"Yes."

"Where did you put her?"

"I'm in the bedroom down the hall from him," Ava said not wanting to be spoken of as if she wasn't there.

Jackson looked at his brother and started to laugh. "Really?"

James nodded.

Ava looked at them confused. "What's so funny?"

"Nothing," James said, but Jackson couldn't remove his grin.

"Tell me about that room," she asked him.

Jackson looked at James. "Can I?"

He shrugged.

"She may get upset."

"She's already upset."

Ava scowled. "Don't talk about me as if I'm not here."

James pointed at her. "See?"

"It's his other room," Jackson said.

"Other room?"

"Yes, it's the room he used to say was his when he invited someone over, because he doesn't like anyone in his real room."

Ava looked at James. "So you lied to your girlfriends?"

He thought for a moment. "I wouldn't call it lying. It is my bedroom, just not the main one."

Jackson smiled. "And now it's yours."

Ava wanted to say something to remove Jackson's smug expression, but Flo came into the room and stopped her.

"Ava? May I see you for a minute?" she said.

She hesitated sending the brothers a considering glance.

Jackson's smile grew. "Scared we'll talk about you? Don't be. You can bet on it."

She narrowed her eyes. "Then you shouldn't be scared of what I will say to your mother."

Ava stood in triumph when she saw his smile disappear.

CHAPTER 17

"What happened?" James asked the moment Ava was out of the room.

Jackson sighed, wishing he could tell his brother the truth. "I got into trouble with a guy I owe some money to."

"For *hours?*"

"You're lucky I'm still in one piece."

James expression changed to concern. "Do I need to do something about him? Do you need money?"

"No, it's fine. That's why I sent you the text. I'm sorry."

"That's all you've been saying lately."

"I'll make it up to you somehow. I promise."

"At least Mom's happy. Ava agreed to this charade for at least six months."

Jackson leaned back and grimaced. Six months! "That's something."

"Did Sylvia get in contact with you?"

He sat up. "Why?"

"She let me know, thinking I was you, that she's looking

into Ava."

Jackson pulled out his cell phone. "I haven't gotten any messages."

"What did you expect to find?"

"Not sure, just guard your accounts."

"We signed a prenup and there will be one joint account. Everything else will remain separate."

"Good," Jackson said through tight teeth.

"You sound like you don't like her."

"I don't."

James sent his brother a searching look. "You did before. A lot. Why the sudden change of heart? I thought it was just cold feet."

He glanced up then lowered his voice. "I did too until—"

"Your mother is so sweet," Ava said, coming back into the room and taking her seat next to James. "She just wanted to make sure that I felt welcome." She looked at them. "Did I interrupt anything?"

"Yes," Jackson said.

"No," James said.

Ava nodded. "I guess I'll believe my husband."

Jackson shot her a look. "We'll see how long that lasts."

"Jackson was just filling me in on what happened after the wedding," James said, trying to ease the tension between them.

Ava lifted a brow. "How interesting. Tell me about it."

"Bookie troubles," Jackson said.

"Gambling is a vice. You should be careful."

"I plan to be. You should too."

"I don't gamble."

Jackson grinned. "I wouldn't say that."

James cleared his throat. "What am I missing?"

"Nothing."

"We're family now," Ava said. "Let's be cordial."

"We're alone. Let's not pretend that any of this is real."

"We still have to be careful," James said. "The walls have ears." He stood. "I'm heading to bed."

Ava waited for James to leave, checking the hallway to make sure no one could overhear them, before she turned and glared at Jackson. "You're not supposed to be back yet."

"I gave you enough time."

"What are you trying to do?"

He looked bored. "Nothing."

"You're making your brother suspicious."

He shrugged. "Can't help it. He knows me. We don't keep secrets from each other."

"You will this time."

"He will find out the truth eventually."

"But not yet."

"Don't worry, you're still in control...for now."

"Pull another stunt like that and I'll make my threats real. You should have seen your mother's face when I told her how much I loved her son. But if you want, I can just as easily tell her the truth." She leaned forward and lowered her voice. "You're going to be nice to me the next time we meet my dear brother-in-law." She stood and left.

Jackson watched her go, resisting the urge to trip her. He secretly hoped she'd have a tumble down the stairs or have an accident in the kitchen. He had to get rid of her some way. He'd been played. They'd all been played, his stepfather the most, and there was nothing he could do about it. Yet.

But a lot could happen in six months and he wouldn't squander a minute. He wouldn't let her win without a fight.

A shadow went past her window. She wasn't one to believe in spirits or ghosts but her bedroom had an eerie feeling at night.

She heard something shuffle in her closet.

"Who's there?" she called out then noticed that the light in the closet was on.

She was sure she'd turned it off. She crept over to it and went inside to see if something had fallen. The closet door closed behind her. She spun around and tried to open the door, but it was fastened shut. How had she managed to get locked in? She banged on the door then screamed.

Moments later it swung open and James stood there wearing grey cotton pajamas. "What's going on?"

She dashed out of the closet and looked around the room. "I couldn't get out. Someone locked me in."

"I didn't see anything," Jackson said, coming into the room dressed in a green and black stripped robe, "and it locks from the inside."

Ava looked at him surprised; he should have left and gone to his apartment by now. "What are you still doing here?"

"It's called a family house for a reason."

Ava turned back to James. "I didn't make it up. Someone locked me in."

"Why would someone do that?" James asked.

"To scare me."

"There's no reason to scare you."

"Who would want to do that?" Jackson asked.

"Sure you don't know?" she challenged him.

James frowned. "Why would he want to lock you in a closet?"

Jackson shoved his hands in the pockets of his robe with a smug grinned. "Yes, why would I want to do that?"

Ava glared at him, knowing she couldn't share his motive without revealing what she'd done to him. It was a petty revenge, but it worked. "Never mind."

"Perhaps it was a nightmare," Jackson said. "I can relate. I feel like I'm living one right now."

"Go back to bed," James said to him. "I'll stay with her."

"No," Ava said quickly. "That's okay. I'll be fine."

"I'll stay until you fall asleep." James sent his brother a look. Jackson nodded then left.

"It's embarrassing enough," Ava said when Jackson closed the door behind him. "You don't have to do this. At least I didn't wake up anyone else."

"Hmm." James sat on the edge of the bed, like a looming dark presence in the bright white room. He looked up at her, thoughtful. "You and Jackson know something that I don't. What is it?"

Ava rubbed her arms, feeling suddenly bare in her pale blue cotton nightgown. "Nothing."

"I know Jackson locked you in the closet. He did it to me once when we were kids."

"Why?"

He measured her with a cool look. "I made him mad."

Ava shook her head. "You don't have to stay. He can try to get rid of me but it won't work."

"Why would he want to get rid of you?" James asked in a soft voice.

She'd said too much. Damn Jackson and damn James for being so observant. She searched her mind for the perfect lie. "Before I knew you'd switched places, at the rehersal dinner I may have said something that I shouldn't have. I thought he was you after all and..." Her words trailed off.

James nodded encouraging her to continue. "And what did you say?"

"I..." She chewed her lip, hoping to look properly contrite. "I said James—you—dressed better than him. That he had the flair but you had the taste. I'd hoped you'd talk to him and convince him to tone it down a little. It's not my fault that he was really Jackson."

James nodded and Ava felt her tension easing as she watched him swallow her lie. "That would do it. His style means a lot to him."

"Yes."

"You're lucky I convinced him not to wear the red suit he really wanted to wear to the wedding."

"Red?"

"He called it crushed mauve or something, but it just looked like red to me."

Ava sat on the single reading chair that faced the bed. "That would have been ridiculous."

"It would have matched your dress."

"My dress?"

"Yes." James nodded with a faint smile. "He initially had ideas about that too. Mom persuaded him otherwise. He likes to put on a show."

"That's true."

"But it's his style that first caught your eye, right?"

Ava felt her tension return. Was James questioning her motives? She had to be careful not to criticize Jackson too much; she had planned to marry him after all. "What?"

"On the cruise. I noticed you watching him."

She blinked trying to remember. Edgar had invited her on a night cruise and she'd met Jackson for the second time, as she'd planned. But she didn't remember James. "You were there?"

He nodded.

"No, you weren't. I would have noticed you."

"Really?"

"I would have remembered if there had been two of you."

"But you didn't."

She frowned. "How could I have missed you?"

"Think back to the balcony. Did you notice anything about that moment that was strange?"

Ava let her mind drift back to the time on the cruise. She'd spent time flattering Edgar and was heady with a chance to meet his stepson again. She took a break to get away and enjoy the sea air, the breeze toying with the hem of her silk blue dress. She'd been surprised to see Jackson alone on the deck.

"How did you get up here so fast?" she asked him.

He turned to her surprised and opened his mouth, but she waved his words away. "Never mind. I don't care. It's nice to see you out of that jacket. What are you trying to be, eh? A disco ball?" She held up her hand again. "That was a rhetorical question. I know you're into fashion more than I am."

She was about to say something else, but he suddenly grabbed her and pulled her to the side just as a young man reached the railing and lost his dinner over the side.

"I guess someone had too much to drink," Ava said, wondering why she suddenly felt nervous. There was something different about Jackson, steadier, more in control. His arm around her shoulder made her body warm in a way it never had been before.

"We should get back before we're missed."

"You go first," he said.

She remembered returning to the lower deck and seeing Jackson in the hall. "Did you run here?" she asked him amazed.

"What are you talking about? I've been looking for you."

She looked up towards the stairs. "Why were you looking for me when we were just—"

"I have someone I want you to meet," he interrupted and then she forgot her confusion and pushed the incident from her mind. Now she understood as she looked at James. "That was you."

"Yes."

"Why didn't you say anything?"

"You didn't give me a chance, for one."

"For one? What's the other reason?"

He shrugged, his heated gaze holding her still. "At that moment I wanted to be him."

She folded her arms and looked away not trusting herself not to fall prey to his invitation. "You should probably go back to your room. I'm fine now."

"You haven't broken my rules yet so you're still safe."

"I don't feel safe."

He stood. "I'm a man of my word."

Ava also rose to her feet, not sure what he would do next. She wanted to be prepared. "When you're not lying."

He smiled and patted the bed. "Go to bed."

She scuttled past him and got under the covers. But the extra sheets didn't make her feel any less vulnerable. "You don't have to stay."

He took her seat in the reading chair. "I'll leave in a minute."

She closed her eyes, pretending to sleep, but when she lifted her head moments later, the chair was empty. She hadn't heard him leave.

For two weeks Ava studied the Fortune family, learning their habits and routines. Her days at BioMed Solutions didn't take up much attention, since her tasks were easily managed and she'd studied the entity for years, but understanding the family dynamics at home had become a new part of her plan. To her relief, Jackson stayed at his apartment. She sensed James had a hand in convincing him to leave after the closet incident, but she would never ask him.

Rudy was the easiest to keep track of. His routine was the most unchanged. A week ago he'd returned from an adult resort camp with lots of stories and presently worked hard on his business. He wanted to take the bus (for some reason he found buses fascinating), but his family provided him with a driver.

His craft business was created out of necessity and was the only opportunity for employment. Although he had achieved a university degree in History and had strong computer skills, no company would hire him for even the most basic tasks. Edgar had briefly created a position for him at BioMed Solutions, but Rudy had felt stressed and unhappy. In response, his family encouraged him to create his own business. At first he ran it online from home until he expanded to a boutique in town, which he shared with two other artists.

For the past five days he'd been moody and more aggressive than he'd been before. Because Ava had been studying everyone so closely she noticed his behavioral change first.

At dinner she noticed he wasn't eating, which was strange because food was one of his loves. His family worked hard to manage his weight knowing that obesity and diabetes were high in people with Down syndrome.

The following day, after Ava had returned from a meeting with Edgar at headquarters, she found Flo talking to Rudy in the great room. "Come work with me in the garden," Flo said to him. She had a vegetable garden on the vast property out back that she and Rudy liked to tend.

"No,"

She reached for his hand. "Just for a little while. You know I like your help."

"No," he said with more force, pushing her away. She lost her balance and fell.

Edgar pushed past Ava and rushed over to them. "What is wrong with you?"

"Honey, it's all right," Flo said quickly, taking his hand.

"Your mother is sick and this is how you treat her?" Edgar chided him. "I thought you were a grown man. That's not how a grown man behaves."

Rudy gripped his hands into fists and stared at the ground.

"Apologize."

"I'm sorry."

"Now go to your room."

He bit his lip and stomped away.

"He's usually not like this," Flo said a little embarassed when she noticed Ava watching them. She took a seat looking worn. "But he can get into moods sometimes."

"Do you think something's wrong?" Ava asked.

"What could be wrong?" Edgar said. "He's got everything he needs and his business is doing great."

"Maybe it's me," Ava said. "Maybe having me in the house has upset his schedule."

"No, that's not it. We've had family guests before and he's fine, plus you haven't changed anything here."

"He just needs to have some time alone to calm down," Edgar said.

But Ava wasn't so sure and at dinner that evening when Rudy continued to let his food go cold without touching it, her concerns grew.

"Eat your food," Edgar said.

Rudy continued to stare at it.

"Are you feeling sick?" Flo asked.

He shook his head.

"Hey kiddo," James said.

Rudy looked at him.

"Just a couple of bites." He nodded to Rudy's plate trying to coax him with a smile from across the table.

Rudy didn't move.

"You know how I feel about wasted food," Edgar snapped. "Eat or you don't go to the next resort camp in the summer."

Rudy stared at him with wide eyes. "But I have to go. I have to."

"Then eat your food."

"We're going to Mexico and I've never been there before. You said I could go."

"Stop acting this way and behave."

Rudy took a bite of his sautéed carrots then pounded both fists on the table over and over again, rattling the dishes and shocking everyone.

James jumped up and raced over to him. "Rudy, it's okay."

He continued pounding, causing his glass to tip over and stain the tablecloth with purple grape juice.

James wrapped an arm around his brother and lifted him out of the seat. "Come on, let's go."

He screamed, but didn't fight him, tears streaming down his cheeks.

James led him out of the room.

"No," Edgar said when Flo stood to follow them, her face creased with worry. "He'll be okay."

She sank back into her seat.

Edgar cut his carrots. "I told you that we didn't need the tablecloth."

"I thought it was a nice touch," Flo said. "We usually don't but," Flo said to Ava by way of explanation. "I thought it would be nice for you."

"I don't want you to go through any trouble. I've been here long enough that you don't have to do anything special."

"See?" Edgar said. "It was a waste."

Flo's face fell.

"It wasn't a waste," Ava countered, annoyed by his cutting tone. "It was a nice gesture."

Edgar sniffed. "I'm glad you think so. Our dinners are not always so eventful."

"I've been around long enough to know how things are." She turned her attention back to Flo. "You don't have to worry. I'm not going anywhere."

"Sometimes people get frightened," Flo said, smoothing out the napkin on her lap. "But he's harmless. He wouldn't harm anyone and—"

"Stop making excuses for him," Edgar cut in. "Or apologizing. Ava knew the kind of family she was marrying into."

"I like Rudy," Ava said.

James returned to the table. Flo looked at him anxious. He offered her a smile. "He's okay now."

James wouldn't elaborate even when they were briefly alone after dinner and Ava asked him for more details. For the past few weeks they'd lived separate lives and James made no move to change that, so she went to Rudy's room on her own to find some answers. In the Fortune family, Rudy was a true innocent and she was worried about him.

She stood in front of Rudy's bedroom and lifted her hand to knock then stopped herself. *This really is none of my business. No matter how much I like him, if the family isn't worried, why should I be? James said everything was okay.*

She began to turn away, but the sound of crying caused her to pause. She turned back to the door and knocked. The crying stopped but he didn't respond. She slowly opened the door and saw him in a corner, curled up on the ground.

"Are you okay?" she asked gently, knowing it was a silly question. He clearly wasn't. He looked miserable. She walked over to him.

"I want to go to Mexico," he said.

She sat down beside him. "I'm sure you will."

"But Dad said I can't because I didn't eat and I wanted to, but I don't want to."

"Why not?"

He shrugged.

"None of us like to see you so unhappy."

"Me too," he said and Ava paused when she noticed that his breath had a slight odor it shouldn't have.

"Could you open your mouth for me?" she asked.

He did.

"A little wider?"

He did and winced.

"When's the last time you went to the dentist?"

He shrugged.

She touched the side of his neck. "I don't want you to cry. You're going to get to go to Mexico with your friends and have a good time."

He looked at her with hope. "Really?"

She nodded and patted his hand. "Trust me." She left his room and gasped when she saw James standing there.

"What are you doing?" he asked in a cool tone.

"I was talking to Rudy."

"This is a personal family matter."

"Right, and I'm family."

"I overheard what you told him." James folded his arms, his eyes hard and filled with warning. "Don't make promises you can't keep. Life is hard enough for him."

Ava fought to keep her composure under his penetrating gaze. "I know that and I think I know how to help him. I was going to talk to your parents right now." She turned.

James grabbed her wrist and spun her back to him. "You can tell me first. I don't want you upsetting my mother either."

"She needs to hear this. I have an idea." Ava sent a pointed look at his hand on her wrist. Do you mind?"

He released her and said in a low voice, "Your idea had better be a good one."

"A dentist?" Edgar said, doubtful.

"I'm not a doctor," Ava said as she sat across from him in the library. Flo sat quietly beside him and James stood by the wall. "But I think there might be something wrong with his mouth. That's why he's not eating and being miserable. I also detected some swelling under his jaw."

"We have to schedule him right away," Flo said, her voice anxious.

Edgar frowned. "There's no need to panic."

"I could be wrong," Ava said.

Flo took out her cell phone and checked her calendar. "For his sake, I hope you're not."

The dentist discovered Rudy had a major abscess that needed to be expressed. Once it was taken care of Rudy was back to his old cheerful self giving Ava a big hug when he returned home from the procedure and found her waiting to greet him in the foyer. "I get to go to Mexico like you promised, Dad said I could."

"I'm glad," Ava said with a smile.

"And I want you to have this." He pulled a sterling silver necklace with an amethyst pendant from his pocket.

"Oh, it's beautiful."

"I know. I made it. Let me put it on you," he said, unclasping the latch.

"But it's too pretty to wear now," Ava said, looking down at the unflattering pant suit she wore.

"You can wear it with anything." He draped it around her neck.

"Are you trying to make moves on my woman?" James said, coming down the stairs.

Rudy giggled pleased.

"It's the nicest gift I've ever gotten," Ava said.

Rudy gave her another hug, kissed her on the cheek and said, "I love you," before heading to his room.

"Thanks," James said.

"I wasn't pretending," Ava said, staring down at the necklace. "I really do like the gift. No wonder your brother's business is so successful. Just wait until Camy sees this."

James shook his head. "Not about that, about what you did for him."

"It was nothing," Ava said suddenly feeling shy.

"No, it wasn't. He's not articulate and sometimes things like this get missed. It could have been worse." He paused. "I'm sorry I doubted you." He looked at her for a long, powerful moment, desire clear in his gaze. She felt it too, a longing to touch and taste him again, wondering how she could close the gulf that had come between them. But she knew that keeping him at a distance was the only way to keep her traitorous heart safe. She could care for Flo, even for Rudy, but caring for James could destroy her.

As Ava had predicted, when she sent a photo of her necklace to Camy, her friend wanted one of her own and promptly went to Rudy's website and ordered two, as did a number of her friends until the design was sold out.

To Rudy's delight, that Saturday, Ava came and visited his boutique, which was located on a side street lined with other high end specialty stores. He showed her around the exquisitely decorated bright room and shared some of his other ideas.

She treated him to lunch, remembering Flo's warning that he wasn't allowed to overindulge, then after returning him to the boutique, left him to go run some errands.

She was halfway to her car when she saw Edgar across the street, standing near his black Mercedes in front of a nondescript building. At first she thought he was coming to pick Rudy up, since there were no stores in the vicinity that would interest him, then she noticed a woman in a flowing yellow dress step out of the passenger side of his car. The woman was probably a decade younger than Flo with light skin and medium length brown hair.

Ava scrambled to get her cell phone from her handbag and took a picture as he and the woman hugged in a manner that was far from professional. Such evidence would come in useful eventually. Her heart turned cold as she watched the pair disappear into one of the stores.

She looked down at the photo of them embracing. This was the reminder she needed. This was why she was here and why she needed to focus solely on her task. Edgar was a true bastard. He had a woman on the side while he had a dying wife at home. Ava put her cell phone away, her heart breaking for Flo. She couldn't be swayed by his care for Rudy or the image he liked to portray to the world. This was the real him. He deserved to go down.

"You're still acting like a single man," Flo said as she placed a basket of lettuce, okra and red bell peppers she'd picked from her garden, on one of the two islands in the large kitchen. The smell of the spring day seemed to follow her with the scent of sunshine and fresh soil.

James looked up from his position at the kitchen table where he'd been reviewing the data of one of his projects. "What?"

"Ava doesn't seem to be comfortable here and I rarely see you two together. After what she did for Rudy she should feel like she's part of the family now, but you two act like strangers. You live different lives."

"You know we married for business reasons. Edgar's happy that—"

"I thought you married for love."

James paused; he'd briefly forgotten *that* part of the story.

"She knows I love her," he said pleased he didn't stumble over the words. "She's fine."

Flo took a seat in front of him. "Have you asked her?"

He sighed. "Mom, trust me. We're happy."

"That's how marriages fail. It's because the man is clueless. Show her some affection. Your brother Rudy is more affection than you are."

"He always has been."

"It wouldn't hurt to show a little tenderness once in a while."

"I do...you just don't see it."

"Hmm," Flo said, but she continued to worry that her son was neglecting his new wife. It had been nearly a month and she sensed something was amiss between them. Perhaps they'd had a martial spat early on and neither one wanted to address it. She knew she had to do something before it got out of hand.

She found Ava reading in her bedroom. Her new daughter-in-law was almost always there only coming out to be with the family at dinner. She never ventured to the back patio or even the library, which Flo thought would be much more comfortable. She knew Ava had grown up as an only child, but found it strange that she didn't feel comfortable using any other rooms in the large house.

"May I talk to you?" she asked.

Ava set her book aside. "Sure."

Flo hesitated then sat on the bed. "I'm sorry James put you in here."

"I like it."

"Really?" Flo shivered a little. "I find it so cold. Distant."

"I like the minimalistic lines and lack of color."

Flo laughed, pleased. "I guess that's why you fell for him."

Ava frowned not understanding her response. "What?"

"James." She gestured to the room. "This was one of his projects."

"Yes," Ava said in a grim tone. "His special guest room. I'm surprised he told you about it."

Flo sent her an odd look. "Why wouldn't he?" Before Ava could respond, she grinned, "Have you tried the bed out yet?"

"The bed? Of course. I've been sleeping on it."

"No, I mean really tried it out. Didn't he tell you that he had this room designed for me?"

"No," Ava said, drawing out the word. "He lied and said..." She shook her head. "Never mind."

"He didn't tell you the truth?" Flo said surprised.

Ava shook her head.

She sighed with regret. "It's probably because I hurt his feelings. I didn't mean to."

"I don't understand."

"After my diagnosis James had this room redesigned for me hoping for a calm sanctuary that would help me heal. He made the bed appear weightless so that I could feel as if I were floating and the view from the window changes with controls and the bed..." She shook her head.

Ava leaned forward curious. "What about the bed?"

"It actually frightened me."

"Why?"

"It's attached to a mobile device and embedded with software that knew too much about me. When you lay down it is programmed to adjust to your body temperature, read your heartbeat, adjust to the curve of your body, it even comes with a virtual reality headset. Want to try it?"

"Okay," Ava said uncertain.

Flo pushed the side of the bed frame, opening a hidden

drawer. She pulled out the headset and gave it to Ava. "You wouldn't believe how long it took me to figure this out." She watched Ava put on the headset then said, "Are you ready?"

"Yes," Ava said. Seconds later a hillside landscape, lush with greenery, seemed to surround her. "Oh, it's lovely." She looked around at the clear sky feeling as if she could touch the green grass beneath her feet, then a dark shadow rose from behind one of the hills. As it raced closer, she felt the ground beneath her feet move and soon the shadow gained form. It became a large monster with black fur, seven eyes and razor sharp teeth inside a black foaming mouth. Its eyes pinpointed her as if ready to eat her alive. "What am I supposed to do?"

"Grab the sword."

"There's a sword?" Ava asked, frantically searching for it until she found it down by her side. She struggled to pull it from its sheath as the creature continued to come closer "Why didn't you tell me before?"

"It's been a while. I forgot."

She held out the sword. But it seemed like a twig in comparison to the monster, but she still used it to try to slice the monster before it got any closer. "It's not scared," she said noticing that the monster's pace hadn't slowed.

"You have to kill it. Quickly."

Ava reached out and tried to battle the monster, but it jumped on her and opened its large dark mouth, salvia dripping down as it prepared to sink its teeth into her neck. She screamed and tore off the headset. She stared at Flo her heart racing. "What was that awful thing?"

"The cancer. James worked with a friend to develop a game to help patients find an outlet to fight their diseases. Unfortunately, his monster is too real."

"Perhaps for true gamers it would be better." Ava wiped sweat from her forehead. "It's not too bad if I'd been more prepared."

"It was scary."

"Terrifying," Ava admitted, handing Flo the headset. "But still impressive. Perhaps if he changed the look of the monster or created different levels and gave people the option as to whether the bed would also move or didn't, as if you were there, then it would be better."

"Maybe, but after one moment in that world and on this bed, I had nightmares in this room and never returned. I prefer my meditation and yoga."

"And your gardening," Ava mentioned with a smile.

"Yes."

Flo hesitated then said, "I'm telling you about the bed so that you can understand that James means well even if he doesn't show it the way he should."

"I know."

She took Ava's hand and held it between both of hers. "You joined our family just in time. When I think of what could have happened to Rudy if you hadn't—"

Ava touched one of Flo's thin shoulders. "It's okay."

Regret made her eyes sad. "If I hadn't been so tired I would have paid more attention. I used to worry about Rudy. We have him taken care of financially. Edgar promised me he'd do everything he could." The sad look left her eyes, replaced with joy. "But now I know Rudy has someone like you also looking out for him and it puts my mind at ease."

Ava hugged her hoping Flo would never really know the truth about her husband.

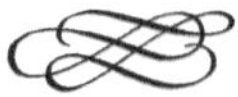

Flo left Ava's room and lay on the bed in the master bedroom, sweeping her hand over the plush bedspread; she closed her eyes remembering when she had felt like a stranger in the elegant room.

Neither she nor Edgar had married for love. And in the beginning they had separate bedrooms and lives, much like Ava and James, only coming together when Edgar requested her company. Flo didn't expect much else.

And for five years they lived that way until one night after they'd been together, Edgar said, "It's late, you can stay."

Flo halted halfway out of the bed not sure she'd heard him correctly. "What?"

"I said you can stay."

Flo hesitated not sure she wanted to. At first she'd dreamed of being a true wife to him, of turning their formal arrangement into something more, but over the years he'd made it clear that wouldn't happen. But now this. She stared at his hard profile; he wasn't a man to jest. She cautiously slipped back into bed, gripping the bed sheets to her chest, not quite sure what to do.

He sighed annoyed. "You don't have to stay if you don't want to."

"I do." She swallowed, releasing her grip on the sheets. She glanced at him again before she reached and turned off the lights.

"Are you happy?" he asked, his voice sounding deeper in the darkness.

What a strange question to ask. "Yes," she said not sure of his strange mood.

"And the boys?"

"They are happy too. You fulfilled your promise."

He didn't reply and she didn't expect him to. She'd gotten use to his silences. She bit her lip and inched closer to him. When her skin touched his, she closed her eyes and waited, wondering if he'd turn or push her away. Instead he drew her closer, his arm felt warm and solid around her. He pressed a featherlike kiss on her forehead. "You can stay every night if you want."

It was then that their relationship changed, that she finally understood him. He wanted her to stay, but he'd never admit it. She searched her heart, amazed by how buoyant and happy it felt and realized that he was no longer a stranger to her; she could accept him fully as her husband. Until that moment she hadn't realized how much she wanted to.

"Do you want that?" he asked.

She nodded and whispered, "Yes." And she stayed for the next twenty-three years.

Flo opened her eyes and looked around the bedroom with a smile that slowly faded as she thought of the fate that awaited her. Was it fair to him to keep sharing this room? This room filled with memories of their marriage? She glanced at the beige wingback chair where Edgar had stayed for hours after his uncle died; the window where they'd stood arguing about Rudy's future. She had initially been against Rudy starting his own business, but Edgar had been adamant and she was glad she'd listened, but it had taken a lot of persuasion on his part.

She'd had more fight in her back then. Others had been afraid of him, but not her, although she never let that truth show in public. She was keenly aware of Edgar's reputation and wouldn't do anything to jeopardize it, but in private she could be fierce and knew he secretly enjoyed it.

But she wondered if he took any pleasure in her anymore. Her weight loss had stolen some of her beauty; her energy wasn't what it once was. Did he at times regret his decision? Did he sometimes want space?

She'd once broached the subject about moving into another room, but he'd swiftly dismissed the idea and she'd never brought it up again. However, she knew there would come a time when they wouldn't be able to share a room or a bed and she wondered how she would be able to bear it.

"You lied to me," Ava said when she found James on the large, curved back patio, listening to the tranquil sounds of the water rippling from the pool below.

James turned a page of the report he was reading. "I know."

"About the bedroom."

"Oh, that." He briefly looked up at her. "I didn't lie. Jackson did."

"You went along with it. And at first you said it was a special guest room."

He nodded in agreement. "It sounded more interesting."

"You could have told me the truth."

He closed the report and sat back in his wooden chair. "That I created something that gave my mother nightmares for weeks? I don't think so."

"Weeks?"

He opened the report again.

Ava sat in front of him. "I was telling her that if you changed the look of the monster you may be on to something."

"You think so?" he said sounding bored.

"I like how it corresponds with the bed."

He shrugged. "I've moved on."

"I can't believe you designed that bedroom. I always wanted a floating bed."

He looked at her surprised. "Really?"

"Yes, ever since reading—"

He shook his head. "Don't say it."

"*Robot Chronicles.*"

He closed his eyes as if in pain. "I can't believe you said it."

"Why?" Ava said perplexed by his response. The books were very popular in her childhood and considered classics now. "Didn't you like the series?"

"Couldn't stand them," James said with feeling, "but Jackson had to read every single one."

"My father didn't let me read them so I had to sneak them. He said they were filled with junk science."

"He was right."

"That's why it's called *fiction* and the storytelling was amazing."

James returned to his report. "I'll have to take your word for it."

"Have you tried the bed yourself?"

"No."

"You should."

A slow smile spread across his face and he lifted his gaze to hers. "Is that an invitation?"

Ava cleared her throat, feeling suddenly warm. "I mean you should try it after I'm gone."

"Oh," he said sounding disappointed. "That doesn't sound as much fun."

"What doesn't?" Jackson said, stepping through the sliding glass doors to join them.

"Nothing," Ava and James said in unison.

Jackson took a seat and sent them a suspicious look.

"I found another fan of those boring books," James said.

Jackson frowned. "Boring books?"

"*Robot Chronicles.*"

"What do you mean *boring*? Those were the best."

"I know," Ava said.

Jackson looked at her amazed. "You liked them too?"

"They got me through school."

He stood and did the mock salute of one of the characters. "Are you ready to serve?"

She stood and did the same. "All the time all the way." She clapped her hands then pointed to the sky.

Jackson laughed, impressed. "You remembered that?"

"Of course. I disappeared into those books as well as my manga collection."

Jackson snapped his fingers. "Oh right. I still have one of your *Fullmetal Alchemist* copies. Volume–"

"That's okay." She'd loaned it to him when they were dating. "I started another series set in a post-apocalyptic world where humans live inside cities surrounded by these enormous walls."

James shook his head in mock dismay. "How old are you two?"

"Good stories know no age."

"Comic books."

"They are not—"

Jackson waved his hands. "Don't try to convince him. He doesn't get it."

James smiled. "Something else you two have in common."

"Something else?"

"Yes, I know you're both sharing a secret."

"No, we're not," Ava said when Jackson looked away.

James shrugged, nonchalant. "I'm not worried. I will find it out." He nodded at his brother. "What are you doing here?"

"Stopped by to see Mom and Rudy." James looked at Ava. "Heard what you did for him."

"Yes," James said. "I guess we're lucky to have her."

Jackson rested his elbows on his knees and smiled at her. "You'd like us to think that, wouldn't you?"

Ava stared back at him determined not to be provoked. "I don't care what you think."

"How come there's not much about your life before Canada?"

"What?"

"Are you looking into her background?" James asked.

Jackson kept his gaze on Ava. "Just curious."

James lowered his voice. "We're doing this for Mom. There's no need to stir up trouble."

"We're already in trouble."

"What does that mean?"

"It means that I hold all the cards and he doesn't like it," Ava said, stopping Jackson from saying anything else.

"Could you excuse us for a minute?" James said then shook his head when she opened her mouth. "I'm not really asking."

She shot Jackson a dirty look before she left.

"You're doing it again," James said once she was gone.

"What?"

"Every time you're around her you go for the jugular. What is going on?"

"I just don't like this set up."

"It's working right now. Mom is happy and so are Edgar and Rudy."

"And what happens to Rudy and Edgar if something happens to us?"

"What could happen to us? I'm the one who committed the fraud. If she wants to bring up fraud charges against me for what I did, I'll face the consequences. It has nothing to do with you. Until that time I'm trying my best to make this work."

"Maybe I don't want it to work," Jackson muttered.

"You're not making sense. Ava and I have an agreement. We keep this up and then we'll get a divorce and I'll—"

Jackson shook his head. "You're going to have to do more than that. She's been meeting with Edgar a lot lately and her interest in the company is intense. Almost obsessive."

"It always has been." James sat back and studied his brother. "I know she's up to something if that's your concern."

Jackson rubbed his chin. "But what and why? We have to do something."

"Like what?"

"Her life begins at age three in Canada. Don't you think that's strange?"

"I really don't care."

"It means she's keeping secrets."

James drummed his fingers against his knee. "What do you want me to do about it?"

"We need leverage. She's winning over our family."

"And what's your solution?"

"You have to make her fall for you."

James laughed. "I can't make that woman do anything."

Jackson sent his brother a hard look. "Yes, you can. I've seen you do it before."

James's good mood died. "That was different." He'd used his limited charm in the past to get what he wanted. Only his brother knew that his past breakups had always been strategically designed so that the other party felt that they had made the decision.

"I think you've let your guard down and have forgotten what this is really about."

James shrugged. "I'm willing to listen. What is it about?"

"The two things Edgar taught us were important—business and power. If we continue to stay in control we keep the upper hand."

James sighed. "Why do I get the feeling that you have something in mind?"

"Because I do."

James motioned him forward. "Go on. Tell me."

"You've got to up the stakes and steal her heart."

CHAPTER 24

James didn't argue with him.

Jackson took that as a victory when his brother left the patio and returned inside. He closed his eyes and rested his head back, letting the sun warm his skin. He'd lied when he'd told his brother why he'd come to the house. He'd really come to see how Ava would respond to his questions about her past. A smile touched his mouth as he thought of how he'd gotten the information he needed from Sylvia.

"You call that a quickie?" Sylvia demanded when Jackson rolled away from her and grabbed his jeans from where he'd tossed them over the couch in her apartment. "That was barely even a second."

He playfully slapped her on the bottom. "What do you have for me?"

She pulled a face. "How come you always make me feel used?"

He zipped up his jeans and winked at her. "You like being used."

She pulled on her large T-shirt, which she found crumpled on the ground. "We could make a great—"

He shook his head. "It would never work."

She pushed away an empty can of soda and a bag of caramel popcorn with her foot and reached for her skirt, brushing off some dust bunnies that clung to the pale, worn fabric. She should have cleaned up before he arrived, but she hadn't known he was coming until he was halfway there and she didn't want to turn him down. "It's not like you to be afraid of commitment."

"I don't trust my taste in women." He sat down beside her and nudged her with his elbow. "Present company excluded."

She pulled up her skirt. "Thank you."

"But I'm on a fast. No commitment for the near future."

"And what do you have against Ava?"

He playfully tweaked her chin. "Tell me what you found."

Sylvia sighed, knowing he wouldn't tell her. She liked him unfortunately their timing was always wrong. She'd first met him when she was still married to the man she fondly liked to call Her Greatest Mistake. By the time she divorced, Jackson had gotten burned twice and then fallen for Ava.

Although his relationship with Ava was now over, she suspected Jackson was right; she and he would never last. He had another side she couldn't reach, but she knew she'd enjoy herself in the meantime.

"I don't know why you need to use a lowly cop like me when your father likely has bigger fish on the hook to get the information you want."

He affectionately kissed her on the cheek then said, "Tell me."

"Not much. She has no past starting in Canada."

"What do you mean?"

"I mean that she doesn't have anything before the age of three. Her life before that is nowhere."

"That's impossible."

"Not if you know what you're doing."

"But—"

"I think I might know why," Sylvia interrupted, "but I can't tell you yet until I'm sure. I don't want to accuse someone of something until I have more evidence."

Jackson tapped his finger against his knee, pensive. "Is it big?"

"Could be."

"I knew it."

"Or it could be nothing so don't jump to conclusions. But if it is something, she was a child and may not know anything about it either. It could surprise her."

"I don't care," Jackson said in a grim tone.

"You should. She's married into your family, right?"

"Don't worry. I'll make sure that James and Ava don't stay married for long..."

James and Ava. He didn't like how cozy they'd looked together on the patio and he remembered the excited voice of his mother telling him how much she liked Ava and all that she'd done for them. Jackson opened his eyes and stared over the vast property, lingering briefly on his mother's vegetable garden. If James did what Jackson told him to, Ava would regret she'd married him in the first place.

His brother's idea was just as ludicrous as wanting to switch places, James thought as he poured himself water from the fridge. He'd fallen for Jackson's idea once—no twice!—he wouldn't do it again. Even though it was tempting. He knew Ava responded to him and it would be fun to see how he could manipulate her.

But they had an agreement and their arrangement worked for now. For the past several weeks they'd been cordial and he'd managed not to think about her too much. She stuck to his rules and he stuck to his cold showers.

Lots of cold showers. Like the one after he saw her in the garden, running her hand up and down an okra's short stem, or at the dinner table when her legs brushed against his. His work kept him busy and that would be enough for now. James finished his water and left the kitchen.

"She's alone right now," Flo said, grabbing James's arm as he passed her in the hall.

"Who?"

"Who else?" she said with impatience. "Ava. I convinced her to sit in the library."

He frowned not understanding her reasoning. "So what?"

"Go to her."

"Why?" James asked, letting her drag him towards the library so she wouldn't expend too much energy. "I don't have anything to say."

"Make up something. Sit with her for a minute."

"And do what?" he asked just to tease her. He found the situation amusing. His brother and mother both wanted him to do the same thing but for different reasons.

"Do I have to tell you?"

James peeked into the room. "She's reading. She probably wants to be alone."

"Go and put your arm around her. Ask her how she is."

"Mom, I really don't—"

"You're going to lose her at this rate. I may not be around to see any grandkids but I would like to believe in the hope there's a possibility." She shoved him forward. "Go."

James stumbled into the room and offered Ava a look of chagrin when she lifted her head in question. "Sorry about this," he said in a low voice, taking a seat beside her. "Just pretend to be happy to see me, my mother is watching."

Ava caught a glance of Flo before she disappeared behind the wall.

James stretched his arm behind her head. "Don't stiffen like that I'm only doing this until she goes away."

"I'm not stiff. What did Jackson say about me?"

James frowned down at the book in her hands. "What are you reading?" He leaned forward. "Is that—?"

She slapped him in the stomach with the back of her hand. "Shut up."

He looked at the manga graphics. "The drawings are impressive."

"I said shut up. I don't want to hear your comments on my reading material."

"There aren't many words though."

"Be quiet, James."

He slid his arm to her shoulders and lowered his voice, "I either keep talking or I kiss you. Your choice."

For a moment Ava didn't move, not sure how to respond.

James pointed to one of the illustrations, the movement bringing her body closer to him. "I really like that one."

Ava bit her lip, resisting the urge to lean in. He smelled good. But what had he and Jackson talked about? Why had Jackson brought up her past? Was James here because of his mother or for another reason?

She looked down at his free hand resting on his lap, swallowed and made a bold decision. She covered and held it.

This time James didn't move, but his voice deepened. "You're breaking the rules."

"I know. What are you going to do?"

His mouth covered hers.

And she totally forgot about Jackson. Or breathing. His mouth left hers burning with fire. Then she felt his tongue, not sure if she'd made the initial invitation or not, but surrendering to its persuasion. Her hands reached for him.

"Hold on," James said, waking her from her dream. She looked down and saw that she'd unbuttoned his shirt. "Your bedroom in two minutes."

"Why not yours?"

He pressed a finger against her lips. "I'll make it one. Are you scared?"

She searched his gaze, her heart racing, realizing what she faced. What she'd done. She should be horrified. She'd lost herself. Her dignity. Her inhibition.

She didn't care.

She wanted him and he wanted her. She jumped to her feet and ran.

Once she reached her bedroom she quickly searched it to see if there was anything visible that would ruin the mood, but it looked fine. She didn't know if she should strip down, let him undress her or do it herself.

She covered her face and made a sound of frustration. No, she couldn't have these questions. She had to get back in control. If he knew how much he could dazzle her she would be at a disadvantage. This was just sex. Nothing more. She didn't really like him, just wanted him. A lot. More than a lot if there was such a thing. She was a straight, healthy woman with a handsome man who wanted to sleep with her, she was not making a mistake.

It was just physical. It didn't mean anything. So she was attracted to him, that didn't mean it had to be anything serious. For weeks she'd been secretly lusting after him, and now she could finally get him out of her system.

CHAPTER 26

James didn't know what to expect, but the sight of Ava in a pair of heels wearing only black lace panties and bra wasn't it.

He wasn't sure how to read her expression. She was up to something but he wasn't sure what. He slowly closed the door behind him and removed his shirt. "You don't waste any time," he said, placing it over a chair.

"No." She walked up to him and tugged on the waist of his trousers. "I like it quick, hard and a little rough. Think you can manage that?"

James smiled, finally understanding what she was up to. "Yes." He removed his socks and shoes and placed them together near the chair.

She frowned. "What are you? A neat freak?"

"Is that a problem?"

"No." She folded her arms. "So you know what to do."

He nodded, removed his trousers and placed them over the chair as well.

"Good."

"But I don't take orders."

She paused. "What?"

He cupped her chin in his hand, his eyes dark. "Somehow you've confused me with someone you pay for."

She removed his hand. "Do you want to sleep with me or not?"

"I will sleep with you tonight," he said, his voice holding a note of promise, "but on my terms not yours. Remember you broke the rules."

"But you're the one who's scared," she shot back, meeting his eyes. "Scared you can't handle a simple request from a woman like me."

He sniffed. "A woman like you?"

She nodded.

"What makes you so different?" he challenged, taking an aggressive step forward, inwardly pleased when she took a step back. "Do you think you're my first? Do you think you're somehow special?" He took another step forward; this time she held her ground, but not for long. "Is that what men have been telling you? Have they been telling you that you're so strong and independent that you frighten them?" He held her gaze. "Do I look frightened?"

She turned away. "You can leave—"

"I can see through it all, Ava. I can feel how you respond to me. Is it fear or something else?"

Ava hugged herself, annoyed that he'd been able to intimidate her. She shouldn't have backed away no matter how uncomfortable he made her. He was too close to the truth, but if she wanted to control him he couldn't know that. She forced herself to look at him again. "It's not fear. I just don't—"

"Want to be alone with me too long?"

Yes. "I like my space."

He swept her with a considering look, his gaze feeling like a heated caress over her body. "You want it quick, hard and rough?"

She nodded, not trusting herself to speak.

"You're sure?"

"Yes." She knew it was a challenge and didn't expect him to do it right. Most men didn't. If he did what she expected him to—try to prove himself, his manliness and power—he'd be another unmemorable bedfellow to ease some frustration. And she always liked a little pain with her pleasure; like salt and sugar on popcorn. She hoped to end up with some bruises, maybe a tiny scar. She wondered if he'd use his teeth, scrape her skin with his nails, grab her throat and squeeze.

But he tricked her, not in the way she expected. He was quick—having her naked and on the bed within seconds—and he was hard, big and solid as he entered her. He was also rough —she felt the raw passion of his entrance as she prepared herself to ride him into climax, but then he slowed the pace and kissed the curve of her neck.

"What are you doing?" she asked with a note of panic.

"A compromise," James whispered, his breath hot against her skin.

"But I said I wanted it rough."

His eyes captured hers. "I can be rough and smooth."

And to her surprise he showed her how.

Making himself memorable in the most wonderful, exciting and frightening way. He wasn't a quick lay she could forget, he made an imprint and she was helpless to stop him because as much as she wanted to pull away, she craved more.

No man had ever taken so much time to explore her body, to find her pleasure points, to touch her so tenderly, but also with reckless abandon. She didn't think he had it in him. She'd been wrong. She'd offered him a challenge and failed.

But what a glorious defeat.

She knew once wouldn't be enough, even when he stopped she craved more.

She'd never known the true pleasure of a man's tongue before, the feel of it between her toes, against her navel, touching the tip of her center with wet, warm delight, leaving her languid with desire.

It wasn't supposed to be like this.

She wanted it to always be like this. She enjoyed him with equal hunger, dragging her nails down his back, tightening around him, inviting him deeper inside her. She wanted to devour him, using her teeth against his chest, wondering if she could frighten him a little. It only seemed to excite him more and that thought—that she couldn't scare him—thrilled her and she knew she was in danger of falling in love.

James lay on his side and looked down at her. "Well?"

Ava turned her head on the pillow and stared up at him. "Well what?"

"Did I succeed?"

She frowned. "You know you did, smug bastard."

He smiled. "Just wanted to make sure."

"Where did you learn to do that thing with your tongue?"

He bit his lip. "I probably shouldn't tell you this."

"Why not? Embarrassed?"

"A peach."

She blinked. "What?"

"A peach. My brother and I used to practice on a peach. We'd cut it in half, remove the pit and do the rest. An older cousin of ours told us the sensation was kind of the same." He winked. "Warm, sticky, sweet."

"I don't believe you."

He shrugged. "It's the truth. I haven't had any complaints yet."

"You must like peaches a lot."

He only smiled.

"Clearly you've perfected your skill."

"Glad you noticed. I would hope I would be better than I was at eleven."

She sat up and stared at him shocked. "You were doing that to peaches at eleven years old?"

"Late bloomers I know."

She pulled the bed sheets to her chest. "You're making this up."

He shook his head. "No, it's the truth. I tried plums once, they were a disaster. And forget about the kumquat. I'd gotten too ambitious."

"Horny little bastard."

He grinned.

She rested her head on the pillow and pulled up the sheets. "I'm ready to go to sleep."

"You'll miss dinner."

"That's okay."

She felt him reaching for something. "You're right," he said.

Ava turned to him when he didn't leave. She saw him

reading one of the mangas she'd left beside the bed.

"I can see why Jackson likes it," he said. "You could cosplay this any day." He pointed to a sexy image of a warrior princess.

Ava smiled at the thought of him wanting her to dress up as one of the characters. "Be careful what you wish for."

James squeezed his eyes shut and moved his lips without saying anything.

"What are you doing?"

He opened one eye. "Wishing very hard."

She playfully slapped him. "I told you I'm ready to go to sleep."

"Go ahead. I won't bother you."

She stared at him confused. "You can't stay here."

"Why not?"

She blinked, dumbfounded. "Because I don't—"

"Relax, I just want to look at a couple more pages."

"You can take the book with you."

"I know. I don't want to. I'm comfortable where I am."

Ava hesitated. He couldn't stay. She'd never spent the night with a man. She hadn't had many relationships, but when she did the guy was usually gone the moment they finished, having James linger felt strange, even more intimate than what they'd just done. His room was only down the hall; he had no reason to stay. Why was he still there? The manga was interesting, but not enough. It didn't make sense to her.

He set the book aside. "I thought you said you wanted to sleep."

"You're leaving now?"

He lay down beside her and drew her close, holding her

snuggly. "Let's try this for a minute, if you don't fall asleep in five minutes I'll leave."

That sounded reasonable. She wouldn't sleep. She'd count every second. She didn't cuddle. It was unnecessary. She licked her lip. She wished her heart didn't feel as if it were going a hundred kilometers an hour, but once he was gone it would return back to normal.

Normal. Why did his arms around her feel so normal, ordinary, and right? She felt as if she was right where she belonged. But that was wrong. He was one of them. The dreaded Fortunes. She wouldn't close her eyes, she wouldn't lean back against him, she wouldn't fall asleep...

CHAPTER 27

"James and Ava are late," Edgar said with irritation as he, Rudy and Flo sat at the dinner table. Jackson had gone home.

"We can start dinner without them," Flo said, a private smile touching her lips as she filled her plate.

Edgar looked at her wondering what her secret expression meant. Her smile was always a mystery to him. It was one of the first things that had intrigued him even though he'd sought her out for very different reasons.

"I could help you win more favors and funds if you changed your image," his business mentor had told him as they stood together in the formal living room of a mutual friend. The cocktail party was lively and filled with influential people, but Edgar wished he were elsewhere.

"What do you have in mind?" he'd asked, feigning interest.

"Not what, but who."

The 'who' had captured his interest and moments later he

was introduced to Flo who smiled prettily at him with that same secretive smile. He still wondered what she'd thought of him that first meeting. He knew he'd been less than gracious, giving her little opportunity to reject his advances, confident in his ability to impress her.

His friend had been right. Flo and her three boys had given his image the boost he needed, especially Rudy. That had garnered him extra bonus points. Rudy was the only one of his stepsons who called him Dad, but it was expected since Edgar was the only father he'd ever known. He made sure that their biological father didn't reappear, now that his sons were provided for(persuading him with a handsome financial incentive and soft threats). It had taken three months to convince Flo to marry him. He'd anticipated token resistance, he knew women liked not to appear overeager, but she'd made a surprisingly easy, conquest agreeing the moment he'd shown her the ring.

And now she was dying.

Fortunately, the boys were grown. It would have been more of a hassle if they'd been younger. He'd adopted them after all and they would have been his responsibility, but a good boarding school would have taken care of that problem.

He told himself that at least they'd had good years together, he'd given her a good life. But the guilt still remained.

He needed a cigar.

After dinner he went to the back patio, grabbing his coat from the closet. Although the sun still lingered in the sky the evening was cool. He no longer smoked inside the house because of Flo's illness. He stepped outside and put on the coat a faint scent drafting around him. The smell of Lynn's perfume. He wished she wouldn't wear such a strong scent, he'd warn her next time. He lit his cigar and took a puff.

He didn't want anyone getting suspicious. Now wasn't the time for anyone to know what he was up to. It would ruin his image, one he'd taken years to build. He couldn't let a woman destroy it. He couldn't let his true weakness be discovered.

CHAPTER 28

Ava woke up with a start. She opened her eyes and saw the room cloaked in darkness. She'd fallen asleep. She sighed and squeezed her pillow then paused when she realized the warm, solid form wasn't her pillow at all. She had her head on James's chest, her arm draped across him. She quickly sat up.

"What is it?" he mumbled.

Her face burned. She'd never done something like this before. To have him stay was one thing (Why was he still here?), to even let her hold him was another (How could she have let herself fall asleep in his arms?), but for her to cling to him? That was completely foreign. For a moment she didn't know herself. What if he'd wanted to leave and she'd forced him to stay because he hadn't wanted to wake her? She turned on the side light. "You should have pushed me away."

James squinted against the glare and stretched his arms above his head. "Why would I want to do that?" A slow smile spread on his face. "I know you like me." He pointed at her with mock severity. "Don't try to deny it."

She grabbed his finger. "I liked what we did. It's nothing personal. Don't get confused."

He pulled her down and locked her in his arms. "It's personal all right." His voice deepened into huskiness. "Very personal."

Ava didn't move. There was no point in lying. Would he taunt her? Tell her that he'd warned her not to fall for him?

"How would you like to get away for the weekend?"

"Alone? With me?"

"Of course with you," he said with a laugh. "Who else?"

She bit her lip. "What are we doing James?" she asked, knowing their relationship had changed.

"If you say 'yes' I'll show you."

SHE NEVER IMAGINED THAT SAYING "YES" would lead her to the Caribbean.

James flew her to Grenada, a small island that lulled Ava into a tropical embrace where for three days she thought she'd touched paradise. They spent every night in each other's arms. During the day, they snorkeled in the clear blue waters and sailed against a cloudless sky, took a tour along one of the waterfalls, inhaling the fragrant scent of nutmeg trees.

Ava indulged in the rainfall shower and luxurious soaker tub of their cottage, and lounged on the private patio where they had every meal delivered—Breakfast (fried bake and saltfish), lunch (callaloo soup), afternoon tea and dinner (chicken stew and pumpkin mash). They wandered in the market where farmers sold fresh fruit and spices and walked hand-in-hand along the boutique lined roads of the French-colonial capital of St. George's where James bought her a multicolored, spaghetti strap dress, wedges and an off-the-shoulders floral blouse to wear over jeans.

At a small village they stopped to listen to the sound of steel drums and joined the festivities of a weekly fish fry. For a sweet treat, James bought her Grenadian ginger fudge and coconut drops.

"I know the owners of the resort," James said on their last day on the island. They walked barefoot along the white sand beach mere steps from the patio of their private cottage and marveled at the natural beauty around them, "They pay careful attention to the environment, recycling plastic bottles to a local medical clinic, using produce from local farms, even using hot water solar heating and more. I like to patronize businesses like this." He turned to her. "In case you were wondering why I didn't choose a hotel."

Ava looped her arm through his; surprised he'd think she could be disappointed. "I love it here. This has been a wonderful holiday."

"I guess we'll have to come again."

Her heart skipped a beat. Another time. Would there be another time for them? She sighed, saying what was truly in her heart for the first time, "I'd like that."

CHAPTER 29

"Someone is looking extra pretty today," Flo said one morning when she found Ava in the kitchen with James as they finished strawberry covered pancakes and scrambled eggs before they headed for work.

Ava blushed.

"Leave it, Mom," James said.

"At least you're finally acting like the newlyweds I expected you to be," Flo said without apology. "And when I'm gone, don't forget how easily it is to put your work before each other."

He sighed. "I hate when you talk like that. You haven't gone anywhere yet."

"But I will," she said with a resigned smile.

"We'll remember," Ava said before James could argue, sensing how much the conversation hurt him.

She sat down in front of them. "And don't forget me either."

James put down his fork, his patience thinning. "Cut

it out."

"I'm trying to let you know that you don't have to worry about me anymore."

James lifted his fork and continued eating. Flo looked at him, sadness in her eyes. Ava realized his mother didn't know that James found her words painful rather than comforting.

"I'm going to go to work late, today," Ava said. "I'd love to spend some time with you in the garden."

Flo's eyes brightened. "Really? Aren't you busy?"

"No," Ava said pleased she'd eased some of the tension between mother and son. "I can make the time."

LATER THAT EVENING, Ava saw James sitting in the great room reading another manga. He had his back to her so she walked up behind him, wrapped her arms around his neck and planted a quick kiss on his cheek.

"I know your mother's words bothered you this morning, darling, but she really wants you to know that she's okay." She pressed another kiss against his neck, then touched a location where last night she'd made a faint scar. "You must be a fast healer," she said surprised. "I'm afraid I was extra rough last night, but you know that about me." She touched the smooth surface again. "But it almost looks like it was never there."

Never there.

Something clicked in her mind and her heart turned cold when she looked down and saw that James's trousers weren't his usual grey but rather a deep purple. She hadn't kissed James, she'd kissed Jackson!

He turned to her and flashed a knowing smile.

"The witch has a heart," Jackson said with a cruel laugh.

Ava took a step back, horrified. She should have been more careful.

"You're in love with him."

"No, I'm not."

"Put your arms around me again, maybe I was mistaken, *darling*."

Ava gripped her trembling hands behind her back, it was her fault for laying her heart bare for him to stomp on and mock. She'd never called anyone 'darling' before. Nobody had ever been as dear to her as James, and now she was having that fact thrown back in her face. She deserved it. She'd forgotten her place and why she was there. From the triumphant look in Jackson's eyes, he knew he could hurt her if he wanted to.

He clicked his tongue in pity and stood. "Don't worry. I won't say anything." He patted her on the shoulder. "I'll save you the humiliation."

Ava pulled out her cell phone and showed him a picture of her with a smiling Flo. "I make her happy."

"I know. That's the only reason why you're still here." He left the room, leaving the manga behind.

Ava sunk down into the seat, staring at the illustrated cover that soon grew blurry as tears built behind her eyes. She buried her face in her hands.

She soon felt arms around her. "Ava, what's wrong?"

She knew that voice, that touch. He'd grown too precious to her. How could she have been so foolish as to fall in love with him?

She let her hands fall and met his kind gaze before she caught a glimpse of Jackson's smug smile as he passed in the hallway. *I'll save you the humiliation.* She had to remember that none of this was real. James would enjoy her as long as she kept his mother happy. Once that was over...plus she had to remember Edgar. Edgar was why she was here. She wiped away her tears and smiled. "How embarrassing." She lifted up the manga. "A favorite character died," she lied, feeling as if some part of her had died too.

CHAPTER 30

Pain.

Ava sat cross the dark booth in the cheap, mostly empty restaurant her father had found so that they could speak without being seen.

Although Ava knew her father loved her, she always associated him with pain. Pain from regret, betrayal, misery. He'd had a hard life. She knew it was her fault that his marriage had dissolved. Her mother and him had great plans for her, believing her to be brilliant until the year she turned three and failed the entrance exam to a prestigious pre-school. That's when they realized she was just ordinary.

Her mother couldn't bare her disappointment and left, a sting Ava still felt. She worked hard trying to prove herself, wanting to be great enough so that her mother would come back one day and say, "I was wrong", but that day hadn't arrived yet.

Because of her mother's desertion, her father never remarried, although at times Ava dreamed of him doing so or finding a woman with children of her own so that she could have siblings to play with. Instead, it was always just the two of them living in a cold dark apartment wherever he managed to get an appointment because of his erratic behavior from one university to another, before having to move on.

Every moment he could he told her about the Fortunes—how they were the reason she was without spending money, how they were the reason she'd have to work after school, how they were the reason his life, and thus hers, was one of struggle. Growing up she'd envied the Fortune's familial bond based on the stories her father managed to share about them, plus the online clippings she read of their various accomplishments and over the years her desire for revenge grew.

After the mistake with Jackson, Ava was more cautious and was eager to finally put her father's plan into action; she'd been preparing for the role for years. (She knew she didn't have much time.) Before meeting Jackson she'd spent hours learning as much as she could about him—what he liked, didn't like—and used it to seduce him. His betrayal by switching places with his brother was very clever; but marrying James as a countermeasure had proven to be more of a problem than a solution. Yes, she was now a member of the Fortune family, but she hadn't planned on her feelings.

Her heart would give her no relief. As much as she wanted to continue to despise James, fueled by years of hate, he seemed to dilute her resolve every day with a word, a touch or a look. And the nights she'd spent with him had proven to be dangerous.

For the first time, when he took her to Grenada, she felt guilty. She'd never felt that way before, not with Jackson and she knew she owed the Fortunes nothing. They owed her.

But as she spent time with Flo and Rudy she kept wondering where the monsters were. Where were the beasts her father had described all these years?

Ava picked up the paper menu that was missing a corner and was stained with ketchup. "Let's order something."

Her father snatched the menu from her, motioned to a waiter, and said, "Two coffees," before handing the menus to the young man with tiny hooped earrings. "I didn't come here to eat," Walter said. There was no anger in his voice, but it was reflected in his angular, handsome face. He had skin the color of caramel, but there was nothing sweet about him.

"I just thought—"

"It's been nearly two months."

"I'm still—"

"You haven't spoken to Lortis yet," her father said.

"I will."

He shook his head. "That's not what I want to hear."

"I'm still settling in."

"You've had more than enough time."

"Rudy was sick and I was worried about Flo—" The feel of her father's hand against her cheek stopped her words. Ava stared at him stunned. He'd never hit her before. He'd pinch her as a child, until he brought tears to her eyes; he'd sometimes kick her in the ankles when he felt she was talking back or not paying attention, but he'd never slapped her.

His eyes burned. "Have you forgotten who you belong to? You may have married a Fortune, but you're a Hughes. Is that clear?"

"Yes."

"You will fly to New York within two days."

"I can take the train."

"You will fly and secure the shares we need. Understood?"

"Yes."

"And if I see you grow soft like that again, I will finish this myself."

She nodded.

He softened his tone and reached out and touched her hand. "You're all I have. I can't let them take you away from me too. I'm sorry." He tenderly touched her cheek. "I'm sorry. I shouldn't have lost my temper."

"It's okay. I won't disappoint you." It was her fault. Her father provided for her and was good to her. She'd let him down, just as she had years ago as a child. James would forget her, but her father was all she had. The only person who truly loved her.

CHAPTER 31

"What happened to your face?"

Ava jumped when she entered the foyer and saw James. He wasn't supposed to be home yet and her dark skin hid bruises well. Only a sharp eye would notice. How could he see it so quickly? She lightly touched her cheek. Was there swelling?

"What are you doing home?"

He folded his arms. "What happened?"

She thought of telling him that she'd been clumsy but knew he'd see through such a lie. She had to make him angry instead. "I told you I liked it rough and I found someone who liked it too."

His eyes darkened with an emotion she couldn't read—she wanted anger but what she saw looked like something too close to hurt and disappointment. She inwardly grimaced hoping it was the former. If he hated her, that would make her job easier.

He nodded then walked away.

Ava let out a breath and headed towards the stairs.

James grabbed her wrist and spun her to him, his eyes blazing. "I will let you get away with that once, but while you're married to me you stay exclusive. Understood?"

She welcomed the hard grip of his hand, the rage in his eyes. *Yes, hate me James. Hate me for your own good.* She blinked, pretending to look bored. "Understood."

"Do you think I'm kidding?"

"No."

"I think you do." He lifted his hand to strike her then stopped and swore. "You lied."

Her heartbeat throbbed in her ears. "What?"

He wrapped his arms around her and held her close. "I'm sorry," he said with feeling. "I had to see for myself."

Mixed feeling surged through her. What was he doing? Why was he holding her like this? Why did she want him to? Why did she want to bury her face in his neck and cry? She steeled herself against the desire and kept her voice steady. "What are you talking about?"

He drew away and met her gaze. "You're not used to being hit in the face. I just saw fear in your eyes."

She pushed him away, feeling exposed and vulnerable. "I said I won't be with anyone else again. At least until we end this charade."

"Who did this to you?"

Ava turned away. "I have lovers. There's no need to be jealous."

James grabbed her chin and searched her eyes. "There's that look again. That fear. What are you hiding?"

She struggled to release herself. "Let go. You're hurting me."

He tightened his grip. "Why? I thought this is what you liked."

She tried to spin away; he pulled her back against him, but his grip didn't hurt. He trapped her with casual restraint, but not pain, and that hurt more. She wanted to free herself from his tender embrace.

"Tell me who hurt you," he whispered, his voice warm against her ear.

She blinked back tears. *Don't pretend to care about me, I can't bear it.*

"Ava? What are you afraid of?"

She searched her mind for another lie. "I told an old lover I didn't want to see him again. He didn't take it well and that's all you need to know."

James fell silent for a moment then said, "Why did you lie to me?"

"Because...I was embarrassed."

"Will he bother you again?"

"No."

He kissed her behind the ear. "Tell me his name."

"No."

"Please."

The childishly insistent tone of his voice made her reluctantly smile. "No."

He released her. "Okay."

She bit her lip then turned to him. "I have to go on a business trip, but I'll be back in a day or two."

"Okay." He gently touched her bruised cheek. "Could you give me his initials?"

She playfully pushed his hand away. "I'm a big girl. I can take care of myself."

"I know that." His smile fell. "But I'm a big boy who doesn't like his things being touched."

"I'm a thing?"

"You're my woman."

"In name only."

James shook his head. "No, I didn't say my wife. I said my woman."

"There's a difference?"

He looked at her for a long moment then he kissed her on the forehead. "Have a safe trip."

CHAPTER 32

Someone had hit her and she'd lied to him. He didn't know which bothered him more.

James walked into the library and sat with a book he'd pulled from the shelves, but couldn't settle his mind to read. He closed the book and set it aside.

"What's on your mind?" Jackson asked, picking up the book. He read the complicated scientific title and frowned, "Are you trying to put yourself to sleep?"

James took the book from him and replaced it on the shelf, annoyed. His brother had never stopped by the house as many times as he had over the past couple of months, but James suspected the reason. "Ava's hiding something," he said.

Jackson's brows shot up. "You're only figuring that out now? She's a conniving, manipulative—"

James pinned him with a look. "What are you hiding?"

"Nothing."

"I get this feeling that you two know something I don't."

Jackson shrugged.

"Is she in trouble?"

"No."

"Are you?"

"We all are, but I don't have proof so don't ask me any more questions. Just be careful. Don't fall for her."

"Why not?"

"That's a joke, right? She told me..." He stopped and shook his head.

"What?"

"Forget about making her fall for you. She told me how much she feels trapped having to pretend for Mom."

James's brows rose in amazement. "She said that?"

He nodded.

James accepted the stinging truth of his brother's words. No matter how much he cared about her, being with him and part of his family wasn't what she'd bargained for. Was that why she'd lied to him? She wanted to be free, but he didn't want to let her go.

Jackson watched his brother take another book from the shelf, feeling a twinge of guilt. He'd never seen a lie have such an impact. He hadn't meant to hurt his brother, but knew James was becoming too attached to Ava. He hadn't realized how much until that moment.

Jackson glanced at a light fixture, making a personal note to remind Abigail to have it dusted, then stole a look at James again. He told himself he was lying for James's sake. That it was the only way to keep him safe. He'd rather hurt his brother than let Ava get the chance to.

Success!

Ava returned from her trip to New York brimming with joy. She stepped out of the car and stared up at the Virginia mansion, seeing it in a new light. It wasn't her home, it was just another step to her true destiny. One day her father could afford a place like this and he'd be happy again.

She had a lot to tell her father and was eager to find her way back into his good graces. He hadn't spoken to her since they'd seen each other at the restaurant, now she had a reason to make him proud.

The trip had given her the distance she needed to see everything with clarity. She'd gotten too close to the Fortunes and that had clouded her view. Especially, James. She'd become a little too complacent. Now she was back on track. Victory was in sight.

Abigail met her at the door with a somber expression. "I hope your journey was good?" she asked, taking her bags.

"It was great, thank you."

Abigail began to turn then James stopped her. "I'll take these." When she hesitated, he said, "It's okay."

She nodded then left them alone.

Ava opened her mouth to offer him a greeting, but he looked away and set her bags in the corner. "There's no need to unpack."

She put up her guard, sensing something was wrong. Had he found out something? Had they discovered the true reason for her trip to New York? Had someone leaked about her meeting with Lortis? "Why? I don't understand."

James rested his hands on his hips. "We don't have to pretend anymore." His gaze lowered as did his voice. "Mom died yesterday."

CHAPTER 33

"But that's impossible," Ava said, refusing to believe what she'd heard. "She was fine a couple of days ago. I was just with her in the garden."

"Ava—"

"I even called her from New York and she sounded great. Full of life. We laughed about—" Her throat tightened and she fought against tears. "You said six months. It's barely been three, how could this have happened?"

"It was an infection. It caught us all off-guard. We thought it was a minor cough, but it quickly progressed to something else and spread faster than anyone expected. She passed peacefully. Just tell me where you want me to send your things."

She hesitated not understanding his cold words and behavior. They'd parted as lovers and now he was treating her like a stranger. "But I don't have to leave yet."

"It's up to you." His cell phone rang. "Excuse me," he said before he turned and walked away.

Ava stood frozen in the foyer, not knowing what to do, where to go or what to think. Flo wasn't supposed to be dead. She'd even bought her a gift, a silly little T-shirt with a picture of Lady Liberty holding a garden cushion and hoe. She was supposed to have more time. How could Flo be gone? Why did she feel so bereft? Wasn't this what she wanted? Now she could focus on her main goal. Ava grabbed her bags without thinking, needing something to do, and headed to her bedroom.

She hesitated when she walked past Rudy's bedroom and saw him sitting on the bed staring down at his hands.

"Are you okay?" she asked him.

He looked up and shook his head.

"I'm sorry about your mom."

He pursed his lips. "I'm angry at her."

Ava set her bags down in the hallway, entered the room and sat down beside him. "Why?"

His voice cracked and tears filled his eyes. "She left without telling me she was going to heaven. I don't know why she didn't tell me first."

Ava hugged him, hoping to offer him comfort. "It happened so fast she didn't know."

An hour later, after sitting alone in her room, trying to decide her next move, Ava returned downstairs and found James sitting alone in the great room. She took the time to make sure it was really him, scanning his clothes and the way he sat just to make sure. But although she knew it was James she felt as if a chasm had suddenly formed between them and she didn't know when or how.

But his pain was palpable.

Maybe that was it. This loss changed everything and she felt helpless.

She'd slept with him, but didn't know how to comfort him. She'd never comforted someone before.

"After the funeral we can announce our separation," James said without turning.

She started; surprised he knew she was there. She entered the room and sat in front of him. "Let's not discuss that right now. How are you? What do you need?"

"Nothing."

"Anything you want?"

He closed his eyes and a smile spread across his face. "Peaches."

Ava frowned. "I was being serious."

He looked at her. "Me too. My mom used to take me to the farmers' market to buy them when they were in season. She'd show me how to choose them, and I remember how she looked when she smelled them." His smile fell and for a moment he looked like a little boy who'd lost his mother and that tore at her heart.

"I've never selected peaches before," Ava said, not knowing what else to say. Desperate to ease the pain in his eyes.

"Really?"

"Most of my fruit comes out of the can."

James glanced at his watch. "Then let's go now. The market's still open." He stood. "I don't want to leave Rudy alone right now. Do you mind if he joins us?"

"No, of course not. I'll get him."

Ava enjoyed the unfamiliar sights and sound of the farmers' market under the warmth of the summer sun. For the new adventure, she wore the floral print blouse James had bought her in Grenada. When he saw her, his gaze lit with appreciation for a brief moment then disappeared to something more distant, confusing her.

At the market she listened patiently while both Rudy and James showed her how to pick different fruits. Back at home, they made a peach crumble, scenting the kitchen with the smell of sweet peaches, cinnamon, and brown sugar. James teased Ava about using the metric system to measure the ingredients. They served the dessert with vanilla ice cream, sat together and laughed while remembering Flo.

"I wish she were here now," Rudy said, scooping up a large portion of his dessert. "She'd like this." He sniffed. "I miss her."

James patted him on the back. "It's okay to be sad. I miss her too."

"Are you sure she's not coming back?"

James nodded. "I'm sure."

He picked up his bowl and stood. "I'd done. Thanks Ava." He kissed her on the cheek. "I love you."

She smiled. "I love you too."

James watched his brother leave the kitchen then sat back in his chair. "Thanks for today. I needed that."

"I did too. I learned a lot."

He carried his plate over to the sink. "I'd like to stay friends."

"I'd like to stay married."

He spun around and stared at her in surprise. "But you told Jackson that—" He stopped and turned on the faucet.

Ava walked over to him. "I told Jackson what?"

He shook his head. "Doesn't matter now." He rubbed the back of his neck. "You want to see this through?"

"At least for another three months."

"Why?"

I don't know. I don't know what I'm doing! "Because it doesn't feel right to end things yet."

James looked at her for a long moment then nodded. "Rudy?"

"Yes, but–"

"You're worried about how the stockholders will feel about a funeral and divorce so close together."

"No, that's not—"

"It makes sense. You're thinking more clearly than I am. Edgar would be proud."

She sighed. She'd gotten what she wanted, more time with him, but it felt like a hollow victory.

CHAPTER 34

"This is the perfect time to strike," Walter told her over the phone once she'd shared the news about Flo.

Ava sat in her car staring up at the BioMed Solutions headquarters standing tall against the cloudy blue sky. "I just don't think—"

"Are you getting soft on me? Have you forgotten what they have stolen from me? Stolen from us? This is your chance. They are weak and it will make it easy for you."

She sighed. To hurt them at such a painful time may have seemed smart three months ago, but now it felt cruel. She couldn't hurt James this way. But Edgar? Edgar was another target entirely. And she kept waiting for Jackson to strike, but he hadn't yet. When he'd arrived for dinner the evening of the funeral, she'd managed to get a moment alone with him on the patio.

"Don't say anything to James yet."

Jackson leaned against the railing. "Why not? Mom's gone so you can't hurt her."

"James has already gone through enough."

Jackson sent her a cold look. "When did you start caring about him? About any of us?"

"I liked your mother."

"Sure. That's why you were sleeping with her son and conning her husband right under her nose and with her blessing. I stayed quiet but I'm not going to anymore."

"What do you want?"

His eyes pierced hers. "You. Out. Of. Our. Lives. Especially my brother's. You've been able to toy with him long enough."

She felt frantic. She didn't want to lose James; she didn't want him to know the truth. Not yet. "I'm not toying. I really—"

"Love him?" Jackson finished. "That's your problem not mine."

"I will be out of your lives in—"

"Tonight. That's all the time you have," he said then left her alone on the patio.

She had to do something before he did. Perhaps she could please her father and protect James by revealing who the true traitor was.

Dinner that evening was somber, even though Jackson had joined them and tried to make Rudy laugh, Flo's absence felt like a heavy weight around the room. Ava thought of her as she gathered the courage to do what she needed to do. She turned to Edgar. "I didn't want to say this, but I saw you with another woman. Now that Flo's gone are you ready to tell us her name?"

Edgar didn't look up from his plate of rice and stir-fried vegetables. He continued to eat as if she hadn't spoken.

"Or are you going to keep her in the shadows a little while longer for the sake of appearance?"

He wiped his mouth with a napkin. "Rudy, go to your room. You can finish your dinner there."

"But Dad—"

"Now."

Rudy shuffled away.

"He'll find out eventually," Ava said. "You can't shield him from the truth forever."

"What are you talking about?" James asked.

"I was hoping your stepfather would tell you," Ava said, staring at Edgar's calm expression. "Since Flo is gone it doesn't matter anymore."

James turned to him. "What is she—"

Edgar shook his head. "I don't know."

"I saw you with her," Ava said.

"You were seeing another woman?" James said.

"No."

"Yes," Ava countered. "An attractive younger woman." She sniffed. "I'm not surprised to hear you deny it."

"There was nobody else," Edgar said firmly.

Ava took out her cell phone and held out the picture she'd taken of them. "You call this nobody?"

Edgar's jaw twitched. "You were spying on me?"

"I saw you both by accident. I shouldn't have seen it at all. I knew you could be heartless but to cheat on your dying wife—"

Edgar grabbed her phone, slammed it on the ground and crushed it under his heel. "The matter is closed."

"Who is that woman?" James asked.

Ava reached to pick up her broken phone, but Edgar

kicked it away. "I was never with another woman."

James nodded. "I believe you, Dad."

It was the first time James had ever called him that. Edgar didn't know if it was a slip of the tongue or a strategic move, but it affected him. He hung his head in shame and despair. "Her name was...is Lynn. She is a healing psychic. She promised me that she could heal your mother. That she'd done it for many others before. There was proof. I met some of her clients. Your mother wouldn't see her, but Lynn said that she didn't need to touch whoever she helped."

James shook his head. "But—"

"I know it sounds strange, but people pray for loved ones faraway, don't they? Is it wrong to want help?"

"How much did you pay her?"

"I'm not proud of what I did. I know what investors would think if they knew the truth. That's why I kept it a secret. I didn't use any company funds. No money can be traced to her."

"How much?"

"For a while it seemed to be working. You saw it too, didn't you? Your mother had more energy and seemed so happy. And the pain wasn't what it had been."

"Just give me a range," James said.

"It doesn't matter. I would have paid her millions if it would give your mother one more day." He turned to Ava with cold eyes. "I loved my wife. So much so I didn't tell her the truth about you. I made sure not to let her know what you've been up to behind our backs."

Ava felt her skin grow cold. How could she have been wrong about him? Everyone knew the marriage had been one of convenience. Edgar Fortune didn't love anything but money, right? He was lying. There was no psychic healer and what could he possibly know about her? He was trying to shift blame and confuse her. "I was only thinking about Flo when I saw you with that other woman. I didn't mean to—"

"You can stop the act. I know you've been trying to buy up shares. I had a very informative conversation with Lortis who likes to keep me up-to-date about things. Your pathetic little purchases won't do much harm. I don't know the reason, but whatever you're planning won't work."

Ava kept her voice level. "I'm not planning anything."

Edgar rested his elbows on the table and clasped his hands together. "In boxing there are many great moves. The Haymaker, The Bolo Punch. I really like the Jab and Grab, which is a mixture of offense and defense. You lead in with a jab and quickly proceed to grab your opponent. It helps to neutralize any more attacks coming at you." He leaned forward. "But my favorite is The Body Drop Feint. It's a move of distraction. It allows your opponent to think you are about to do one thing, like punch him in a certain way, while you switch it up with another punch aimed at a different spot. You really should have thought carefully before trying to tussle with me."

"I know—"

"I taught my boys the same. James was a master at distraction. I'm sure you've seen some of his moves, but not all of them. Do you really know who you're in love with?"

"Not now," James said in a warning voice.

"Do you think he needs your protection?" Edgar continued. "He's the strongest of all of us. I thought I was tough, until I met this kid. This kid knows where his allegiance should be. You will not come between us."

Jackson flashed a cruel smile. "Did you really think you were part of this family? Did you really think you were the only one pretending for Mom's sake? She was the only reason you lasted as long as you did. James is a master player and he played you. You think that trip to Grenada happened by accident?" Jackson tapped his chest. "I helped him choose the spot."

"That's enough," James said.

"He wanted to make Mom happy, but with her out of the picture, there's no longer a reason for you to stay."

Ava didn't dare look at James, afraid to see what would shine in his eyes. Had it all been a lie? Grenada was just a plan to seduce her? She remembered his first warning, *When I seduce a woman she doesn't know it.* She now saw all his care and tenderness as an act.

"Ava," James said. "That's not—"

"You don't have to console her," Jackson said, "or worry about getting a divorce. You married an imposter."

James turned to his brother. "What?"

Jackson nodded. "Your marriage isn't legal because she married you under a false name. Her real name is—"

"What are you talking about?" Ava said. "Ava is my real name."

"Sure it is. And you haven't been buying up stock either, right?"

"I admit to that. My father is Walter Hughes and he once worked with your stepfather in the early days. But Edgar stole his ideas and took everything from him, forcing my father to flee the country and start over again. I just wanted my father to have a taste of the revenge he deserved."

"What's her real name?" Edgar asked Jackson. "I want to

understand what's going on."

"Amelia Bremmer."

"And her father?"

"Walter Bremmer."

Edgar nodded then turned to Ava with pity. "Your father lied to you."

"My father would never—"

"He did work briefly with me as did your mother. She was a talented office manager and I respected her. When she asked for my help I agreed. I know that doesn't fit my reputation, but it's the truth. Your father, at the time, made your mother very unhappy."

"My father was a brilliant man. He gave you ideas. I saw his notes."

"Maybe, but he didn't share them with me. There was no exchange of ideas. He had nothing to do with the founding of BioMed Solutions. He'd briefly worked in one of the labs that was all. Whatever he's told you is from his imagination. The last time I saw your father it was in a courtroom. Your mother had divorced him and wanted to get custody of you. My testimony helped her win that case and your father never forgave her. Or me. He kidnapped you and disappeared."

"No." Ava swallowed hard, bewildered by his words. "My mother left me. She—"

"She's been looking for you, for years."

Ava jumped to her feet. "This is all a lie. My father would never hurt me like this."

James rose too and took her arm. "Go upstairs. I'll be there in a minute."

She yanked her arm away. "Don't pretend to care," she said before she stormed out of the room.

CHAPTER 35

Jackson stared at his brother outraged. "You're letting her stay here? You should have kicked her out immediately."

James sat down and glared at him. "Keep your voice down."

"Why? She's dangerous. Didn't you hear what I just said?"

He looked at Jackson then Edgar. "I know, but we must also think about Rudy. He's gone through a lot and is already struggling with depression. More change could—"

"Don't you care what she's done?"

"Of course I care."

"Maybe not enough," Edgar said. "You let her get to you."

James turned away. "That's not it."

"She forced you to marry her," Jackson said.

"I know that."

"By having me locked up in a room with two thugs and telling me that I had to disappear for two days." Jackson nodded at his brother's look of surprise. "Yes, that's the secret she wanted me to keep hidden from you. She was no innocent in this mess. I would have played my role and arrived at the reception as we'd agreed if she hadn't interrupted our plans."

"What plans?" Edgar said.

"It's a long story," James said. He looked at Jackson. "I still think you went too far. You shouldn't have mentioned Grenada."

Jackson's brows shot up. "Are you feeling sorry for that thing? That creature from the Black Lagoon?"

"That's enough."

"One of her thugs even punched me."

"I'm not saying what she did was right, but she's a victim in all this too. Her father stole her from her mother and has been lying to her for years."

Edgar shook his head. "She won't believe anything you say. Walter Bremmer was a master manipulator. That's how he first tricked her mother into marrying him before showing his true colors. He even charmed the judge, but I was able to break through his façade." He fixed James with a look. "I'll tell you this only once. She doesn't deserve you. Getting her out of our lives will be the best thing for everyone. I want her out by tomorrow."

James sighed resigned, then went to Ava's room not surprised to see she was already gone. She'd left her ring behind on the pillow.

CHAPTER 36

Edgar retreated to his bedroom surprised by what he'd just heard. He sat on his bed and shook his head. Walter Bremmer had resurfaced in his life. Flo would have been shocked. He wished she was there to see how everything had unraveled. How the quiet little girl they'd briefly seen, had grown up. He hadn't wanted to get involved initially, but when he told Flo about his office manager's request to help her get custody of her only child, she was the one who'd urged him to testify in court against Walter. She had such a good heart.

He grabbed her pillow, held it close and cried. He fought not to make a sound as the depths of his sorrow bubbled out. His joy and peace. His life. He'd married her for gain and lost his heart instead.

He remembered kneeling by her bedside one last time. The light touch of her hand on his face, her weak smile. With all his money he couldn't make her well.

"Don't look at me like that," she said.

"There's something you should know," he said, ready to reveal the truth that had been a guilty thorn in his heart.

"I know Rudy was the real reason you married me. I know you wanted a child with special needs to improve your image and make you appear as someone you weren't. I know you also chose my sons so that you could have them look up to you, depend on you and serve you. I know I was the last part of your plan, a wife that would an accessory to your ambition." She took his hand. "I knew all that and I fell in love with you anyway. What does that say about me?"

He took her hand, pressing it against his lips. "I was not a good man and this is my punishment."

"No, my darling. Think of all the years we've had together. Think of the man you've become. Take care of our boys for me."

"Always."

"And could you do something else for me? I know it will be hard but—"

"Anything."

"Say the words."

He swallowed. He'd never realized in all the years they'd been married, he'd never said the words to her. The words that had lingered in his heart since the first day he'd told her she could stay the night with him. He closed his eyes against tears. The words were hard, words he'd never said to anyone. "I love you."

He opened his eyes, childishly wishing his words would have a magical affect and make her well again.

"Thank you," she said with a tired smile, but her eyes glowed with the light of youth and joy and he knew he'd made her happy with a gift that was priceless.

Edgar remembered that gaze as he held her pillow, his tears as fresh as the pain in his heart, but he also felt gratitude. He carefully set the pillow back down, as if it were precious. He'd been able to say goodbye, to tell her how he felt. No one else had loved him like she had, it was a debt he would forever repay. And that meant keeping her boys safe, which he would do until his last breath.

CHAPTER 37

Walter stared at his daughter with a bored expression. When she'd arrived at his apartment, brimming with anger, he'd expected a fight and was ready.

"What do you want?" he asked, opening the door wider.

She marched past him into the dark, cramped room and slammed the door behind her, the sound echoing down the hallway. "They told me."

"What?"

"The truth."

"What truth?"

"About Mom."

Walter sniffed. "That's one version of the story. The same story he used in court against me."

Ava stared at him. "So it is true?"

Walter hesitated, he hadn't imagined that she might have been doubting Edgar's story. Now he'd confirmed it. He slapped the wall with the flat of his hand. "I had no choice! He stripped me of my life. I wouldn't be surprised if he wasn't sleeping with her at the time."

"That's not the kind of man he is."

"You think you know him better now?" He sat down on a torn green couch the previous apartment owner had left behind. "You got used to the sweet life and you want to stay close, is that it?"

Ava quickly looked around the dingy room. "You don't have to live this way. I told you that I could help you get a better place."

"Now you're looking down on me?"

"You're lucky I'm still talking to you at all. You lied and said that Mom left."

He shrugged. "You were better off without her. She didn't realize how bright you were. You would have had a dull life with her. I wanted more for you. I gave you everything you needed."

"Except tenderness."

He winced at the word. "You didn't need that. That would have made you soft."

"I thought so too, at first until I met—"

"You were dumb enough to fall in love with him? He tossed you aside, didn't he?" He looked at her with disdain. "You should see yourself. Look at how his soft touch has made you weak. Pathetic. That's what your mother did too. Coddled you."

Ava looked at him with sadness. "You can't say it, can you?"

"Say what?"

"I'm sorry."

"Why would I say something I don't feel? You have a lot to

thank me for. I hope one day you'll see it. They did steal my life. They damaged my reputation. And now they're trying to steal you away from me. Will you let them?"

"No, Dad. I'm not being taken from you because you can't lose something you've never owned."

CHAPTER 38

"I don't know what to say," Camy said, her voice filled with dismay over the phone. "I always thought there might be something fishy about your father's story, but I never imagined this. He actual kidnapped you?"

Ava sat alone in her apartment on her hard couch, gripping her cell phone as if it were a life line. "Yes."

"What are you going to do?"

"I don't know where to begin. I want to find my mother, but I'm scared."

"What are you going to do about James? I know how you feel about him."

"It's over now."

Camy paused. "Give it time. Maybe—"

"There's too much to overcome. I have no one else to blame but myself. I had many chances to turn back and I didn't. You should have seen how I accused his stepfather of cheating and when Jackson tells him what I did to him after the wedding, I'm sure he'll never want to see me again."

"You know you can always come and visit. Actually I'll be entertaining another of my aunt's students. You're welcome to join us."

Ava smiled. "Thanks, but I don't think I'd be good company."

"Whenever you're ready, I'm here."

"Thanks."

Ava disconnected and hugged herself, looking around the room. her apartment was a big improvement from the place where her father was staying, but not by much.

She'd never felt so cold. So alone. She hadn't realized how used to warmth she'd become. A warmth that had always been empty from her life, so she never missed it. She missed it now. Craved it. Wanted to fight the bone chilling ache inside her. She had no anger to fuel and warm her, leaving her hollow.

She felt as if she'd lost the only home she'd ever known. Even though it hadn't been real, it had felt real. It had felt safe. She missed James holding her, the feel of him in bed beside her, a feeling of belonging.

She began to drift off to sleep when she heard a soft knock on her front door. She looked through the peephole but the person was out of range. Was it her father? Had he come to apologize? Or was it Jackson coming to gloat?

"Who is it?"

"James."

She rubbed her hands together, trying to bank down her excitement. She couldn't jump to conclusions, she didn't know why he wanted to see her. She took a deep breath and opened the door. "Yes?"

"Can I come in?"

She hesitated then silently stepped back.

He sent a wary look at the couch then turned to her. "Why do you have a couch made up of textbooks?"

"My father and I used to move a lot and he didn't much care for furniture. But his books were his treasure so I learned to make use of them and he didn't complain. I guess I got used to it. I could get you a chair."

He shook his head and sat down. "I don't want to get too comfortable." He shook his head again, looking perplexed. "I don't know what I'm doing. I shouldn't even be here."

"Why not?"

"Because we're not going to work."

Her heart fell. She knew he couldn't forgive her. She sat down beside him, but looked straight ahead. "I see."

"Lies," he said with a tired sigh. "That's all we have between us. And now we've added my family's distrust. Do you think you can survive that? Do you want to?"

"Yes."

He turned sharply to her, amazed. "What?"

"I said yes." She licked her lower lip. "I want to be with you."

He covered his eyes. "Then I need to find a way to fix this. Any ideas?" He glanced at her when she didn't respond. "Why are you smiling?"

"You really still want to be with me?"

He nodded.

She closed her eyes and sighed with relief. She felt some warmth slipping back into her and leaned against him. "I thought I'd lost you."

"You may still lose me."

She straightened and stared at him, the cold, lost feeling returning.

"I have responsibilities," he said in a grim tone. "Do you think my brother Rudy can take any more changes? Do you think I want to live the rest of my life alienated from my brother and stepfather? It's not a choice I can make lightly."

"I understand," she said, even though it hurt.

"No, I don't think you do. I don't think you know what it's like to be ripped in two. To always try to do the right thing even though it kills you."

"I lived most of my life believing a lie. Hating the Fortunes, it felt like a betrayal falling in love with you, but I did."

His eyes narrowed suspiciously. "How do I know that this isn't part of your plan too?"

"What?"

"You wanted the Fortunes destroyed," he said in an even tone. "This could be the ultimate way to do it. I run off with you and then months from now you leave and my family is divided forever."

Ava gasped, shocked by his words. "If you think I'm capable of—"

"No," he said softly. He lightly touched her cheek. "I'm just throwing out a theory. Unfortunately, my stepfather is adamant that we can't be together."

"I could try to win him over."

James flashed a sour grin. "That would take a miracle. Once you've lost his trust, there's no way back."

"How about *your* trust?" He fell silent and his hesitation hurt her, but she fought not to let it show. "You don't have to answer that. All I ask for is some time."

"Time?"

"Wait for me," Ava said, resting her head on his shoulder, wanting to be close, even though he still felt far away. She had a renewed sense of purpose. "I'll win over your stepfather no matter what it takes." *And I'll fully win your heart too.*

CHAPTER 39

She was bold. He had to give her that.

Edgar studied Ava as she sat in his office. He tapped a finger against his large oak desk, ready for a match. His assistant had announced her arrival and he'd considered ignoring her request, but then succumbed out of curiosity. It had been a week since she'd left the house.

"You have five minutes."

"I only need two. As you know I've been studying BioMed Solutions closely."

He steepled his fingers and nodded.

"And I have a proposal." She placed a report in front of him.

Edgar briefly flipped through it then stopped on one page. "You want me to cut two of my divisions?"

"I believe you can sell them off for a large profit, and then focus your company's efforts on its highest performing divisions, while also incorporating the new product my company has developed. I believe by doing so you could increase profits a hundredfold."

"I don't need you for that. We signed an agreement, you can't back out now. Your company has already been folded into BioMed Solutions. I got what I wanted for the business. And let's not forget that you have benefitted financially and will continue to do so."

"I'm still legally married to James. Ava Hughes *is* my legal name. My father completed all the correct paperwork."

"Divorcing James won't be too painful. There's still the prenup. Once you leave you get nothing." He smiled. "What's your next move?"

"Flo."

His smile disappeared. "Don't you—"

"I'm sorry. I was wrong about you and I shouldn't have accused you, especially in front of your family. But I'll admit that I'm not really here for your sake or even mine, although I do love James. I'm here because of her." She glanced at the framed picture of Flo on his desk. "She taught me so much, but one thing she showed me was that it was okay to be vulnerable. That strength comes in many forms. Her love for her family made her strong at her weakest moment. I know she taught you that too."

Edgar shook his head. "It won't work. I don't want you near my family."

"Why not? You and I are the same. We both married for selfish reasons and we both lost our hearts. The difference is...I didn't have to wait years to find out."

Edgar rose to his feet. "You should go."

Ava remained seated. "You stood up for me once. I don't know what my life would have been like if I'd been raised by my mother, but it's good to know that someone was looking out for me. If nothing else, let that little girl pay you back."

Edgar slowly sat down. "You're definitely tenacious," he said with reluctant admiration. "A knockout punch."

"What?"

He held out his hand. "You have a deal."

CHAPTER 40

"What should I do with this?" Abigail asked James as he and Jackson sat watching TV in the great room. He looked up to see what she was holding in her hand and saw it was one of Ava's mangas. "I found it under the couch in the library."

"Thanks."

He reached for it, but Jackson snatched it first. "I'll make sure she gets it," he said.

Abigail nodded and walked away.

James glared at him and held out his hand. "Give it back."

"No."

"I want to return it to her myself."

Jackson returned his attention to the TV. James reached for the manga, but Jackson held him off. James grabbed him by the collar. "I'm not playing."

Jackson grabbed him by the throat. "Neither am I."

"You really want to fight me for this?"

"If I have to."

James pushed him away in disgust. "You can't stop me from seeing her."

Jackson smoothed out his collar then returned his attention to the TV.

"What are you doing here anyway?"

"Making sure she doesn't come back. I heard she visited Rudy's shop and had a meeting with Edgar."

"So what?"

"That means she's up to something."

James opened his mouth to reply, but another voice cut him off. "He's right."

The two men turned and saw Ava standing in the entryway. Before they could speak she walked up to Jackson and said, "I'm sorry. I'm sorry I had you kidnapped and held and that Camy's boyfriend punched you."

His brows shot up. "That was her boyfriend?"

"You weren't really in any danger, I just wanted you to think so. Will you ever forgive me?"

Jackson frowned, but not as fierce as he had in the past. "I don't know—"

"You might as well surrender," Edgar said, coming up behind her. He rested his hand on her shoulder. "She's not one to give up easily and you might as well get used to her. She's still part of the family." He looked at James. "Of course how *long* she stays that way depends on you."

Ava looked at him, anxious, not sure what he would say. "I know I need more time to win your trust," she said quickly, "but let's talk alone before you say anything."

James stood and sighed. "I don't want to talk." He held out his hand. "I want to be by your side when you're finally reunited with your mother."

Tears sprung to her eyes as she took his hand, happiness filling her. "Because that's what Flo would have wanted?"

"No," James said, pulling a ring from his trouser pocket. He got down on one knee and gazed up at her with his heart in his eyes. "Because I love you." He slid the ring on her finger and stood, drawing her close. "And I want to stand by your side...always."

DARA GIRARD

A Seductive Arrangement

DEDICATION

For Kemi
Rest in peace

"Your wife is here."

Jackson Fortune lazily rolled onto his side and squinted up at his personal assistant. The bedroom in his apartment was so bright it felt like a thousand lights had burst into his room all at once, trying their best to sear his pupils.

He closed his eyes with a groan and waved towards the lamp. "Turn that off."

"It is off."

Jackson carefully opened one eye wondering why the room was so bright then realized he hadn't closed the blinds last night. The morning's sun rays ate up every shadow in the room. He feebly gestured to the window, desperate for relief. "You know what to do."

He heard his assistant's steady gait as he walked over to the blinds. "These blinds are the least of your worries. You have a very urgent matter to deal with right now."

Jackson absently rubbed his forehead, wishing his assistant

didn't feel the need to use so many words so early in the morning. "Yeah...right. What did you just say?"

The painful sunlight disappeared as he heard the blinds close then his assistant return to the side of his bed. "I said your wife is here."

Jackson blinked waiting for the punch line. Before he could respond, he heard the bed sheets shift next to him and felt a warm, smooth leg brush against his. He turned to his bedmate and blinked. He'd forgotten he hadn't been sleeping alone. She was pretty with light cocoa skin and dark hair that was pleasantly tousled around her head and her name was...

She had a name. Of course she had a name. They always had a name. What was her name?

Her eyes narrowed. Not a good sign. "I didn't know you had a wife."

Jackson blinked quickly, trying to clear his fuzzy brain. Right...a wife. That's why he'd been shaken awake when he'd hoped to sleep in a few more hours. He turned back to his assistant. At least he knew his name. It was Reginald Bowler, but he called him "Bo" because he didn't like the sound of his surname and thought his first name had too many syllables. Bo hadn't worked for him very long. Was it eight months now? The length of his service was about as unremarkable as the man. He wasn't very tall, had a slightly ruddy complexion, tufts of grey hair and serious features. Serious was good.

His previous assistant had disappeared without explanation. Just left a resignation letter on the kitchen countertop without even the decency to at least let the chef know what to prepare for dinner. That had been annoying. The entire reason he had an assistant was to handle the issues he didn't want to. He had better things to do with his time.

Perhaps Bo had a hidden sense of humor and was playing a joke on him. He could take a joke.

Jackson yawned and rubbed his eyes. "I don't," he said, flashing her a smile. "Bo's just teasing."

Reginald cleared his throat and shook his head. "Teasing isn't part of my job description. I left her in the living room."

Jackson became a little more awake. "A woman's really here?"

"Yes."

He sat up. "Saying she's my *wife*?"

Reginald nodded.

"Tell her she has the wrong address."

"I also came to that conclusion, but she's very insistent. She won't leave until you see her."

Jackson slid back under the covers and rested his head on the pillow. "Then make her feel comfortable until she comes to her senses." He was too tired to deal with a crazy woman right now.

"Is that all?"

"Yes."

Jackson heard Reginald's footsteps leave before he closed his eyes. He sighed in frustration when he felt his bedmate nudge him with her foot.

"What?" he mumbled. He just wanted to sleep. It had been a wild night.

"What are you doing?" she asked.

He pulled up the sheet to his chin. "Do I really have to answer that?"

"Aren't you even curious?"

"Curious about what?"

She pulled the sheet down to his waist. "The woman."

Jackson rolled onto his back and looked up at her. Ooh... pretty eyes. Nice breasts. Damn what was her name? "No."

"There's a woman in your living room claiming to be your wife and you can just lie here and try to go back to sleep?"

"You say that as if it were a problem."

"Are you sure you're not married?"

"Of course I'm sure..." He stopped and bit his lip, wishing he could come up with a name. He'd sound more sincere that way. He swore. What was her name? She had a West African look and her accent sounded French. So he knew she was from one of those French speaking countries.

"I'm not sure I believe you." She turned her back to him and swung her legs over the side of the bed. "I'm going." She stood and began to change.

The bed felt cold without her and he hated feeling cold. Did she have a French name? Estelle? Coline? Marie? Probably not. Perhaps if he could remember what country she came from that could give him a clue. Was it Benin? Burundi? Niger?

"You don't have to go yet. It's all a misunderstanding I'm sure. I enjoyed last night." *What I can remember of it.* "And I'd like to see you again. Are you traveling back home to..." He let his words trail off hoping she'd fill in the blanks.

She zipped up her formfitting red dress. "No, I have work in Sweden."

Damn. "I'd like to see you again."

"Take care of your wife first." She stepped into her matching heels.

"I told you I don't have a—"

She grabbed her black clutch from off of his dresser. "*Adieu.*"

He felt the finality in her word. "Don't you mean *Au revoir?*"

"No." She left and closed the door behind her.

Damn and he still didn't know what her name was. Too bad. He pulled the sheets back up and closed his eyes. It didn't work. He couldn't go back to sleep. This stranger, possibly some tipsy ex-girlfriend of his that Bo couldn't identify, had ruined a perfect morning. Jackson kicked the bed sheets off in frustration. He just wanted to sleep.

He wasn't a morning person; he could barely function before ten and it was...

He glanced at his clock and saw it said ten thirty-six. Okay, but it was Saturday and he usually got up after twelve on a weekend. Plus, he'd had a late night. He wasn't like his brother James who would be showered, dressed and have solved the mystery of the confused woman who thought she was his wife by now.

Another couple of minutes and then he'd deal with her. If he was lucky, she'd give up and go home. The thought brought a smile to his face as he reached over, pulled up the sheets and sunk back into his pillow.

An hour later he woke up feeling refreshed. He took a shower, grabbed a robe and headed for the kitchen ready for something to eat.

He walked past the living room and paused when he saw a woman sitting there reading a book. A woman! A woman he didn't recognize because her head was lowered and her long dark hair framed her face, putting it in shadow. He swore. He'd forgotten about her. He dashed into the kitchen before she looked up and spotted him.

He rushed over to Reginald who stood at the sink washing a glass. Jackson gestured to the living room. "Who is that?"

Reginald set the glass on the drying rack before turning to him. "Your wife."

Jackson's brows shot up. "That lunatic is still here?"

"You told me to tell her to wait."

"I was kidding."

"You didn't tell me that."

"I didn't think she'd stay." He rested his hip against the counter. "Did she tell you what she wanted?"

"Only to see you. I told you she was insistent."

Fine. He'd deal with her after he'd eaten. Maybe waiting a little longer may encourage her to leave.

But she was still there after his breakfast of avocado toast with egg. He walked into the living room, annoyed when she sent him a quick disinterested glance before she returned her gaze to the book. He could tell by the colorful imagery it was a graphic novel. She was probably mad at him. Served her right for playing this prank. He sat down in the soft recliner in front of her.

"What do you want?"

She closed the book but didn't lift her head, keeping her face hidden. "You don't remember me, do you?" she said in a low voice.

That voice stirred something deep inside him. It had a sensual, husky edge that made him think of hot wax and black silk sheets.

He looked her up and down. Her voice was more memorable than the rest of her. She did a disservice to the purple mohair velvet sofa which she sat on and the 1920s Persian carpet her heeled boots rested on. She looked like she was dressed for a job interview in a straight black skirt, blue satin blouse and black boots which suited Virginia in the fall. She was pleasantly proportioned with brown skin and clear manicured nails. If he could see more of her face, maybe he'd remember something.

"If you'd look at me that may help."

She lifted her head and tossed her hair over her shoulder. She wore more makeup than a drag queen.

Nope, that didn't help. She seemed a little familiar but something was off. He could pretend, but then she'd know he was lying. "No."

She tossed the book on the oval shaped table with a sigh. He noticed it was a graphic novel he hadn't finished reading yet. "I was afraid of that."

"Are you sure you haven't confused me with someone else?"

"No, Jackson. I know who you are."

She knew his name. Of course she knew his name. She also knew where he lived and the way she said his name felt familiar. Felt good. There was something very familiar about her. Something he couldn't pinpoint. Yes, that voice...and those lips and that body...but it was also unfamiliar too.

He rubbed his forehead. "Lay it out for me. Why did you say we're married?"

"Because we are. We got married in Las Vegas."

She held up her hand and flashed the ring on her finger. "Don't worry, I only just put it on to show you. I haven't worn it since that night."

That night. Suddenly, it all came flooding back to him. Sort of. He remembered the threat of tears (hers not his). A lot of liquor (definitely him). A limo ride and not much else.

"When?"

"Two months ago."

He stared at her, stunned. "Two months ago and you're just telling me now?"

"Yes, well the thing is..."

Two months ago. He couldn't believe it. Wow. Okay, he had to think. Two months ago...hmm...two months...two months. Two months ago he remembered waking up alone in a hotel room in Las Vegas and catching a flight back to Kirkland before his stepfather gave him the riot act for missing a sched-uled meeting. He did remember taking a ring off his finger and briefly feeling victorious for some reason, but it had been a crazy weekend and he was ready to go home so he hadn't thought much of it.

"If we really did get married, why didn't you stay around and—"

"That's what I was trying to explain, if you were listening."

"I wasn't. Sorry. Start over. Why didn't you stay the next morning?"

"That was not part of the deal."

"Deal? You're sure you married me?"

She showed him the papers.

He briefly scanned them then nodded. "Clearly we both made a mistake. What do you want? An annulment? That's fine with me. I'll squash this before anyone finds out."

She bit her lip. "Might be too late for that. I came to apolo-gize. I didn't know who you were—are, and—"

Warning bells rang in his mind. She seemed nice and harmless, but he had to be careful. His tone sharpened. "You want money?"

"No."

"Blackmail?"

"No," she said losing patience. "I will explain everything but first you should change."

"Change?"

"Get yourself together."

"I am together."

She gestured towards him. "You always go around in just your robe?"

He glanced down amused. "Yes." He smiled at her. "Don't worry you're not going to see anything you shouldn't. Now start talking."

"What do you remember?"

He leaned back and rested his arm along the back of the couch. "Clearly not enough."

"I am really sorry about this. I thought I should get to you before someone else does. It was a mistake. I should have erased the pictures from my cell phone. I am willing to get a quick annulment and disappear from your life. At least I would have done that. I didn't expect my sister to see the pictures of us and then—"

Jackson shook his head. "Hold on. You're not making any sense. Who would get to me?"

"You haven't gotten any calls?"

"No."

"How about—?"

The sound of the doorbell stopped her words.

Jackson stood. "I wonder who that is?"

She sent him a wary look. "Trouble."

CHAPTER 2

For a moment Toyin thought she was hallucinating.

First there was one Jackson and now there were two. Except the man on the other side of the door seemed meaner and darker somehow. They both had the same tall, powerful physique; elegant, clean shaven features and smooth brown skin. But the other man wore a black sports jacket, somber colored grey shirt and trousers—a direct contrast to Jackson's stripped red and yellow robe.

"What have you gotten yourself into?" the man said then stopped when he saw her. "I'm sorry. I didn't realize it was true."

"What's true?" Jackson asked.

The man held out his hand to her. "I'm James Fortune by the way."

"Toyin. Toyin um..." Dear God she'd forgotten her last name. Why did this guy scare her? She already knew she was in trouble but the presence of this man made it all feel worse. "Jacobs."

He gestured to the sofa. "How long have you known my brother?"

She sat down, although she felt like running. "Not long."

"I see." He sat down beside her and turned to Jackson. "When were you going to tell us about her?"

"There's nothing to tell," Jackson said with a shrug. "I hardly know her."

James motioned to Jackson's robe. "You always entertain strangers like that?"

"I was with someone else when she just showed up out of the blue and—"

James surged to his feet. "You did what?"

"I didn't expect her to come."

James turned to her with regret. "I apologize on behalf of—"

"No, it's okay," Toyin said quickly, waving her hands. "It's my fault. I surprised him."

"He surprised all of us."

"It wasn't like that," Jackson said. "I wasn't cheating on her. I—"

James offered her a small smile of regret. "Will you excuse us for a minute?"

Toyin nodded, knowing it wasn't a question. She watched him take his brother's arm, lead him into another room and close the door.

"Would you like anything more to drink?" the ruddy faced man who'd told her to call him Reginald asked her.

"No, thank you."

"They may be a while."

"I should have just told him the truth an hour ago."

"This serves him right," Reginald said with a sly smile. "He shouldn't have kept you waiting."

"I'm sure it wasn't on purpose."

He sent her a look. "Jackson doesn't like to confront things."

"I can't blame him. At least about this. No one was supposed to know about it. It was just a stupid lark. But I'll find a way to fix it."

"You're not the only trouble he's gotten into so don't be too hard on yourself."

Reginald was being kind but she still felt guilty. If her nosy sister hadn't gotten hold of her cell phone her secret would have been safe. A reckless, crazy secret no one was supposed to know about. Something she'd even forgotten about until her sister stopped by her apartment to cheer her up.

"When's the last time you've left this place?" Maryam had asked her yesterday morning as she opened the closed blinds of Toyin's apartment, dust particles dancing all around her. She waved them away then brushed off her tailored white top and green trousers. Her hair was perfectly set in a pixie cut that complimented her oval shaped, earth brown face and small frame.

Toyin lay on her stomach on the couch dressed in a pair of old jeans and a pale blue sweatshirt. She stared at the TV feeling like a beached whale in comparison. She'd lived on the couch the past week. Unwashed dishes sat in the sink and clothes littered the ground along with two empty pizza boxes. She wouldn't cry but she had the right to fall apart. She'd returned from Las Vegas and discovered that the woman she'd hired to run TJ Studios, her web development and animation company, had lied about everything. She'd lied about the distribution opportunities she'd secured, the authors and illustrators she'd hired, the future business opportunities had been a mirage; she'd let contracts slide, and now Toyin was in deep financial trouble. She'd misled her for months!

Toyin had thought the dip in business had been due to competitors not from her manager siphoning off clients and then starting her own rival business. For the past two months she'd been scrambling to recover, but had stopped trying.

Toyin felt on the verge of a nervous breakdown, but she wouldn't cry about it.

"We're worried about you," Maryam said, pushing aside three Chinese and Italian takeaway cartons from the coffee table. "I realize that what happened with TJ Studios is hurtful—"

Toyin pushed up her glasses and glared at her. "Hurtful? You call an employee stealing your clients and designs *hurtful?*"

"Okay, a big betrayal, but you can fight this."

"I'm running out of funds." *And energy and the will to go on.*

"You still have your store to run."

It was small comfort. New Worlds, her comic and pop-culture shop, paid the bills and was something she enjoyed. It was female focused; designed for women to feel comfortable in. A contrast to more known places that had a grimy, leechy, male dominated energy. At New Worlds, women could ask questions without fear of condescension, where as in the larger comic world a woman without an encyclopedic knowledge of the industry is sometimes treated like a pathetic outsider.

With its clean, airy atmosphere, bright colors and knowledgeable friendly staff, New Worlds, had become popular and profitable with a robust online presence that helped maintain their visibility worldwide.

But TJ Studios, which she had set up in the space above the store, had been her passion and now it was over. She had no new projects and no energy to develop them or seek out new clients. "I have a manager who runs the store. I don't need to be there."

Maryam looked around the apartment in dismay, briefly scrunching her face at the sight of a large poster of Wonder Woman and another of Storm from X-Men. "This isn't like you. You can't live like this. It isn't healthy."

"I don't care." She didn't care much about anything since Shanna's deception and she didn't even want to think about Lance...

"Where's your cell phone?"

Toyin pulled her phone out of her back pocket and handed it to her. "Why?"

"I need to find someone you can talk to."

She groaned. Maryam could be irritating. An electrical engineer by trade and a pain in the ass by nature, her sister didn't know when to give up. "I'm talking to you, aren't I?"

"You need someone else to help you out of this funk."

"I don't want to talk to anyone. That's the point." Toyin motioned to the door. "Now go away."

Maryam searched through Toyin's cell phone. "It's amazing how many pictures you have on this thing. Do you even remember them all?"

Toyin sighed and pointed to the door. "If you're going to judge me, go home."

Maryam gasped and paused. "Who is this?"

"I don't know," Toyin said with little interest as she

grabbed her TV remote to search for another show to binge watch. Preferably something with more than fifty episodes. She didn't want to think.

Maryam enlarged the image and peered closer. "You have to know."

Something in her sister's tone told Toyin something bad was about to happen. She reached for the cell phone. "Let me see."

"Who is this man?" Maryam said, holding up the phone so Toyin could see the screen, but keeping it out of reach.

Toyin's heart constricted in horror as she stared at Jackson's face. She'd forgotten all about him and Las Vegas. "He's nobody," Toyin said, hoping her calm voice didn't make her sister suspicious. She returned her gaze to the TV hoping to look disinterested, her mouth suddenly dry. "I'll talk to Tansy later so you don't need to worry."

Maryam continued to look at the photos. "You did a great job with Photoshop."

Toyin closed her eyes wishing she hadn't taken so many pictures with him. "Yes, Photoshop is amazing."

"Except I don't think you would have manipulated so many pictures unless you had a strange obsession with this guy since you and Lance broke up."

"Right."

"Tell me the truth. Are these pictures real?"

Toyin hesitated.

"Don't tell me these pictures are real."

Toyin decided to be defensive. If she was defensive her sister may apologize and change the subject. It was the only tactic she could think of. She sat up and folded her arms. "Why wouldn't they be real?"

Her sister sent her a long, considering look and Toyin quickly realized she'd used the wrong strategy. Maryam had a more devious mind than she did. Because Maryam had chosen the more traditional route in life—graduate degree in engineering like their parents, marriage and children—no one in the family knew that on her study abroad in Belgium she'd had two lovers; she sometimes shoplifted small items and had a tattoo on her right inner thigh. She'd championed Toyin's career choice and finally helped their parents see some merit in her career as a cartoonist, illustrator and store owner.

"You don't know who this is," she said with a knowing grin.

"Of course I do," Toyin said, now feeling defensive for real. "You're the one who asked me."

"Because I was surprised to see him on your phone."

"It's nothing. He's just some guy I met in Las Vegas."

Maryam narrowed her eyes. "You're not telling me something."

Toyin held out her hand, motioning to the cell phone. "Did you find what you were looking for?"

Maryam held the cell phone close, her eyes wide with interest. "What happened?"

Toyin cleared her throat, folded her arms and glanced down; pushing an empty soda can aside with her foot. "Nothing."

"Then why are you two in front of a chapel?"

She shrugged, gripping her arms tighter. "The chapel was just there."

Maryam leaned forward and lowered her voice. "What did you do?"

Toyin met her sister's eyes then sighed in defeat. She could never stand up to her sister's lethal stare. That piercing look always made her feel as if she were five-years-old on the verge of being grounded. "I got married."

Maryam fell back in her seat as if dodging a punch. "You did *what?*"

Toyin threw out her hands. "I was depressed. He came along and cheered me up. We both had too much to drink and thought...*Screw the world let's do something crazy* and we did. I haven't gotten around to contacting him and fixing things because I got home and—"

"You got married?"

"Yes."

Maryam pointed to the photo, her hand shaking. "To him?"

Toyin sighed and nodded. "But you can't tell Mum and Dad."

Maryam waved the cell phone. "Are you *sure* you married this guy?"

Toyin rolled her eyes. "Why do you keep asking me that? Yes. I'm sure. Positive. One hundred percent." She snatched the cell phone and showed another image of Jackson kissing her on the cheek. "See? This is not something I could make up." She thought of a comic she'd created about a woman who could talk to the dead with a ninja squirrel as her sidekick. Her family knew she had a wild imagination. "Okay, scratch that, I could make it up, but I didn't."

"You're amazing."

Toyin tossed the cell phone on the table and lay back down. "I know."

"You don't know who he is."

Toyin growled in frustration. Why wouldn't her sister listen? "Yes, I do. His name is Jackson Fortune."

Maryam shook her head. "No, who he *really* is."

Toyin frowned. "He's not Jackson Fortune?"

"Yes, but he's more than just a name. This is why I've told you to read the business section and the articles I forward to you. How you can expect to run a lucrative business and not do so is beyond me."

Toyin stuck out her tongue.

"Does his family know about you?" Maryam asked.

"No, nobody knows about this. What are you doing?" she asked when her sister picked up her phone and started typing.

"I'm going to help you."

She sat up and reached for the cell phone. "I don't need your help."

Maryam moved the cell phone out of reach and continued typing. "Yes, you do. You've got a golden ticket and you don't even know it. Fortunately, I do. This is what big sisters are for."

Toyin stood up to grab it. "Maryam—"

Maryam jumped out of her seat and backed away, her gaze never leaving the screen. "You leave this to me. You need money and he's loaded."

"Wait. No!" Toyin grabbed her sister's arm. "He helped me out already and—"

Maryam pushed "Send" with her free thumb then handed the cell phone to Toyin with a big smile. "That's the problem with you. You're too nice. Opportunities like this don't come every day."

Toyin stared down at her cell phone horrified. "What have you done?"

"Changed your life."

For better or worse? Toyin now wondered as she looked around Jackson's stylish bachelor pad, her gaze spotting an original Basquiat painting and vintage French coffee tables. She buried her face in her hands. Her life had changed enough as it was. She didn't need any more change.

How was she supposed to know that the drunken stranger she'd married was the stepson of the founder of BioMed Solutions? A multi-million dollar company. How could she have imagined that her bossy sister had been able to create a major social media storm with a few choice words and interesting pictures? Weren't most things posted online ignored? Weren't millions of things posted every day? How could this stupid story have gained any traction?

But it had and that was why she had to warn Jackson because Maryam's action hadn't only changed her life, she'd changed his too.

CHAPTER 3

Laughing would probably be a bad idea, but the look on his brother's face made Jackson want to laugh anyway. His brother's expression reminded him of the time he'd covered a bagel with frosting and sprinkles to make it look like a donut. He really didn't think anyone would fall for it. James had and he hadn't found it funny.

And Jackson knew what was happening now wasn't funny either, but he still had to bite his lip.

James stood in the middle of the bedroom with his hands on his hips and glared at him. "Why didn't you tell me you had a wife?"

Jackson opened his dresser drawer. Putting on some more clothes was probably a good idea. "I didn't know I had a wife. I mean I forgot I had a wife. I don't know what's going on. I woke up with..." Jackson closed his eyes and pounded his forehead with his fist. "I should know her name."

"Yes, you should," James said in a dry tone. "It's Enomwoyi."

Jackson stared at him. "En-no what?"

"En-nohm-WHO-yee."

Jackson swore. He'd never have guessed that. "How did you remember that?"

"She introduced herself to me at the party last night, but that's not the point. Who is *she*?"

Jackson tapped his chest. "You just told me. She's someone I met last night." The charity party had been more interesting than he'd expected it to be. He couldn't stop a grin as he walked into his closet. His brother liked to tease him that it was the size of an Olympic swimming pool. "She was amazing. She could do this thing with her lips that—"

"Not Enomwoyi," James said with a frown as he followed him, "your wife."

Jackson folded his arms and let his gaze skim over his selection of shirts then sweaters. "Oh, right. Her."

"Yes, her! Mrs. Jackson Fortune. Do you realize what you've done?"

"Right," he said absently. Should today be an orange or yellow day? He turned sharply when he heard his brother swear before he grabbed three shirts and put them in another location. "What are you doing?" Jackson demanded. He took the shirts and put them back in place. When it came to his clothes he had a precise order. They were arranged by size, color, season and material.

"Getting you to pay attention."

"You're the one who told me not to go around in my robe."

James reached for another shirt.

Jackson held up his hands in surrender. "I'm listening. I'm listening."

"What happened?"

"I'm not sure yet."

"That's not good enough. You need a good story to tell Edgar."

Jackson sighed at the mention of their stepfather. Their stepfather, Edgar Fortune, was founder of BioMed Solutions, a company that manufactured joint replacements. While not a sexy business, with a growing aging population with more active lives, business was booming.

Edgar had eclipsed any memory they'd had of their Grenadian father who'd left their lives a year after their younger brother Rudy was born with Down syndrome.

Edgar had adopted them and they'd lost their last name "Brownson" and had become Fortunes. Edgar liked to constantly remind them, "I gave you my name for a reason. It means your fortunes have changed. So you owe everything to me." He had drilled into them the importance of maintaining a good reputation. Jackson hadn't always been as diligent as his brother, but he'd never gotten into trouble like this before. Neither of them liked displeasing him.

At six-years-old Jackson had been in awe of the Jamaican born-US raised man who loved Cuban cigars, boxing and fast horses. His awe soon turned to affection, although it had taken years to warm up to him. Edgar was a driven, ruthless man and a hard man to get close to and had surprised many by marrying a woman with three kids. After their mother's passing last year, he'd softened a little, but not enough to look past a mistake like this.

Angering Edgar was never a good idea. "I will give him the perfect story."

"At least tell me you got a prenup," James said.

Jackson rubbed his forehead.

James read his expression and swore. He stormed farther into the large closet, grabbed a bunch of shirts and threw them on the ground.

Jackson raced after him and gathered them up like they were precious gems. "Not the clothes. Not the clothes! Take it out on me."

James grabbed him by the lapels of his robe and shook him. "You want Edgar to kill you?"

"Relax," Jackson said with a nervous laugh, "this is what lawyers are for. Trust me. I can handle this. I'll pay her off and get rid of her quietly. No one needs to know."

James patted him on the cheek and flashed a sour grin. "You haven't woken up yet, have you?"

"What do you mean?"

He rested his hands on his hips. "Why do you think I'm here?"

"I don't know."

James pulled out his cell phone then showed Jackson an online posting with the heading *Fortune Finds a Bride!* and a picture of Jackson and Toyin smiling in front of a chapel.

Jackson stared at the image appalled. "How did this happen?"

"You tell me."

"Why did I wear that shirt? It looks awful against—"

James snatched the cell phone from him. He walked to a silk cream colored shirt Jackson hadn't picked up off the ground and stomped on it, leaving a footprint. "That's not the point." He stomped on it again.

Jackson shook with anger as he stared at the damage. He kept his voice low. "What is wrong with you?"

James's brows shot up. "What's wrong with me? My brother is an idiot!"

Jackson gathered the rest of the shirts and placed them on the bed, separating what would have to be dry cleaned and ironed. "We could just squash it as a rumor. Get the lawyers on it."

"It won't be that easy."

"In the meantime I just need you to do me a favor. Someone needs to deal with her." He pointed to James's jacket. "Let me—"

James laughed. "Don't even think about it," he said, reading his brother's mind. "I'm never switching places with you again. I took care of one wife for you, this time you're on your own."

"I thought you came here to help me."

"No, I came here to warn you."

"About what?"

"Edgar collapsed last night after the event. He's okay now," James quickly said, seeing the concern on his brother's face, "but you know Mom's passing hit him hard. He can't take any more stress."

"So you're saying he doesn't know?"

"Not yet. We need a quick, simple solution."

Jackson grinned. "You leave that to me." When his brother looked unconvinced he frowned. "What?"

"You haven't been yourself since..."

"Since what?"

"You know what."

"I'm fine." Jackson held up the ruined shirt. "Except when my brother goes crazy and does this."

James's blinked, unmoved. "You have six others."

"They're not the same."

"White is white."

Jackson waved his hand. "Don't go there with me." He and his brother never agreed when it came to clothes, food, art or entertainment. "Mom's passing was a surprise for all of us, but I'm moving on. I haven't changed."

James's tone softened. "Three assistants in six months?"

"Bo's stayed so far," Jackson said, seeking some credit. He knew he'd given his past assistants a hard time—changing his schedule without warning, at times losing his temper. "I've improved."

"You call a wedding in Vegas an improvement? What is going on with you?"

Jackson shrugged. "Living life to the fullest."

"Recklessly."

Jackson went into the closet again and grabbed a pair of dark purple trousers. "I don't need a lecture."

"I'm not only here because of Edgar. It's Ava. She's been talking to Edgar about...about possibly removing you as head of marketing."

Jackson sat down hard on the bed as if he'd been punched in the gut.

"It wouldn't be permanent," James continued, "just for a couple of months until you...get yourself together."

Jackson glared at him. "Talk about holding a grudge! That woman has had it in it for me since—"

"I agree with her."

For a moment Jackson lost the power to speak. Words filled his mind but the pain of his brother's betrayal stopped them from leaving his mouth. He swallowed then said in a hoarse voice, "You what?"

James sighed with regret. "I agree with her."

Jackson surged to his feet. "You want to see me kicked out of our company? A company you and I have helped build? You're throwing me over for her?"

"It's not throwing you over. If it were just your personal life then I would defend you, but you've made critical public mistakes that have affected the company. When your choices affect other's livelihood I can't sit back. It's not good for all of us."

Jackson pulled on his trousers. "Mistakes happen."

"Want to say that to Edgar?"

He knew what his stepfather would say. He didn't mind mistakes as long as they weren't lazy ones and Jackson's had been the worst kind. In a rush he'd sent out a typo filled memo and another with an image inserted upside down; at the last minute he'd stopped himself before sending out a huge email marketing push to the wrong subscriber list.

But the worst had been the recent disastrous new logo launch which he'd pushed for to expand the brand, an unnecessary and costly decision. The new logo had lasted an amazing two days before its demise at the hands of a public outcry. They hated the look and what they thought it represented. It was only in hindsight that he realized he'd gotten out of touch with their core base and had ignored the feeling towards the brand. He'd been too focused on the numbers: Blinded by software that focused on customer relationship management instead of what was truly important—the actual *people* behind the data. He wasn't used to feeling embarrassed, but he was and knew his brother had a right to be worried. Which only angered him more.

He selected a purple and white geometric shirt and put it on. "I'm good at what I do."

"You used to be."

James's words hurt, but Jackson knew his brother was right. He hadn't been as topnotch as he'd been before his brother's marriage to Ava and his mother's passing. Both had hit him hard—Ava's initial hidden agenda against the Fortune family and their mother succumbing to cancer faster than they'd expected. He didn't want to admit how unmoored he'd felt since last year. It embarrassed him that others had noticed too. He was thirty-five; he should have his life under control.

"I'm not going to let her force me out."

"She's thinking about the company."

"I don't believe that. She's thinking about her investment. Her reputation." Ava's arrival in their lives, both personally and professionally, had come at an opportune time. The agent Ava's company had developed was a biodegradable solution that allowed replaced joints to stay in place longer and to eventually be replaced by the patient's own cells within two or three years. It had given BioMed Solutions the extra value to please stockholders. And her marriage to James had also given the company's image a boost. Both events had pleased Edgar immensely.

"Maybe it's time to start thinking about yours."

Jackson held up his hand. "Enough. You win."

"This isn't a game."

"Then why do I feel as if I've already lost?"

"Jackson, listen—"

"No, you can't let her—" He took a deep breath, not wanting to show his anger. "You have to take my side in this." He held his brother's gaze, pleading. "This is all I have. What am I supposed to do? Huh? Mom used to tell me how proud she was of me, of us...I won't let Ava take this way from me."

"Then stop giving her ammunition. I told her not to tell Edgar about this marriage fiasco and I've made sure he won't hear about it for at least a few days, but time isn't on your side." James held up his hand before Jackson could speak. "I will give you a second chance and let you stay as head of marketing, if you do one thing. Show me you're the same guy who did Operation Domination."

Jackson couldn't stop a smile. He hadn't heard that phrase for so long for a moment he didn't know what his brother was talking about. Then it all came back to him. The person he used to be. Someone he'd forgotten.

Seventeen years ago, as a freshman in college, he'd wanted to prove to Edgar that he had the skill to be hired by the company in the marketing division. So he'd given himself a challenge and told Edgar about it. He'd pledge the worse fraternity on campus and then turn it into the best. He'd achieve his mission by using valid marketing strategies to increase its membership by hosting four get acquainted parties. He wanted to convince students to join *his* fraternity above all others.

So using his basic understanding of why guys joined fraternities—mainly to meet girls and a sense of brotherhood—he set out to prove that his fraternity had it all. When his first attempts to invite the most sexy and beautiful girls on campus to act as hostesses at parties failed, he decided to hire five of the most beautiful strippers from two local strip clubs. They were eager to pretend to be sexy coeds and hostesses for his parties. He also had the guys practice pretending to be "brotherly" when in most cases they couldn't stand each other. By the time he launched the fraternity's first party they looked like the most connected group of guys with the hottest women around.

He ended up with the biggest pledge class in the school's history, by the time the fourth party occurred they didn't have enough room for everyone and the strippers had such a good time that they invited their girlfriends to come and party too. He'd impressed everyone, especially Edgar. He'd succeeded at both goals.

Could he do something like that again? He knew it wasn't a real question. He didn't have a choice. He flashed his brother a smile and tugged on the cuffs of his shirt, ready to lie. "You can trust me. I've got it all under control."

CHAPTER 4

"You know I want to trust you," James said, following Jackson down the hall towards the living room, "but then you do crazy things like get married and sleep with women whose name you don't remember the next morning, I get worried."

Jackson shook his head impressed. "I don't know how you were able to remember her name, but it wasn't going to be a one night stand. I liked Eno...uh you know. Not only is she beautiful, but she is smart and that accent—"

"The accent is fake," Toyin said.

The brothers stopped in the entryway and stared at her. Toyin looked at their startled faces and waved her hand. "Sorry, none of my business."

"What do you mean the accent is fake?" James said, taking a step forward.

"It's very good, but before she left, someone called her and I overheard her on the phone and her accent was gone."

James hung his head. "Damn. The curse strikes again."

"Curse?" Toyin said.

"It's nothing," Jackson said with a grin.

"Nothing?" James said. "In a vat of a thousand, you'd find the one rotten apple."

"She probably was just trying to impress us."

"Then why did she try to take your USB?" Toyin asked.

"USB?" the brothers said in unison.

Toyin nodded. "Yes, it was on the table and I thought it was strange when she came and briefly talked to me before she left."

James sat down in front of her, intrigued. "She spoke to you?"

"Yes, she was saying how sorry she was. That she didn't know Jackson was married. At first I thought she was truly distressed until I noticed that when she passed by that coffee table—"

"It's a cocktail table," Jackson said.

"They're the same thing," James said.

"No, coffee tables are thicker and sturdier. Look at these fine lines."

James turned to Toyin and pointed to Jackson. "As you can see my brother gets easily distracted by nonessentials."

"It's not—"

"What happened?" James interrupted.

"The USB was gone," Toyin said.

James swore. Jackson sunk into the couch and stared at the table.

"Who does she work for?" James asked him.

"I don't know. I think it was some medical firm. She said she was worried she might get fired if their sales didn't increase soon."

"And that didn't raise alarm bells?"

Jackson looked up at him. "Why would it?"

"What was on the USB?" James asked.

Jackson shook his head.

"Tell me what was on it."

He stood and paced. "A special campaign project the team was working on. I—"

"Don't worry," Toyin said, holding up the item. "She didn't leave with it." She stood up and set the item down on the table.

The same moment James seized the USB, Jackson walked over to Toyin and whispered, "Just play along and pretend that you love me," before he turned to his brother and said, "She's lying."

James looked up at him, startled. "What?"

Jackson turned to her, his eyes dark. "Aren't you?"

Toyin blinked not knowing what to say. Shocked by his sudden change. At first she'd feared his brother now she wasn't sure of him. "I..."

"You're upset because you found me with another woman and you want to discredit her," Jackson said. "Isn't that it?"

She swallowed and licked her lips. "No," she said, drawing out the word, trying to think of what to say in response. "I wasn't lying. I knew she was bad for you the moment I saw her and...don't you remember? That's why you married me."

The two men looked at her openmouthed.

She took that moment to expand on her lie. "You wanted me to keep you safe from gold diggers and users because you thought you were cursed," she added, remembering what his brother had just said. "Of course I didn't think I'd fall in love with you on top of it."

"Wait, sit down," James said. "Are you telling me my brother planned this?"

She nodded, but didn't sit, feeling uncomfortable with Jackson standing so close to her and staring at her as if she'd grown a second head. "He was drunk at the time, yes, so I'm not surprised he doesn't remember, but he asked me to be his secret weapon. He told me how he's had bad luck with women and that he needed a weapon to keep him out of trouble. 'If only I had a wife,' " she said, deepening his voice to mimic his. She shot him a glance. "Yes, that's what you said and I said 'Could it be anyone?' and you said 'Sure'. I was also a little tipsy and recovering from a breakup so we did the deed. No one was supposed to know, but it leaked when my sister saw the pictures on my cell phone. We've been secretly seeing each other for two months."

"I don't believe this," James said. "How long were you going to keep this up?"

"I don't know," Toyin said, wondering how to strengthen her lie. "Jackson thought he needed several months to get over his bad luck. I didn't realize he'd already fallen off track or I would have been here sooner. That's part of why I announced our marriage so that I could keep him safe from other women."

James frowned. "I thought you said your sister leaked it?"

Oops, yes, she'd forgotten about that. Best to stick to one story. "She did, but only because I was thinking about it."

"You didn't come here for an annulment?"

"I don't want his money," Toyin said quickly, wishing Jackson would say something so she could stop digging herself in deeper. "Don't worry about that. I truly do...uh...c-care about him, although I know he doesn't feel the same about me. I just wanted to help."

James clapped his hands together, jumped up and laughed. "You got me!" He hugged his brother. "I should have known this was one of your tricks and if I hadn't been so relieved I would be furious. You really made me believe—" He shook his head, grinned and slapped his brother on the back. "You sly dog. You had me really worried for a minute. She's perfect. Why didn't you just tell me the truth?"

Jackson plastered on a smile. "You know I don't think sharp in the morning."

"It's nearly noon." James turned to Toyin. "You're right. My brother has a soft spot that makes him vulnerable. You're exactly what he needs right now."

Toyin took Jackson's hand and gazed up at him with a look of longing. "If only he felt the same."

Humor touched his eyes and he bit his lip.

She narrowed her gaze daring him to laugh.

Jackson squeezed her hand and looked away, but she saw his shoulders shake.

"This is amazing," James said. "We need you to expand on this."

Jackson looked at him uncertain, all humor gone. "Expand on what?"

"This charade. No more secret meetings. She has to move in with you and you have to make it real." James rested his hands on his hips. "I'm proud of you. A true winner. I don't know how you managed it, but you found a woman who's sincere. She hasn't asked for money, she won't mention anything about Enomwoyi and when the timing is right she's willing to annul this quietly. I think that says a lot about her. She's great for your image. She'll give you a look of stability.

She can keep the gold diggers away. Plus, with Edgar in a bad way right now, he could use good news."

"I'll only do it on one condition."

"What?"

"No suspension. Not even briefly."

"I'll talk to Ava."

"No, I'm talking to you." He held out his hand. "Do we have a deal?"

James sighed then nodded and shook his hand. "We do."

Jackson smiled. "Good."

"I'll get going now."

"Bye. Tell Ava where she can put her broom."

James laughed used to his brother's good natured teasing. "Talk to you soon," he said then left.

"What just happened?" Toyin asked after James had gone.

Jackson turned to Toyin. "You just saved my life," he said then pulled her close and covered her mouth with his.

CHAPTER 5

The surprise alone should have stopped her from responding but her body did anyway. It savored the soft, warm feel of his lips against hers. One arm encircling her waist, bringing her body close to his. One hand soft as it slid down the back of her neck, in direct contrast to his body which was hard. Solid. Hot. The heat penetrating his shirt and hers, making her temperature rise. The sweet, savage assault of his mouth, causing shivers of delight to race through her.

Jackson drew away, licked his lips, as if savoring the final taste of a good meal and let his hand slid down her hip, "Yes," he said in a low hiss. "I remember this." He kissed her again, quick and a little wild before he said in wonder, "I'm in love."

"Wh-what?" she stammered, breathless.

His dark eyes searched her face. "I know you, but you look different."

"Jackson," she said unable to say anything more than his name.

"Why isn't it coming together? I've never felt like this with anyone."

"What just happened?"

"I don't know," he said with feeling. "Let's try it again." He bent to kiss her.

Toyin pressed her hand against his chest, stopping him. "Not the kiss. Your brother."

He drew her close. "Let's discuss him later."

She struggled to free herself, annoyed that she liked the feel of his hands around her. "Stop it. You were just with another woman."

"I know. I'm sorry. I forgot it was like this."

She wiggled out of his grasp and took a hasty step back, desperate for distance. "Jackson, be serious."

"I am. You felt it too, right?"

"No," she lied, wishing her lips didn't tingle. That her body didn't remember every place where his hands had been. "Now sit down and tell me what's going on. Why did you want me to pretend I loved you?"

Jackson looked at her for a long moment then nodded resigned, but he didn't sit down. Instead he folded his arms. "Nobody can ever know about Eno...whatsit."

"Enomwoyi."

His brows shot up. "You remember her name too?"

It was easy to remember the name of the gorgeous Amazon who made her feel as appealing as a tree stump. "Yes, go on."

He rubbed the back of his neck. "I have a habit of finding women who want to use me. In the past it wasn't a big deal, but now I can't afford it." He frowned. "You don't look surprise."

"Why would I be? You told me this two months ago."

He looked sheepish. "I talked a lot, didn't I?"

She nodded.

"So I must have told you about Ava."

"The woman you were supposed to marry, but who ended up marrying your brother instead?"

"Yes, that's her. Recently, I've made some mistakes and that would give her just what she needs to get rid of me."

Toyin paused, surprised. "You think she's trying to get your brother to push you out of the business?"

"No, unfortunately, I don't think it's that simple. The truth is my family thinks I'm a liability and I need to prove that I'm not. I will pay you enough to make this worth your while to play this charade for a couple more months." He motioned her towards him.

She took a hesitant step forward. "What is it?"

"I want to kiss you again and see if I remember anything else."

She was tempted, but knew he was too charming to toy with. Even his casual remark of being "in love" already had her heart racing and her mind running wild. There was no way he was being serious and she couldn't let herself fall for him. "No, it won't help. You wouldn't remember anything by kissing me anyway."

"Why not?"

"Because we didn't kiss in Vegas."

"Really?" He laughed. "I married you and I didn't kiss you? That doesn't sound like me."

He was right. She was lying, but if he could barely even remember who she was she wasn't going to remind him of a kiss that still had her mouth burning even more so than the brief one he'd just given her now. It was clear she was one of many.

"You look both familiar and strange at the same time." He stopped and stared at a napkin she'd left on the table. When Reginald had given her a drink he'd offered her the napkin which, out of boredom, she'd used to sketch a squirrel with numb chucks. Jackson lifted it up then looked at her. "Take off the wig."

Her hand shot to her head; her face burned. "What? How do you know I'm wearing a wig?"

"Because it's not a very good one." He sat down and winked up at her. "You can relax, Toyin. I remember you. I was teasing."

She sat down in front of him and folded her arms. She was not taking off the wig. "Were you pretending the entire time?"

"No, not the entire time. Take off the lashes too." He motioned to her clothes. "Why did you dress up like that anyway?"

It had been her sister's idea. Toyin usually wore jeans and a shirt, kept her shoulder length black hair in twists, wore black, square glasses and barely any makeup. At times, for fun, she would put on a pink or silver wig and lipstick to match. But her sister didn't think that was posh enough, so she shoved Toyin in a fitted skirt and blouse, wig, contacts and false lashes and enough makeup to make her face feel like it was falling under the weight of it. "I thought if I was going to pretend to be your wife I have to play the part."

"Technically you are my wife. So you don't have to pretend."

"I wanted to make an impression."

"It's the wrong one; you look a little too..." He waved his

hand searching for words. "Much. And that's saying a lot coming from me. But we'll work on that later."

"Your brother liked me, remember?"

"My brother thinks there's only one type of white," Jackson said in disgust.

"Technically, he's right," she said, stretching the word "technically" the way he had. "But there are shades of white like vanilla, cream and eggshell. Just as there are shades of brown like chestnut and beaver or orange such as peach and apricot...what?" she said when he stared at her strangely. "Sorry, I know I can go on."

"No, it's nice. You understand me. Most people don't understand the language of color. How important it is."

"I took a course on color theory."

He grinned, his eyes warm. "Me too." His grin fell. "Which is why you should know that wig is too black for your skin tone and drowns out the soft red undertone of your skin."

The way his gaze made a slow descent down her body, made her skin tingle. She didn't know how he managed to make a criticism feel sensual but he did. Her face burned. "I'll take it off later." Toyin adjusted the wig, resisting the urge to scratch, her head felt hot.

"You can at least take off the lashes."

"You'd probably want me to take my clothes off too."

He leaned forward and let his voice drop. "Only if you insist."

She couldn't help a laugh. "No."

His eyes held hers, his dark gaze taking her in. "You're fine just the way you are."

Toyin turned away unable to hold his gaze. He was

dangerous. How could he so easily flirt with her after waking up with another woman?

Jackson clasped his hands together and rested his chin on top of them. "It was just sex."

She looked at him again. "What?"

"I like having sex. That's all it was." He shook his head. "No, I'm not a mind reader, I'm just good at reading faces."

"Then why are you so bad at choosing women?"

He let his hands fall and shrugged. "Don't know."

"So you do remember what happened?"

He grinned. "Enough."

She wasn't sure she liked the gleam in his eyes. That was how she'd ended up married to him in the first place. He was a true mischief maker and she wasn't sure she wanted to be part of the chaos he could create. The offer of money sounded good, but would it be enough to deal with any long term consequences?

"I'll take care of you," he said.

"What?"

"You looked worried and I'm telling you not to be." He offered her a generous financial amount.

Toyin stared at him amazed.

"Will that make everything worth it? I need you. I told you, I have to prove myself. I am also worried about my stepfather's health and...you won't have to do much. I'm sure you could use the money."

"Why would you say that?"

He shrugged. "Most people do."

Her sister was right. She needed the money and this was her chance. She could use the money to hire the lawyers she needed and recoup what was left of TJ Studios and possibly start again. And the landlord had threatened to raise the rent on her store because of its excellent location. He'd ignored her pleas to let her buy the property out right.

She was desperate, but there was also something suspicious about all this. About the casual way he mentioned her needing funds. She didn't remember telling him about her money problems, but perhaps he'd made a lucky guess. She wouldn't overthink it. She could just hear her sister scolding her for giving up a good opportunity. What would be so hard about being married to a wealthy guy for a few months?

"Okay," she said, "I'll do it on one condition."

"Go ahead."

"Never say you love me. Not in jest and definitely not for real."

He laughed. "You're joking, right?"

She didn't smile. "No, that's my condition."

Jackson stared at her for a long moment then shook his head. "Sorry, come up with something else."

Toyin blinked, stunned by his response. "Why?"

"Because I'm going to slip and say 'I love you.' I can't help myself."

"Try."

"No."

"But you don't."

He shrugged.

"I don't like when people cheapen such a powerful word by using it all the time."

He shrugged again, unfazed. "I can't help that I love a lot of things."

"Like women and wine?"

He placed a hand over his heart. "Ouch."

"I take words seriously." When his expression didn't change she sighed. He'd be harder to defeat than her sister. "Fine, you can say whatever you want, but don't expect me to say that I love you."

"No, that's part of the deal."

"I'll act like I love you, but I won't say it."

"I'll pay you fifty dollars each time you say it. A maximum of three hundred a day. Not to be said consecutively. They must be spaced."

"You're not serious."

"I'm offering money, of course I'm serious."

"Who says 'I love you' to someone six times a day?"

"You," he said with a wink, "if it's worth your while."

Toyin briefly hung her head. "I'm not winning this argument, am I?"

"This is a negotiation not an argument."

She lifted her head. "Okay, deal."

"Good, any other conditions?"

"I'm not sleeping with you."

He merely smiled, but his smile said 'yet' and she didn't want to argue. He'd already outmaneuvered her twice.

She'd have to make sure to never sleep with him and under no circumstances to fall for him. Ever. He was certainly handsome and could be charming, but he could also be cunning and reckless. No woman in her right mind would give her heart to a man like him. She could save her business and after the charade was over she'd never have to see him again.

"If you're with other women be discreet," she said.

"There won't be other women."

He sounded sincere, but she didn't dare believe him. "I

don't care what you do. Just don't humiliate me until this charade is over."

She expected him to argue. Instead he took her hand and kissed the back of it. "Your wish is my command," he said then a slow smile spread across his lips.

And her traitorous heart responded. It was that same mischievous expression that had gotten her into this mess two months ago...

CHAPTER 6

LAS VEGAS, TWO MONTHS AGO

She wouldn't cry. Toyin took a long swallow of her whiskey, then set the glass on the laminated plastic bar, ignoring the happy chatter around her. No matter how much it hurt she wouldn't shed a tear. She'd be stoic, resolute.

She would not cry about her boyfriend running off with her business manager and leaving her alone in a Las Vegas hotel where they'd planned to elope.

She wouldn't cry because she'd believed the words he'd told her only a few hours ago.

"I love you more than you know," he'd said after they'd left the comic conference room together that morning. They'd come to the multi-day event in Las Vegas for both business development and a chance to network with other trade and creative professionals in the industry, meeting long-standing and upcoming artists, colorists, inkers, editors, producers and publishers. She'd felt charged by the atmosphere and couldn't wait to go home and use the knowledge and new connections she'd been able to make.

"I know," Toyin said, thinking that the creative buzz had influenced him. "Hasn't it been a great conference?" She watched people dressed up as Captain America, Deadpool and Elsa the Snow Queen walk pass them.

He tugged on her sleeve to get her attention. "We're here. So let's do it."

She looked at him confused. "Let's do what?"

"Get married. Let's do something impulsive. I don't see myself spending my life with anyone else."

And in her madness she'd agreed. They'd been dating for nearly two years. It seemed the right move. He loved her. Wasn't that enough? Plus, pressure from her family had become unbearable. Her Nigerian grandmother had sent her three photos of possible matches. Every time Toyin deleted them from her phone, more kept coming, like a bad infection.

"I'm already in a relationship," she'd told her grandmother before her trip to Vegas. Her grandmother had stopped by her store to scold her for skipping out on her cousin's baby shower. She'd skipped it on purpose because she knew that her grandmother had someone she'd wanted to introduce to her.

Mama Bisi, as her grandmother was affectionately called, was a powerful matriarch. A woman whose beauty was more of an illusion than an actuality. She had a cool grace and stark features and was the mother of three sons (all doctors) and two daughters (both engineers), Toyin's mother being one. She had the height and breadth of a monarch and the gift of a seer. She'd been able to match all her children (Toyin's mother having been advantageously matched with a black British Cambridge student) and now had set her sights on her grandchildren and no one interfered with her rulings.

Mama Bisi had been instrumental in helping her sister,

Maryam get married, and her brother, Kemi, was prepared to be matched with whomever she chose. But Toyin had flouted tradition when she'd fallen for Lance, although her grandmother didn't like him. He was of average height and far from handsome, but earnest and smart. He had a slightly nasal voice that she found endearing. But he supported her and believed in her vision for the future.

"You're not in a relationship," her grandmother scoffed with a dismissive wave of her hand. "You're in a holding pen. Will he marry you or not?"

Toyin looked around the store, keeping her voice low. Hoping no one could overhear them. "Right now I'm still focused on my TJ Studios." She walked towards the back office.

"Why did you have to add to your troubles? A family will keep you busy enough. Your little store and cartoons were plenty and then you get yourself into debt with this other nonsense."

Toyin walked into the office and lifted a box from a chair until she noticed the stuffing coming out from a hole in the seat. She set the box back down and moved books from another. "It's not nonsense. It's something I love."

Her grandmother took a seat, looking around the cramped office in distaste. "You need to find a man to love too."

"I'm with Lance."

"But you don't love him."

Toyin sighed. "I do in my own way."

"I know why you put all your heart in creating a business here a project there and nothing else. It's because you're bored. A woman your age would be. You need another creative outlet and that's what a family is for."

Toyin bit the inside of her cheek not wanting to be rude. Her grandmother had never understood her or her ambitions. She'd been openly heartbroken that she hadn't gone into engineering; although it was clear to everyone she'd never had the interest. "I wanted to do this because it's been a dream of mine."

"Do you want children?"

"Someday."

"Someday doesn't exist on the calendar. You need to grow up."

"I am grown." She hated how her grandmother treated her as if she weren't fully grown without a man and baby on her hip.

"You have to make him marry you or find someone else."

Her grandmother's words echoed in her mind when Lance offered her his sudden proposal. It had come at the best time. She could now show her family that she could be both a wife, a passionate artist and businesswoman. This wedding would prove her grandmother wrong. That she hadn't wasted her time with Lance and that she was an adult and had "settled down" as they so often liked to tell her.

Perhaps the otherworldly feel of the conference—the colorful costumes, the feel of possibility—had also influenced her decision, but against her better judgment she'd agreed to marry him.

The fact that he'd disappeared for the next several hours should have been her first clue that something was wrong. That perhaps he wasn't as committed to a new life together as he'd seemed. But he'd disappeared on her before. Once when she'd sprained her wrist and had to give up a major commission and another time when she'd gotten the client from hell.

Both times, instead of being there for her, he'd sent her flowers and his apologies for being so busy (he was working on his PhD) so she hadn't paid much attention.

After he proposed, he'd told her he had some business to take care of first (he worked for a small publishing company) and that he couldn't wait to see her as his bride later that day when they scheduled to meet. She'd believed him. She'd booked the chapel, extended their hotel stay and planned everything. She even contacted one of the costume retailers at the conference to help her and managed to create a Corpse Bride costume. All he had to do was show up.

Which he did.

With someone else.

Toyin wasn't supposed to catch him in the lobby with the pretty woman by his side. Her business manager, Shanna. Lance had planned to meet her in their hotel room, but Toyin had been eager to meet him. So she'd left a half hour early and decided to wait for him in the lobby.

Which meant she wasn't supposed to overhear him talking to Shanna about his plans.

"Relax," he told her in a sexy voice he'd never used with Toyin. "There's nothing to worry about. If she sees you, just say you attended the conference too."

"You're really going to marry her?"

"It makes sense, but it won't interfere with us. You know I'd never give you up. She doesn't know anything about us and this is the best way to handle it. Once she finds out what you plan she'll be on the warpath. But as her husband I can control her and I'll have access to key information and intellectual property. You wouldn't believe the assets she has that she doesn't know how to manage. We can both live off of her."

"I just don't think it's good that I stay in the same hotel."

"She'll be happy to see you and you'll be our witness. Baby, I've got this all under control."

Toyin stumbled away from the lobby. She wouldn't find out the full extent of the damage Shanna had done until she returned home. For now, all her mind could focus on was Lance's betrayal. She hurried back to her hotel room and lost her lunch, but she didn't cry, her mind spinning on what to do.

She thought of poisoning the champagne and chocolates she had bought to celebrate; stuffing the roses she'd gotten in his mouth and stabbing him with an ice pick. She'd charged everything on a credit card, because Lance had told her he was buried under too many student loans to get into any more debt, and now she had nothing to show for it.

She didn't confront him when he arrived back in their hotel room, wearing her favorite cologne. She kissed him and pretended that everything was fine. She even considered sleeping with him so that at the height of climax she could twist her body in a way that would break his penis. But she decided that would be too dramatic. She didn't want to deal with an emergency room visit. Instead, she said, "How long have you been dipping your pen in Shanna's ink well?"

"What?"

"How long have you been with Shanna?"

He shook his head and sat down on the bed. "I don't know what you're talking about."

"I overheard you in the lobby. Shanna was right, you shouldn't have brought her here. Otherwise I would have never known."

"She's blackmailing me."

"Don't make me laugh."

"It's true, there are something's in my past—"

Toyin gripped her hands together and lowered her head as if in pain. "I don't want to go to prison." She glared at him. "But if you keep talking, I'm afraid I'm going to kill you."

Something in her gaze made him believe her. He slowly stood. "Whatever you're thinking, it wasn't like that."

"I will make you pay."

"Toyin."

"Not tonight, not this year, but you'd better hide because when I get over this...you will wish you were dead."

Lance smiled, his nasal voice taking on an ugly tone. "The trouble with you is that you live in comics. Revenge? Really? By the time you recover from this, we'll both be in rocking chairs. You need me if you want to survive what's in store."

"I don't need you," Toyin said, not realizing the truth of his words. "Now or ever."

Minutes later Toyin found herself at the hotel bar wondering what she would do next. She didn't want to think about his veiled threat or what he and Shanna had been up to.

She dreaded returning home to face it. At thirty-two she was already the family loser and this breakup would prove them right. She pulled out her cell phone and with her finger, sketched herself as a horse inside a stable. Her grandmother had been right, Lance had been riding her until he found someone else to replace her and she'd been left with nothing. The cheating hurt, but why did he have to make fun of her dream? She lived in comics?

He knew that wasn't true. Just because drawing comics was a passion didn't mean she was delusional. She'd thought he'd been different. He was one of the few people she'd trusted with her comic ideas and web animations. Why had he said he loved her? Why did he have to use that cruel lie? She had loved him in her own way. She'd felt safe with him. But he'd used her. Tears stung her eyes.

Toyin blinked them away. No she wouldn't cry. Love was for losers. Falling for him had been stupid. She'd never be stupid again.

Toyin felt a tap on her shoulder and looked up into the dark, magnetic brown eyes of a handsome man who seemed to make the rest of the world fall away. He reminded her of someone but she wasn't sure who.

"What's wrong, Beautiful?" he said.

His words made the world come back into cruel focus, the sound of laughter from a trio in the corner and the clink of glasses against the table assaulting her ears. Great, now someone was making fun of her.

She flashed a sour grin. "Are you trying to be funny?"

He blinked. "No."

"Good, because you failed. Now leave me alone."

"I didn't mean...I'm sorry," he said. "I just wanted to know why."

She rolled her eyes. "Why what?"

"What's a bride doing sitting at a bar all alone?"

"How do you know I'm a bride?"

He tapped the side of his head. "Because I'm psychic."

"Really?"

He motioned to her clothes. "And the wedding dress was a clue."

Toyin looked down at her dress horrified. She'd forgotten to change. She'd left the hotel room wanting to get as far away from Lance as she could. She'd gone around looking like a bride raised from the dead. She must look pathetic. "It's a long story." She looked over his three piece sharkskin metallic blue suit with a flashy red shirt. She couldn't guess what character he was trying to imitate. "Did you attend the conference too?"

"What?"

She shook her head. "Never mind."

"I'm interested in that long story you have to tell. I'll get us a table and you can tell me about it."

She laughed. No way was she going to fall for that act. "I don't have money, I'm not interested in sex and my family isn't rich."

The man frowned. "What does that have to do with anything?"

"I don't know what game you're playing but I'm not interested."

"Game?"

"A gorgeous man picks up a lonely woman at a bar. Wine and dines her. Listens to her sob stories, makes her feel as if he's 'The One' then starts a rebound romance that costs her money and her self-respect."

He leaned on the bar, resting his cheek against his fist. "Wow, I've never heard that before."

"I have."

He straightened. "Well, you did get one thing right. I am gorgeous, but I don't want anything from you. I have my own money, I work for my family business and I've given up women...for a while."

She paused. She hadn't expected that. She looked him up and down again. A man like him, giving up on women? "Why?"

He grinned. "You first."

He had her there. She was curious. Very curious. The storyteller in her found the promise of what he had to say irresistible. It could have been a ploy, but his disarming grin persuaded her that he had a story to tell and she didn't want to sit alone or go back to her room.

He held out his hand. "My name is Jackson Fortune, by the way."

"I've never heard that character before. What's his back story?"

He paused. "Back story?"

"Isn't Jackson Fortune who you're pretending to be?"

"Pretending?"

"Your costume and your name."

He glanced down at his clothes then looked up at her confused. "I'm not wearing a costume. And I just told you my real name."

She felt her face burn. "Oh sorry. I didn't mean...You really...uh look amazing."

"Thank you." He held his hand out again. "And your name is?"

She shook his hand, momentarily entranced by his steady gaze. "Toyin Jackson...I mean Fortune." She shook her head. "Jacobs. Toyin Jacobs."

"Actually, Toyin Fortune has a nice ring to it."

She narrowed her gaze, trying to resist his flirtation. "I thought you were giving up women."

"I am...slowly."

She jumped down from the bar stool. "And I'm starving."

"Order what you want. I'm paying."

After having Lance deceive her she wasn't sure he

wouldn't excuse himself to the restroom and never return. But then he said as if reading her mind, "You can look me up if you want."

"No, that's okay. I'm ready to take a gamble."

Moments later they sat in a restaurant booth with two orders of shrimp scampi, the bread basket filled with hot rolls, and Toyin briefly telling Jackson about her ruined wedding plans. She reached for the salt.

Jackson stopped her. "Don't insult the chef. Try the food first."

"I like salt."

"Probably because you've lost the ability to taste. I bet you soak your sushi in soy sauce."

"I don't eat sushi."

"And the world thanks you. It's best not to eat it than to destroy it."

She studied him for a moment. "Are you a chef by any chance?"

"No, just a man who enjoys food." He nodded to her plate. "Just try it."

She took a bite then set her fork down. "You're right. My taste buds are dead. Can I have the salt now?"

Jackson took a taste of his food then visibly shuddered. "Too much oil, not enough garlic and the parsley hasn't been fresh in years. You're right. There's no flavor."

Toyin lifted the salt shaker. "There will be in a minute."

He motioned to the waiter. "No, wait. We're not eating here."

"We're not?"

"No. I know some place better."

Toyin looked down at their plates. "But we can't waste this food."

"We won't."

They took the food with them and ended up giving it to two very thankful homeless people.

"I'm still hungry," Toyin said as they left the happy pair.

"Be patient. It will be worth it."

He was right. She didn't know such savory culinary delights would be only a few blocks away. At first she hadn't been impressed by the décor of the small Japanese restaurant. It wasn't as luxurious as the hotel and they looked completely out of place in the casual atmosphere. But when the food arrived all her misgivings fell away as she enjoyed rich, chewy udon noodles shimmered in a savory miso broth the scent of garlic and sake wafting towards her, steam rising from every bite, fogging up her glasses.

Jackson stared at her, pleased by her expression of delight. "Am I right?"

"Absolutely worth it." She waved her hand. "Simple but heavenly."

"I noticed you drawing at the bar. Are you an artist?"

Heat touched her cheeks. She hadn't expected anyone to be watching her doing the silly sketch. It was an old habit. "Sort of."

"Sort of?"

"I used to draw comics until I realized there was no money in it. Now I own a pop-culture store called New Worlds and a startup called TJ Studios," she said with pride not knowing what she'd find out when she returned home.

"I'd like to see your work."

"Doesn't matter. I don't draw comics anymore."

"Why not?"

"Because it hurts too much. I briefly had a webcomic that failed miserably."

"So what? Start again."

"I was going to let the domain expire and—"

"Why would you do that? You already have a business making money, what's wrong with doing something else for fun?"

She didn't want to admit that she'd lost confidence in herself. "There are others so much better than me."

"Of course. That's how life works, but that doesn't mean you don't enter the ring. My stepfather is a boxing fan so forgive the reference."

"My work isn't the typical comic stories."

"Even better." He moved his chair next to her and handed her his phone. "Let me see it."

"What?" she said surprised by both his question and sudden closeness. She was flattered by his interest. "Right now?"

He nodded.

She went to her site and opened her archives.

He looked through it. "These are great. You shouldn't stop doing what you love."

Was he just being nice? She didn't want to think so. She liked talking about them. There were so few who believed in her. "I'm afraid to love anything anymore after Lance."

Jackson pointed to the screen. "This will never betray you."

"You sound like you understand."

He returned his seat back in place. "More than you know."

"I don't believe it.

He nodded. "It's true. A woman targeted me to destroy my family business. She ended up marrying my brother instead."

Toyin stared at him for a long moment, shocked. "And he doesn't know?"

"He knows now."

"And he doesn't care?"

"She doesn't want to destroy our family anymore."

"Are you sure?"

"Pretty much. We have a love-hate relationship. But she's not the first woman to use me..." And as she'd hoped he would he shared about the women from his past and the bad luck he'd had with them. They left the restaurant and went to a bar and he continued his tales. At first she didn't believe him, but as time passed and the drinks flowed she felt an affinity with him. He knew true heartbreak.

He spoke about his mother who'd passed around this time last year, but instead of being maudlin, he celebrated her life by sharing all that he loved about her, although Toyin could tell he missed her terribly. His mother sounded like someone she would have liked. She liked him too, surprised by how much, but he was easy to talk to. He made her laugh and she could make him laugh too in a way she felt he hadn't in awhile.

At times, he looked at her as if amazed by how funny she could be. She was amazed too. She'd never been able to make Lance laugh. And their shared laughter seemed to destroy any barrier between them. Jackson freely shared how baffled he was by the women he'd cared for and Toyin was baffled too. He seemed like a great guy. Why would he choose such awful women? *Unless he was a con man with a well scripted story*, a cynical voice whispered.

But then he did something—the slight movement of his

head, the nonchalant way he lifted a shoulder in a shrug, she couldn't pinpoint what—that reminded her of someone she couldn't place— and her suspicions subsided. There was something genuine about him in spite of the flashy clothes and quick smile. She felt sorry for him. And for herself. Why did they have such bad luck?

"You need a bitch barometer," she finally said, feeling buzzed and angry.

"A what?"

"A way to measure whether a woman is a bitch."

He sighed. "First I'd need to find someone I could trust."

"We both could use someone like that."

The two left the bar and went to a club, at Jackson's insistence. Toyin didn't think any club would let them in because of her dress, but they didn't have any trouble and danced for an hour.

"It's been a great night," she said, feeling giddy from drink and dancing as she stopped in front of her hotel room. She hadn't gone dancing for a while and it had felt liberating. "You made me forget about Lance."

Jackson nodded. "But not enough," he said then pulled her into his arms and kissed her.

But not in a sloppy, drunken way she would have expected. He kissed her as if she were the only woman on earth; as if she were fine wine and he a sommelier. As if it had been a moment he'd been waiting for.

She'd never been kissed like that before—with both hunger and tenderness. Fire and velvet. Let alone by a man she'd just met. Toyin pulled away her heart thumping wildly, her skin hot. He left her breathless. Was that an invitation? Did he expect her to ask him to come inside? Did he just want to sleep with her? Had she misread him the entire time?

"Jackson—"

He rested his forehead against hers and whispered, "Marry me."

She paused. "What?"

"Marry me. Please."

"You're drunk."

He sighed. "Doesn't matter. I wouldn't ask you, if I didn't mean it. I need you."

"You need to sleep this off. Where's your room?"

He gathered her close and held her tight. "Please. I'll make it worth your while. You look so pretty."

"I look like a cadaver."

"A pretty one and you should be a bride and I need one. I need one to keep the others away. It won't be for keeps." He pulled something out of his pocket. "I even have a ring." He got down on one knee and opened the box. "See? I mean it. Please."

The diamond sparkled like a star that had fallen from the sky. "When did you get this?"

His eyes gleamed with hope. "Do you like it?"

"It's beautiful."

"It's yours."

"It costs a fortune."

He rested a hand on his chest and nodded. "That's right. I'm a Fortune."

"No, that's not what I said. Get up."

He shook his head. "We can get it resized if it doesn't fit. I've been carrying it around for a long time waiting for the right woman."

"Jackson, you don't know who I am."

"I do. And you know me too. And all night you never once asked me for something. I know that you won't use me. This is my idea not yours, right? You're not even sure about it. That's what makes you different. Others would jump at the chance."

She knelt in front of him. He didn't slur his words and his gait had been steady, but clearly he was intoxicated beyond reason. "Jackson—"

"I like you and you like me. It will be easy and quick. We go through the ceremony, take pictures for proof and then we get it annulled later." His eyes pleaded. "That's all I ask."

He was drunk, she was tipsy. She should have had more sense, but the idea was tempting. She wondered if the liquor had given his voice a sexy, husky edge or if it was just her imagination, no matter the reason she liked the sound of it. It stirred up desires within her.

To have a man, no matter what state he was in, ask her to marry him put her self-esteem back in place. Here was someone twice the man Lance was, a man who was way out of her league who she could use as proof that she wasn't a loser.

She saw a man and woman in casual dress send them curious glances as they walked down the carpeted hall. "They must have come from a costume party," she overheard the man say.

Toyin jumped to her feet and opened her hotel door. She'd been a spectacle enough for the night. "Get up. We can talk inside."

He shuffled inside on his knees.

Toyin couldn't help a chuckle. "You look ridiculous."

"I feel ridiculous. Will you marry me or not?"

She closed the door behind him. "If I do, what happens

after this? How do I contact you? I don't know where you live or—"

"Give me your cell phone. I'll give you my address when this is over. Just come by and say you're my wife. I'll take it from there."

"That does not sound like a well thought out plan."

He held out the ring. "Please. Save me from myself. You can keep the ring and later pawn it if you want. It's real."

Toyin took the ring and slid it on her finger. Surprised that it fit. "Okay."

Jackson jumped to his feet and kissed her. "You don't know how happy you've made me."

She stared at him for a moment, wondering if he was really as drunk as she'd suspected him to be. But he had to be because what he was asking was crazy. Why would he want to get married to her?

He took her hand and opened the door. "Come on. Let's go."

And soon after they were married. He kissed her on the cheek, took photos and acted like a jubilant groom, which made her laugh. She thought he would want to part ways after the ceremony but instead he said 'Let's pretend this is real' and they toured the city in a limo until dawn.

By the time morning came she took him back to his hotel, laughing at his halfhearted pleas to give him a real honeymoon, and did her best to forget the crazy night as she focused on her company and fought to keep her manager's betrayal from ruining her business.

Now Jackson was sober and he still wanted a bride and he could save her business. Love wasn't in the equation and that was perfect.

CHAPTER 8

She'd said "yes".

Jackson pumped his fist in the air in victory. Toyin was still his. He'd avoided a disaster.

Reginald walked into the living room. "Is there something I should know?"

Jackson turned to him. "Know?"

"About Mrs. Fortune. Does she have special requirements?"

"We'll find that out later."

"I'd prefer to be prepared now. Should I get the room ready? Hire—"

"Do what you want to," Jackson said impatient and in no mood to think about details. "I'll play it by ear."

He only wanted to focus on the fact that she'd help him. He'd been afraid she may not continue to agree to this arrangement, but convincing her hadn't been as hard as he'd feared.

The doorbell rang.

Jackson sat down ready to deal with whoever it was. When

Reginald opened the door an attractive woman with dark lashes and short brown hair stormed into the room past him.

Reginald shook his head and closed the door behind her. "Three women in one day, that must be a record for you."

She glared at Jackson.

He clasped his hands behind his head and smiled back at her. "Sylvia. This is a pleasant surprise."

"You are such a pig."

He blew her a kiss. "Feel better now?"

"No. Pig."

"Why is that?"

She folded her arms. "I thought we were friends."

"We are."

"We've even slept together."

He let his hands fall to his lap. "I know."

"And you get married without telling me?"

"Don't worry. I didn't tell anyone. It was a spur of the moment thing. I didn't tell my brother either."

"I thought you weren't going to see women for a while."

He shrugged. "I tried. I failed."

"You didn't try very hard." She pulled a face. "Why couldn't it have been me? I thought we were good together."

"We are. I didn't want to ruin a good thing."

She stood in front of him. "Is this for real?"

"Maybe."

"Why her?"

"I don't know." He lied. He knew very well why he'd chosen the woman sitting alone at the bar in a Corpse Bride wedding dress. He pretended to be a stranger, although he really wasn't, but Sylvia didn't need to know that. Nobody did, not even Toyin, until he was ready.

She rested her hands on her hips. "Are you really off the market?"

"For the time being."

Sylvia straddled his lap and sent him a knowing look. "Do you plan on being a good husband?"

"Yes," he said unable to ignore the soft feel of her bottom against him.

She unbuttoned her blouse. "How good?"

He removed her from his lap. "Very good."

She frowned and re-buttoned her shirt. "Pity." She laughed as a thought came to her. "Speaking of pity, you wouldn't believe what I saw coming up here. Some poor fat girl was helping this older woman who'd dropped her things in front of the elevator. Well, first her skirt ripped when she bent down then her wig got caught when the doors closed and was snatched right off her head. It was hilarious. You should have seen her face. I wish I had recorded it."

Jackson briefly closed his eyes and said in a tight voice, "She's not fat."

Sylvia sent him a strange look. "How do you know? You didn't see her."

"Was she wearing a black pencil skirt and blue blouse, fake lashes and a black wig with waves?"

Sylvia nodded. "But how did you—?"

"She's the new Mrs. Fortune."

"No, she's not."

Jackson nodded. "Yes, she is."

Sylvia pulled out her cell phone and glanced at the image of him with his new bride. "But she doesn't look anything like the photo online."

"She tried a makeover."

"It didn't work." When Jackson shot her a look Sylvia softened her criticism. "I mean I know she put in the effort, but the boxy look doesn't suit her and the makeup—"

"She'll learn."

"Poor Jackson. You must have been really drunk. There's no other way you would have ended up with someone like her."

He stood and shoved his hands in his pockets. "Want to get something to eat?"

"When do I get to meet her?"

"Soon, but she has to meet Edgar and Ava first."

"Together? Do you want to see her get eaten alive?"

He slipped on his socks and shoes. "I'll be there."

"It won't be enough."

He grabbed his coat and keys. "You shouldn't sound so hopeful."

"I'll try to behave myself. Oooh, poor girl."

"She's stronger than you think."

"At least I'm certain of one thing. I no longer need to be heartbroken."

Jackson opened the door for her. "Why not?"

"Because there's no way this marriage can last." She sauntered past him. "You'll come back to me."

Jackson smiled, but when she turned, his smile disappeared and he said in a low voice she couldn't hear, "Don't count on it."

CHAPTER 9

"I heard about the elevator."

Toyin rested her head on her knees as she sat on the floor in her apartment. She almost wished she hadn't answered Jackson's phone call. She'd been in a fetal position for the past half hour remembering her embarrassment. She'd only just recovered. Now her face burned with renewed humiliation. How could he have found out? "Oh God, did someone record it? Is it online?"

"No," he said quickly. "A friend of mine saw you. I'm just making sure you're alright."

"The wig got destroyed along with my pride, but I'm fine."

"Good. I didn't ask if you needed help moving things in."

"No, I don't have much. Anything else?"

"Donate the skirt too, it doesn't suit you." He hung up."

Toyin made a face. "You didn't have to call if you were going to make me feel bad about it." But strangely, she didn't. He made her feel relieved. The outfit her sister had encouraged her to wear wasn't her at all. She went into the bathroom and scrubbed her face clean, took out her contacts, and put on her glasses then looked at her fresh bare face feeling better.

She was lucky that her parents and grandmother had traveled to see family in London and wouldn't be back for another week; otherwise her sister's fiasco would have been more of a disaster. Instead, their days would be so busy they wouldn't check online.

Toyin began to tidy up her apartment, tossing things in a laundry basket to wash before she packed them.

She was straightening her bed when she received a text from her sister.

Warning. Kemi's coming.

Why?

You know why.

This is all your fault.

Will you get paid?

Shut up.

She sighed. She heard her brother's footsteps outside her apartment before he pounded on the door. He was built like a truck with the fists to match. She counted to ten before she opened the door.

"What is the meaning of this?" he asked, storming inside.

He was three years her junior but because he was a male he acted like he was head of the household while their father was away. He had Maryam's coloring, but pointed features that made him look like a weasel when he was angry.

"Don't scrunch up your face like that," Toyin said. "You know it doesn't suit you."

"Don't change the subject." He took a deep breath. "Why didn't you tell anyone?"

"Because no one would understand."

"We thought you were with Lance."

"I did too, but he now belongs to someone else."

"Who is this man? When will we meet him? How did you—"

"When Mum and Dad return I'll explain everything. For now, just let them enjoy their travels and keep this quiet. My name wasn't mentioned so it shouldn't have spread far."

"It's spread far enough. Aunt Gretchen knows."

Toyin screamed.

Kemi covered his ears.

Toyin hand's trembled as she stared at him in horror. "How could she find out?"

"I don't know."

"If Maryam told her, I really will kill her."

"It won't help. She's on her way."

"Here?"

"Yes."

"Then why did you come?"

The doorbell rang and a weasel grin spread across his face. "Because I wanted to hear this," he said before he ducked into another room.

CHAPTER 10

Aunt Gretchen and Cousin Tansy stood on the doorstep with identical big smiles. Their teeth beautifully white against their dark cocoa skin. Aunt Gretchen inherited Mama Bisi's commanding presence and handsome looks; her daughter Tansy was as cute as a kitten.

"My favorite niece," Aunt Gretchen said, kissing Toyin on both cheeks.

"My favorite cousin," Tansy said doing the same.

Aunt Gretchen took off her coat and handed it to Toyin. "I saw the news. You naughty girl! What a story. Your sister explained everything."

"What exactly did she explain?" Toyin asked, hanging up their coats.

Aunt Gretchen took a seat. "The details of how you met this wonderful man. We will have a big party and of course you know why we're here."

Toyin sat in front of them unsure. "Actually..."

"Oh, Mummy let me tell her," Tansy said, bouncing with excitement.

Aunt Gretchen shook her head. "I think it best that it comes from me."

"But it was my idea."

"What was your idea?" Toyin asked with growing dread.

The two women shared a look then said in unison, "A double wedding."

"What!"

"You didn't think you could get away with a simple elopement, did you?" Tansy said.

Aunt Gretchen nodded. "You have to have another wedding."

"And since I'm getting married Saturday—"

"Not this coming Saturday," her mother interjected.

"But the one after that," Tansy clarified. "I had this stupendous idea. Why don't we get married together?"

"That way you wouldn't have to worry about anything except the dress and arriving on time. I've already planned everything for my dear Tansy, it won't take much to add a few details for you."

"And we know all the same people."

"So no one will have to travel again to see you."

"And your parents are returning early. They'll call you when they get home. Your mother was upset—"

"Shattered," Tansy said with a sad shake of her head.

"—but I reassured her that all is well. To think you even thought of depriving your parents of this special moment is beyond me."

"But now you can remedy that."

Aunt Gretchen pressed her hands together. "There's one little problem."

"Only one?" Toyin said.

Her cousin nodded, not hearing Toyin's sarcasm. "You know it's our tradition that Mama Bisi chooses your match. She may be a teeny, tiny bit upset that you didn't include her in your choice."

"In other words she'll be completely put out, but," Aunt Gretchen said before Toyin could respond, "this wedding will show her that we're all standing behind you. You have to do this to keep the peace."

Tansy released a happy sigh. "Isn't it great? You're like a sister to me and we'll have the same anniversary."

They both stared at her.

Tansy nudged Aunt Gretchen. "Mummy, she's speechless."

"I know. Give her time to process this."

"She looks like she's going to cry."

"I...I can't let you do this," Toyin managed to say. "It's too much and I don't think Jackson will—"

"Yes, the groom," Aunt Gretchen cut in. "We've thought of that. Your uncle is already prepared to talk to him to let him know how important this is to us. Where are his people from again?"

"I don't remember."

"Never mind. You can call me later and let me know."

"Why would you need to know that?" Toyin asked.

"The caterer can add one extra meal at cost, of course, but we don't want to exclude him from the festivities."

"This is really all too much and—"

"We've made an appointment to look at dresses tomorrow,"

Tansy said. "We have a tailor waiting to alter your dress so that it will be ready for the big day."

"Which is in less than a fortnight," Toyin said in a flat voice.

Tansy squealed with delight. "Yes. Isn't that marvelous? You won't get any presents, of course, but from what I heard he's loaded anyway so you won't want for anything...Mummy, she looks like she's going to cry again."

"Happy tears, my dear. Happy tears." Aunt Gretchen stood and kissed Toyin again. "You'll make a beautiful bride."

"We both will." Tansy kissed her also.

Toyin gave them their coats then waved goodbye.

Kemi popped out of the other room. "I heard there will be a live orchestra," he said with laughter in his voice.

Toyin closed the front door and spun around. She'd forgotten he was there. She pulled out her cell phone. "It's not funny."

"Who are you calling?"

"Maryam." When her sister picked up she said, "You have to fix this."

"Fix what?"

"Aunt Gretchen came by with Tansy and they're planning a double wedding."

"So what?"

"I can't go through this all over again."

"How much is he willing to pay you to get an annulment?"

Toyin glanced at her brother, she didn't want him to overhear. She walked to the kitchen and lowered her voice. "That's not the point."

"It's the entire point. How much?"

"Actually, he wants me to keep this up a little longer."

"Even better. How much?"

"It won't matter if he changes his mind."

"Why would he change his mind? You're already married. This is just an extra ceremony."

At times her sister's logic was aggravating. "In front of all our family and friends. It's a sham."

"No one needs to know that."

"I don't want another wedding. You started this. You have to talk to Aunt Gretchen and Tansy. Get them to change their minds."

"Oh sure," Maryam said with a laugh, "and while I'm at it I'll stop the sun from rising."

Toyin sighed. Her sister was right. There was nc way to stop this disaster from happening.

CHAPTER 11

"Your wife is on the phone."

Jackson slowly opened his eyes. He glanced at the clock and saw it said eight-thirty. He groaned. It was Sunday morning and he'd hoped to sleep in until twelve. What cruel fate was this? "My what?"

"Wife," Reginald said. "Please don't pretend you don't have one. I'm not in the mood today."

Jackson slowly sat up and rubbed his eyes. "I wasn't pretending." He yawned. "What does she want?"

"That mystery can be easily solved by talking to her."

"Sarcasm doesn't suit you, Bo. She could have left a message."

"She's left three messages. All asking, or rather, imploring you to call her."

Jackson held out his hand. He didn't keep his cell phone in his bedroom, not wanting any devices that could interrupt his sleep. Reginald took the phone off mute and handed it to him before leaving.

"Next time call after ten," Jackson told her.

"This is urgent."

He yawned again. "Go on."

"We have a problem. A serious, horrible, terrible problem."

He rubbed his eyes. "Sounds bad."

"I'm not kidding."

"Go on."

"All yesterday I've been trying to fix it. I've called almost everyone I know to help me, but nobody can."

Jackson fell back on the bed, trying to stifle another yawn. "What's the problem?"

"My aunt and cousin are planning a double wedding. *Our* double wedding. They won't take 'no' for an answer. My parents are flying back early to help me prepare."

Jackson closed his eyes.

"Are you still there?" Toyin asked when he didn't reply.

"Yes, I'm waiting."

"Waiting for what?"

"The problem."

"I just told you the problem," Toyin said. "Weren't you listening?"

"Your aunt and parents are planning a wedding."

"No, my aunt and cousin are. My parents are coming back. Oh never mind. That's not the biggest issue. My cousin is planning to get married Saturday." She raised her voice to imitate Tansy's bubbly tone. "Not this coming Saturday, but the one after that." She returned her voice to normal. "Which means we have to get married again in front of everyone."

"Okay."

"Okay?!"

Jackson held the phone away from his ear and grimaced. "No need to shout."

"What is wrong with you? You're supposed to be outraged. You're supposed to say 'Are you joking?' 'Have you gone mad?' 'Is your family batty?' I have better things to do than plan another fake wedding."

"You just said your aunt is planning it. What else do we need to do?"

"In a couple hours they're dragging me to go dress shopping. You'll have to tell your family and friends, although my aunt did mention that there won't be enough room for too many more people."

Jackson put the phone on speaker, rested it on the bed and crawled back under the sheets. "It will be fine. I'll only add four more people."

"How can it be fine? How can we have this huge wedding and then break up in a couple months?"

"We'll stretch it to six."

"What was that? You sound far away."

He put his mouth closer to the phone. "We'll stretch it to six."

"What about my parents? They'll be devastated that—"

"We'll stay married for a year then."

Her voice cracked. "A year?"

"We go through the ceremony, make people happy then we separate. After several months the excitement should have worn off." He smiled pleased to have come up with such a solid solution so early in the morning. "Unless you have a better idea."

"No, I don't. You're handling this better than I thought you would."

"You don't know enough about me yet."

"I'm really sorry about this."

"Don't be. Just don't call me—"

"Before ten," Toyin finished. "I get it."

"Thanks." Jackson hung up and promptly fell back asleep.

THREE HOURS later he wasn't as confident about his solution as he ate his breakfast. He should have thought about the possibility of another wedding. He always liked a party, but knew that this could complicate things. His family liked to do things a certain way. He knew they wouldn't take kindly to a surprise wedding they weren't in control of. Especially Edgar. He called James.

"I'm getting married again," he told him.

"What about Toyin?" his brother said alarmed.

"I'm getting married to her. Her family wants a wedding."

James started to laugh.

"They're planning it for next Saturday. In two weeks to be precise."

James laughed harder.

"I'm glad you find this so funny."

"More than you know."

"It's going to be a double wedding with her cousin."

"Are you making this up?"

"No."

"Does she have a large family?"

"I don't know that yet. I need a favor."

"Don't worry," James said. "We'll be there. Wouldn't miss it for the world. I'll take lots of pictures."

Jackson frowned. "That's not why I'm calling."

"What do you want?"

"I thought you should break the news to Edgar."

James's good humor disappeared. He swore. "I forgot I haven't told him yet."

"You can tell him now."

"Which part? That you're already married or that you're getting married again in two weeks?"

"Both."

"Why don't you tell him?"

"Because you say things better than I do."

"No," James said unmoved by the flattery, "it because you don't want to do it."

"That too."

"He'll want to meet her first," James said.

"There won't be enough time before the wedding."

"He'll make time."

Jackson nodded. "I know."

"And if he doesn't like her..."

"He won't have a choice. He'll have to."

"I'll see what I can do. I can manage to stall for a week and keep him in the dark. I'll let others know it's for the best considering his health. But after that, you'd both better be prepared."

"For what?"

James's tone turned ominous. "The summons."

CHAPTER 12

He never thought revenge would taste so sweet.

James set his cell phone down and looked across the breakfast table at his wife, taking in her fine high cheekbones and exquisite dark skin. This morning she looked fetching in jeans and one of his blue sweaters. The remainder of their brunch— spinach and mushroom egg baked into a light pastry—sat on the table between them.

"What's the smile for?" Ava asked.

"We've been invited to a wedding."

"Whose?"

"Jackson's. He's getting married."

Her brows shot up. "Again?"

"It's to the same woman. Her family wants a formal wedding. Saturday. It's in two weeks. It's all arranged."

"Do you think he'll go through with it?"

"He'll have to."

Ava sent him a knowing look. "He's skipped out on weddings before."

"One wedding," James clarified. "And he was there…just not as the groom." He shook his head. "Water under the bridge. They're already married so it won't change anything."

"Except that it's a public declaration."

"Jackson likes the limelight."

"Does she?"

James frowned. "What woman doesn't want to be a bride?"

"That's not an answer."

"I don't know. If her family wants it, I'm sure she does too."

Ava's frown deepened. "It's not like you to apply fuzzy logic."

"I don't know her enough to form an opinion."

She playfully slid her foot up his leg and smiled. "That's better."

"You'll get to meet her soon, so you can tell me."

She rested her foot on his lap. "Do you believe him?"

He felt himself respond as she wiggled her toes against him. "About what?"

"That he planned all this. That he's tired of making mistakes with women and wants to use Toyin as a sort of shield?"

He covered her foot with his hand. "Right now I don't care what he does."

"James."

"If you want me to concentrate, you'll stop touching me like that."

Ava put her foot down. "Sorry." She winked. "You can punish me later."

James couldn't stop a grin. "With pleasure."

She took a sip of her orange juice. "Now about Jackson and Toyin."

James nodded, trying to refocus. "Yes. She's like no one he's ever dated before. He picked a good one. She found out that Enomwoyi was a fraud."

"You didn't tell me that."

James swore, he'd meant to keep it secret.

"When?" Ava pressed.

"That same morning. They happened to cross paths."

Ava made a pained expression. "Please don't tell me he was with another woman the same time Toyin showed up."

"I won't."

Ava closed her eyes and groaned.

"But she proved to me that she's not in it to use him. She said she loves him."

Ava stared at him. "So he's staying married?"

"Yes. I told you that."

Ava paused. "And you're not worried?"

"Why would I be worried?"

"Because this doesn't sound like Jackson at all."

"You don't know everything about my brother no matter how much you studied him. Besides, this is a good thing. It gives him the right image and keeps him out of trouble."

"What do you think he's up to?"

"I just told you."

"You don't mean that."

"I'm giving him the benefit of the doubt. You should too."

Ava chewed her lower lip. "What is she like? Professional? Beautiful?"

"No, she's pretty, but not beautiful."

"That's what you mean by saying she's different than the rest?"

James shook his head. "No, it's everything about her. I can't put my finger on it. Just trust me. She's good for him and she'll look out for him. Like I said, she discovered Enomwoyi was fraud, isn't that something?"

"Hmm."

"You don't sound impressed."

"That's like giving someone credit for chewing gum. I noticed her watching him at the charity party. It's no secret that your brother has terrible taste in women."

"Present company excluded of course."

Ava shook her head in disagreement. "No, not really. I could have done a lot of damage if I'd wanted to. He was...is easy to manipulate. We need to find out more about her."

"Why?"

"First I don't buy that those photos accidentally got posted. There was a calculated strategy behind them."

James thought for a moment before he shook his head. "But Toyin doesn't seem the type to—"

Ava held up her hand. "And their crazy elopement seems too coincidental. How can you possibly meet a stranger in Las Vegas, get married then discover that you live only twenty minutes from each other?"

James thought for a moment then said, "Few things are completely impossible. Statistically speaking you can argue that—"

"Improbable then."

He nodded. "Yes. You think she targeted him?"

"It's possible. *I* did."

James sighed. He wanted to be happy for his brother, but

Ava had brought up a good point. What if Toyin wanted something? He liked her, but he didn't know her. "It could be nothing."

"I need to find out more about her. If we want to keep this family safe from your brother we—"

James clicked his tongue in pity. "You're forgetting something."

"What?"

"My brother was part of this family before you."

Ava had the grace to look embarrassed. "I didn't mean—"

"I know. You see the threats because you once were one, but you can relax. We look out for each other. I won't let him get hurt. He's not a threat and although his choices haven't been the best, he's a good man. We agreed that we'd give him another chance. Let's wait and see what Toyin's like. I'm going to talk to Edgar. I don't want you to do anything more. Don't go behind his back or mine."

"I wouldn't dare."

"Yes, you would."

She couldn't stop a tiny smile. "I'll try."

CHAPTER 13

The smell of booze and spicy steak drafted towards him as Jackson sat in a private booth with his four friends that Friday night. His fraternity brothers. They'd put together a hasty post bachelor party as an excuse to get together and drink. Nearly a week had passed since Toyin had reentered his life.

"Man, I can't believe you really did this," Lee Chang said. He was a tall, thin guy who could consume more liquor than a man twice his size. He'd made enough money on bets in college to prove it. He lifted his nearly empty glass and shook his head. "You had us all fooled last time. And I saw this girl's picture, what were you thinking?"

Ari Stanz took a large bite of his steak and shook his head, running a hand over his buzzed hair cut. "Women like that are sometimes wildcats in bed. Am I wrong?"

"She's not his type at all," Jaleel Peterson said, stroking his beard, flashing the tattoo of a serpent on his wrist. "What the heck was she wearing?"

"She's the Corpse Bride," Jackson said.

"I think she's cute," Ari said.

Gary Holland gave a sad sigh as if the world were coming to an end. The heavyset man looked ten years older than the rest of them, although he was two years younger. "You shouldn't have married her. Your sex life is now officially over."

"Speak for yourself," Jaleel said. "I'm a happily married guy."

"Bet you're too scared of your wife to say anything else," Gary said." He sighed. "I am."

"What will we talk about if we can't talk about Jackson's women, right?" Lee said.

Ari nodded. "Even in college you could find the worst."

"At least they were all lookers. Remember those girls you got to come to our parties?"

For a moment the men were silent, lost in happy memories.

Lee nudged Jackson with his elbow. "Be honest. Edgar chose her, right?"

"I don't think Edgar would choose someone like her," Jaleel said.

Jackson just smiled. He didn't mind the insults; he hadn't married Toyin to impress anyone. He actually took pleasure in their disappointment. He didn't like being predictable and it would give people something to talk about. That was always a good thing.

"You cost me money," Gary said. "I bet you'd finally end up with Sylvia."

"We all did." Lee agreed.

Jaleel grinned, waving his wallet in triumph. "Except me."

Jackson shrugged.

Lee frowned. "What's wrong with you? You're quiet tonight."

"A man has a right to be depressed when his freedom ends," Gary said.

"Who wants to bet how long this will last?" Lee said.

The men laughed then placed their bets and enjoyed the food and drinks soon forgetting their uncharacteristically quiet friend.

Jackson looked around the room with little interest. His friends really didn't know him. No one did. He gave them the image they wanted because it was fun and worked...but recently he'd felt lost.

And angry.

Angry that he was a joke. A punch line. The one who got cheated on, dumped, used. Yes, the women were all beautiful, but that didn't matter. It still hurt. Toyin was the first person to listen to him. Really listen and not laugh. She seemed to understand that as funny as the stories may seem to others the pain was real. He didn't care what anyone thought of her because he didn't care what they thought of him.

He briefly closed his eyes knowing that was a lie. He did care, a little too much. He cared that Ava had wanted to see him suspended and that James had agreed.

He'd accepted that she was part of his—their—lives now and she'd made his mother happy, but he couldn't forgive her for trying to get him replaced, even briefly. He'd already lost too much. He couldn't let her take more from him. If he didn't have his job, what would he have left?

His brother's betrayal hurt. He knew James's logic but it wasn't enough. He should have stood up for him. No matter what.

Jackson remembered when he was nine and he'd gotten stung by a swarm of bees when he'd upset their nest trying to get a kite out of a tree. His mother had sighed as she tended his wounds and said, "You always get into trouble. *Why couldn't you be a little more like James?*" The expression on his face must have shown the hurt he felt by her statement because she quickly added, "But you're special the way you are." Unfortunately, her words came too late. Her careless words burned in his heart even now. *Why couldn't you be a little more like James?* Honorable James. Serious James. James didn't get into trouble, he fixed things. He was dependable. He didn't date women who only wanted something from him. He was the smart one.

Jackson was tired of being second best. Of being overshadowed. He watched Lee easily down another large glass to his friends' applause and absently wondered what Toyin was doing right now. He pulled out his cell phone and sent her a text.

Rescue me.

Why?

I'm bored.

So?

I want to see you

What are you doing now?

He looked around at his friends, feeling lonely. In the brief time he'd known her, he never felt that way with her. *Nothing.*

Where are you?

A club with my friends.

And you're bored?

Yeah.

Lonely?

He couldn't say yes, although he was glad she understood. He needed that, but he wouldn't admit it. *No, just bored.*

Want me to come get you?

His heart lifted. Yes. Yes. Yes! He wanted to be with the woman Sylvia called fat; who others didn't think was his type. He wanted to be with the pretty woman whose lips he couldn't get enough of, whose curves begged to be touched and felt perfect against him. He wanted to be with her and no one else. He gave her the address. *I'll be waiting outside.*

CHAPTER 14

Why was she doing this? Toyin asked herself as she pulled her car up to the club. Its big, bright sign punctured the dark sky with neon blue and red lights.

Why had Jackson texted her and why had she felt the need to respond? What was she going to do with him? When she saw him standing outside the club bookmarked by two attractive women, her mood dipped even more. This was not how she wanted to spend her Friday night. It had been a tiring week.

She'd had to endure dress shopping (if it had been up to her it would have taken all of three minutes but with her aunt and cousin it had stretched to an hour and a half!), her parent's scolding, her aunt and mother gushing about the caterer's menu, plus dealing with the lies Shanna had told her lawyer as part of their upcoming case. Now she had to pick up a gorgeous man from a club because he was bored.

The money. She was doing this for the money. She'd already signed the contract Jackson (or James she wasn't sure) had created spelling out the deadline and termination clause, which included a detailed postnuptial agreement. Toyin had been happy to sign to prove she wasn't the greedy opportunist her sister had inadvertently made her out to be. After the contract was finalized, she was able to deposit enough funds to get a great lawyer who'd laid out a strategy to defeat Shanna's claims that she hadn't done anything wrong. Toyin watched Jackson laugh with the ladies and felt her heart constrict. She liked him more than she should. She sighed as she realized the real reason he'd texted her. He was tempted and she was his protection.

If he didn't have her, he'd likely take one—or both—of the beautiful ladies home with him and end up in another relationship that went nowhere.

But she was not going to get out of her car and approach him so that she could be exposed to the scrutiny of those women. She pulled out her cell phone and texted: *I'm here.*

She saw him look at his cell phone and glance around almost eager. She sniffed. He must really be tempted. He looked relieved she was there to stop him. When he looked past her, she rolled down the window and waved her hand. He smiled when he spotted her, said something to the two women that made them frown, then shoved his hands in his pockets and walked to her car.

He looked sad.

That surprised her. Only seconds ago he looked as if he was having the time of his life. Now he looked lost and lonely. Was he disappointed she'd shown up? Regretting that he wouldn't be with one of those women tonight? Feeling trapped by their contract? By the upcoming wedding?

"What's wrong?" she asked him when he got into the passenger seat.

"Nothing," he said, flashing a grin and the brief sad expression on his face disappeared.

"It won't be forever."

"What?"

"This arrangement. In a couple months you can get back to doing what you usually do."

He frowned. "What are you talking about?"

"Never mind." Toyin started her car. "Where do you want to go?"

He rested his head back. "I don't care."

"Are you sure you're alright?"

He nodded then closed his eyes.

But she didn't believe his casual attitude. Something was bothering him. Was he having regrets? Was the madness of the charade finally hitting him? He had seemed too casual on the phone the other day and she hadn't spoken to him for almost a week. Maybe the magnitude of everything had hit him. In a couple of days they had to perform this farce in front of everyone.

"I'm really sorry about the wedding," she said.

"It's okay."

He was quiet on the ride and she didn't want to bother him but he was a hard man to ignore. She felt self-conscious about every aspect of him. Of course it was hard to ignore a man in a green and gold suit. How come he managed to look good in anything no matter the combination? Why did she wish she could loosen his tie...no, take it off completely so that she could use it as a blindfold. Yes, she thought, her pulse picking up speed. She'd blindfold him while she slowly stripped him down, layer by layer until she exposed his smooth brown skin and had a chance to find out if his underwear was as colorful as everything else he wore. And then she'd pull it down and fall on her knees and capture him in her mouth. Then she'd suck him like a big chocolate bar...

Toyin shook her head, her body tense and hot. That was not why she was here. She was supposed to protect him. Not want him, even though she did. So much so she was tempted to pull the car over and jump him. She already knew what it was like to kiss him (delicious), to have him hold her close (heavenly), but there was still so much more to learn. And she'd be a willing student.

Toyin groaned and softly swore. She had to get a hold of herself. She turned the car into the parking lot, happy to have reached their destination. Jackson Fortune had to remain off-limits. "Okay," she said a little louder than she'd planned. "Here we are."

Jackson opened his eyes and looked around. "Where?"

"New Worlds. My store. I've got some inventory I want to go through then I'll drop you home. Unless you wanted to go somewhere else," she added when he hesitated.

"No, this is fine."

HER GRANDMOTHER MADE her office feel like a cramped pantry; Jackson made it feel like a bathtub. She'd briefly taken Jackson upstairs to show him where she had TJ Studios, sharing that she'd been relieved the landlord hadn't raised her rent, before taking him to her office in the back of the store. The space had never felt so small before and every time she moved she felt as if she were bumping into him. "Excuse me," she said for what seemed like the thousandth time when she had to pass by him to grab something from the shelf.

"Who's that?" Jackson asked, pointing to a black and white photo on her wall.

"Jackie Ormes, the creator of the Torchy Brown comic. The first African-American female cartoonist." She motioned to the image of the woman beside her. "Most people know Barbara Brandon as the first nationally syndicated cartoonist, but Ms. Ormes' work was in newspapers years before her." She pointed to two more images of attractive older white women. "And that's Jacky Fleming and Lynn Johnson. Those are names people know but there are lots of women in comics who people don't know."

"Which is why you have New Worlds."

"One reason. I wanted to make a living off of my love of art and pop-culture."

Jackson nodded then picked up a small booklet peeking from underneath her desk. He flipped through it. "What's this?"

Toyin looked at the item and smiled. "I'd wondered where that had disappeared to! It's something I'd done for 24-hour comic."

"What's that?"

"It's a challenge to create a twenty-four page comic in twenty-four hours. We hosted an event here last year and had ten participants. I've tried it four times and the fifth time I finally made it. That is one of my failures."

Jackson started to read the story about three African princesses on the hunt of a mystical medallion. "Why is it a failure? It looks good to me."

"But I didn't finish it by the deadline."

"So what? You can still finish it. I'd like to know what happens."

"I don't have the time. I don't draw comics anymore unless it's for challenges like that. I used to draw them all the time." She didn't tell him that while other kids babysat for money, she had started selling her work at fifteen to a website that nurtured and encouraged the creation of comics by girls. "At eight I fell in love with the watercolor illustrations of Pokémon. But as an illustrator you make much more money doing something else."

Jackson turned another page of the comic. "When did you start drawing?"

"Since I can remember." She hesitated, eager to share more but unsure. Because he wasn't looking at her she felt a little more confident, she took a deep breath before she said in a rush, "I used to tape and freeze frame the cartoon *Pinky and the Brain* so that I could draw them."

Jackson continued to keep his head lowered and nodded in understanding. "That's one smart kid."

Toyin felt her tension ebb, pleased he didn't think she was weird. Surprised he knew the characters she was talking about. Then she remembered the graphic novel she'd been reading at his apartment. "And I used to do the same with the films by Hayao Miyazaki. As a teenager I dreamt of getting the Kim Yale Award for Best New Female Talent by the Friends of Lulu." A sad smile touched her lips. "Never did and never will."

"You could still finish this," Jackson said, nodding to the unfinished comic book. "I'll buy it." He lifted his gaze to hers. "Consider it a commission."

"You're serious?"

He sent her a look.

She sighed. "I know. When it comes to money you're always serious."

He smiled.

"Must be nice to have money."

"It is. You have a week."

She stared at him for a moment then shook her head. "No can do."

"Why not?"

"I'm getting married this weekend."

Jackson laughed. "That's right. I can't believe a week has already passed. Two weeks then."

"I'm amazed you forgot."

He shrugged then said with a big grin, "One day I'm going to get you to draw me."

She looked at him and that strange sense of familiarity gripped her again. But this time she made the connection. He reminded her of a boy named Jacky she used to know. She couldn't understand why he had her thinking about a boy from so long ago. A boy she hadn't thought of in years. She'd thought she'd forgotten him. She'd only been six at the time, but he'd made an impression. She remembered how he would always come around her. It used to annoy her at first. He was always bouncing around, the teacher scolding him because he'd jump out of his seat and had a hard time staying still.

"Wow!" he said when he caught her drawing during play time. "You can really draw. Draw me. Draw me." He held out his arms and struck a pose. "I'm really strong."

"I don't want to."

"Please. Please."

"No."

His arms fell to his side. "Do you want to be my girlfriend?"

"No. You have three. My mom says you can only have one."

He shrugged. "I like them all and they like me."

He was right. Jacky and his three girlfriends were always sitting together at lunch time. Most people liked him. Even the teacher. But Mrs. Lorquette hated her. Toyin feared her. She always seemed to choose her when she didn't know the answer. She once caught Toyin sketching an answer to one of her questions and had ripped the sketch from her and said, "You're supposed to be paying attention."

"I was...that's my..."

"I don't care. You're to behave as everyone else does."

She hated going to school. When everyone else had their hand up to respond to a question she could feel Mrs. Lorquette's gaze land on her. "Toyin, what is the answer?"

She hung her head feeling stupid.

"I know, I know," Jacky said, waving his hand and bouncing in his seat. "It's—"

Mrs. Lorquette frowned, but her tone was patient and soft. "Jacky, it's not your turn. I didn't ask you."

"But Toyin told me the answer," he said pointing to her drawing. "That's how I know it." Then he gave the proper answer and the matter of her drawing pictures during class was settled. For one day at least. School was still awful for her because she was a child who expressed herself better with gestures and pictures than with words.

She still found Jacky annoying but as a thank you for that day, she drew him on an elephant. Elephants were her favorite animal to draw. She remembered his bright smile when she gave it to him.

She looked at Jackson now, that boy's smile lingering in her thoughts. "It's strange," she said. "But when you smile like that I feel as if I know you from somewhere."

"Really?" he said, sounding bored. He left the office and his disinterest wiped Toyin's nostalgia from her mind.

She finished her inventory check then locked up the office and watched Jackson stroll around the empty store. "You have a great place here," he said. "Do husbands get discounts?"

She didn't know why the mention of the word "husband" affected her but it did. He was her husband. She had a husband. A sexy, gorgeous husband who liked her drawings. How had that happened?

"Yes. Five percent."

"Fifteen."

"Okay, ten."

"Fifteen."

She threw her hands in the air. "Will you ever let me win a negotiation?"

"Fifteen."

She grabbed a bag from the food display in front of the cash register. "Ten and I'll throw in coconut chips."

Jackson took the bag and opened it. "Fifteen."

"Fine."

He kissed her cheek. "Thanks, honey."

Toyin touched her cheek, feeling oddly moved. "You're good at this."

"At what?"

"Pretending we're married."

He tossed some chips in his mouth. "We are married."

"That it's real."

He nodded. "By the way you're on the clock."

She frowned. "Clock?"

"If you wanted to say that special phrase to me."

Toyin searched her mind then remembered that he'd pay her for telling him she loved him. "Nobody's listening."

"I'm listening."

"It's not the same. You don't need a woman to tell you she loves you in private."

Jackson looked at a display of collectibles. A brief sad expression crossed his face again before he pointed to one of the objects and said, "How much?"

"What happened?"

He kept his gaze on a premium Batman statue before shifting to look at Rey and BB-8 from Star Wars. "Nothing."

She walked over to him, cupped his chin and forced him to face her. "I love you. Feel better now?"

He grinned, desire lighting his eyes. "A little."

She swallowed hard and turned to head back to her office to double check that she'd locked it. "You're a strange man."

Jackson stopped her, wrapping his arms around her waist. "Thanks for rescuing me," he whispered, his breath warm against her ear.

A delicious shiver coursed through her. "I didn't do anything."

"You came back into my life when I needed you most."

"How much have you had to drink?"

He turned her to him, his eyes studying hers with curious intensity. "Las Vegas wasn't a mistake."

She laughed, trying her best not to feel hypnotized by him. Desperate not to fall under his spell. "You believe in destiny?"

"Toyin—"

"I wasn't going to tell you but a pretty woman who walked like a cop stopped by."

His expression grew guarded. "Sylvia. What did she want?"

"She said she wanted to meet me." Toyin lowered her gaze, her voice faltering. "She let me know that you two are *very* close."

"Not as close as she wants us to be. She's not one of the ones who broke my heart." Jackson touched her cheek with a tenderness that had her craving more. "Still thinking about Lance?"

Toyin blinked, surprised by the question. "Not as much as I used to."

"I can help you forget him completely," he said, his words a velvet promise.

She knew what he was offering. A night with him. A night she wanted. This was why she'd answered his text. Why she'd come to see him.

Her cell phone rang, breaking the spell.

"I'm sorry," Toyin said, checking the number. "I have to get this."

Jackson smiled. "It's okay. I'm very patient."

Edgar Fortune used to only dream of ambition. Now his dreams were filled with her. His darling wife Flo. At times he wondered when the pain of loss would ease, but other times he feared that it would because his longing made him feel alive. His pain made his love for her feel even sweeter than it had felt when she was by his side.

"Edgar?"

He opened his eyes at the sound of his stepson's voice. He hated feeling weak. The health scare last week had been an embarrassment, but after a few tests he was sent home and told to rest. For the past several days people had tiptoed around him as if they expected him to break. It had been annoying. He sat up in his bed. He'd rested his head for a nap that had lasted longer than he'd meant it to.

The sun sat lower in the sky, signaling that Saturday evening was closing in. He hadn't been as productive as he'd hoped to be but planned to be back in the office Monday. He looked at his stepson's dark trousers and dark green shirt and knew he was talking to James. "What is it?" He held up his hand. "And don't ask me how I am. I'm fine. I gave you a little scare to keep you on your toes. I'm not planning to go anywhere yet. Even if I tried, I'm sure your mother would send me back to finish what I started."

"Yes, well...there's been a development."

"What kind?" He swung his legs over the side of the bed and grabbed a cigar from his cigar box. "Has something happened?"

"The business is fine as always," James said, guessing his concern. "It's Jackson. He's...getting married."

"Married? Did you say married?"

"Yes, the wedding is this Saturday."

"Today? How can you—"

"No, this coming Saturday."

"To who? Where? Who's arranging it?"

"Her family."

"Why haven't I heard anything about her before? Can we delay it in any way?"

"No, there's no point. They're already married. This is just a formality."

Edgar rolled the cigar between his thumb and forefinger, agitated. "Already married?"

"It was quick and from what he told me, was sort of whirlwind."

"Your brother picked up a bad habit from you and Ava," Edgar said referring to their own wedding last year when James had eloped with Ava to Vegas.

James rubbed the back of his neck. "It's not quite the same."

"How long have you known?" He crumbled the cigar in his hand. "Why wasn't I told sooner?"

"We weren't sure—"

Edgar let the ruined cigar fall to the ground and wiped his hands. "This is a disaster."

"No, she's good for him. A good influence."

James's cool tone helped ease some of Edgar's anxiety. "What is she like? What does she do? Dear God, please tell me she's not a stripper."

"Jackson has never dated a stripper."

"But that woman with the blondish hair and tight—"

"Was a dentist."

Edgar sniffed. "She didn't look like any dentist I've seen before."

"Things change," James said simply.

Edgar shook his head. "Your mother and I had someone we'd hoped...but that doesn't matter now. What do you know about her?"

"She's the middle child of three and attended the—"

Edgar waved his hand impatient. "Don't care."

"She's pretty. An artist."

"She's an artist? What's the use of an artist in the family?"

"She also owns a comic and pop-culture shop and a separate startup called TJ Studios so she's business minded."

"How business minded can she be with a comic book shop? What is that anyway?" He continued before James could reply, "Why have something like that when people can buy what they need online? Aren't bookstores dying like flies? Why would a niche store like that survive? It doesn't sound as if she has much sense."

"Her business is doing very well. She has a solid online presence."

"Hm...you also mentioned Something Studios. How is that going?"

"It's still growing."

"Which means she's struggling. Probably needs someone else to keep her afloat. I've warned you two about women like that. Never get caught by a woman who wants to get her hands on your willy and your wallet."

"I don't think—"

"You know what your brother is like. This woman could suck him dry. Have you looked at the prenup?"

James cleared his throat and made a noncommittal sound.

"Make sure you do. I'm depending on you. We can't let ourselves become vulnerable to anyone. I want to meet her."

"She's busy with the wedding planning so—"

Edgar sent him a hard look. "I don't care. Make it happen. Now."

CHAPTER 16

Thursday.

His brother hadn't been able to delay the meeting with Edgar any further than that.

"It's close enough to the wedding day to rein him in," James explained. Jackson had thanked him for the help then told Toyin the news. She tried to come up with alternative dates that he patiently countered until she finally agreed.

He heard the nervousness in her voice, but felt rejuvenated. He'd regained the trust of his team at work after his latest missteps and ideas filled his mind. He'd met the week with a focus and vigor he hadn't felt in a while. If getting married made a man feel this way, he was ready for more. Sylvia had discovered how much when he'd invited her out for drinks the Saturday night after his Friday post bachelor party.

"I heard you met Toyin," he said in a neutral voice as she finished her martini and ordered another.

She stared at him as if she'd been caught stealing. "I was in the neighborhood and wanted to see what her store was like."

Jackson rested his chin in his hand and continued to study her. "I find threats boring, don't you?"

"I wasn't trying to..." She began but Jackson's unwavering stare made the words die on her lips. "I'm sorry. I was curious. I couldn't believe..." She sighed. "I'll leave her alone."

He smiled. "Good girl."

Sylvia traced the base of her glass with her finger. "She was nice and looked much better this time. Pretty." A reluctant, knowing smile spread on her face. "But you don't care what I think, do you?"

His smile remained.

"You don't care what any of us think." When he again didn't reply she nodded in resignation. "I guess I need this more than you." She raised her second glass. "To friends."

He touched her glass with his and softened her disappointment with a wink. "Always."

The next day he sent her flowers. That Tuesday he returned home ready to go over some marketing plans when Reginald opened the door as he was about to open it.

"There's someone here to see you," he said.

Jackson handed him his coat and keys. "Who?"

"She's waiting in the living room."

"And you let her in because...?"

"She'll explain herself." He turned.

Jackson walked in and saw a tall older woman sitting as still as a statue. "Hello, I—"

"I am called Mama Bisi. Forgive the intrusion," she said in a clipped English tone. "Please sit."

Jackson did, not daring to refuse her.

"I wanted to talk to you about my granddaughter Toyin."

He nodded.

"She must never know I came to see you."

He nodded again.

Her dark eyes studied him for a moment then she sat back and sighed. "It won't do. She is no good for you and I say this out of love for her." She pointed a finger at him, her long red nail fashioned like the tip of a sword. "You have the eyes of a fox and the heart of an elephant. It is steady and true. Such a contradiction will cause you pain because most people won't see it. Yes, I can see by your eyes that I am right. No woman has been worthy of your heart yet. Yet you give it out freely. Too freely."

Jackson cleared his throat, uncomfortable. "Madam, I—"

"Is your mother still living?"

"No."

"Yes, so you're even more vulnerable. Take heed of this warning. You do not want a woman who has the heart of a dragonfly. It cannot hold tight to someone who cannot rest in one place. Do not continue with her."

Jackson fell silent a moment before he said, "And if I do?"

She narrowed her eyes. "I see the fox is stubborn and a little selfish too." She stood. "I can only warn you."

"Why not tell me how?"

She looked at him surprised. "How?"

"How to win her heart."

Mama Bisi shook her head. "You can't without sacrificing your own."

CHAPTER 17

She couldn't escape.

Jackson's call had stunned her. His stepfather wanted to meet her before the wedding—at all costs. She'd tried to tell him that her week was busy—coming up with false excuses—but nothing worked. Thursday was D-day. It wasn't fair. Jackson had managed not to meet her family yet, why couldn't she have been as lucky? The closer she got to her wedding day the less she thought she had any good luck at all.

But she couldn't escape it. Her first impression had to be good.

Toyin emerged from her bedroom with her hair pulled back wearing a simple white and black dress. Jackson would soon pick her up.

Maryam frowned. She'd stopped by to offer advice and support. "You look like a nun. No, a novice."

"It's not funny."

"Which is why I'm not laughing. You're not attending a funeral."

It feels like it. "I'm trying to look sophisticated."

Maryam went to Toyin's closet and pulled out a patterned dress with a West African flair and European accent. Toyin briefly smiled picturing Jackson in a matching suit. He would love the bold yellow, red, green and orange colors. But would his stepfather? Could she take the risk?

She shook her head and adjusted her glasses. "It's too much."

"It's perfect. Besides, you don't have much time."

Toyin took the dress. At least she knew Jackson would be pleased. She wondered what combination he'd show up in. Metallic silver with purple accents? Plush mauve? She changed into the dress. "I'm only in this mess because of you."

Maryam rested a hand on her hip, unapologetic. "You're married to a wealthy man. You're going to have a big wedding, where's the mess in that?"

"Now I have to lie to his family."

Maryam grabbed Toyin's cheeks and spread her lips into a forced expression. "Just do it with a smile."

"I HOPE YOU DON'T MIND—" Toyin began when she opened her front door. But the words died on her lips. She hadn't expected to see James. He wore a dark suit and blank expression. "Oh, I thought Jackson was picking me up."

He nodded. "He is."

"Where is he?"

"You're looking at him."

She looked at Jackson's somber suit. "What happened to you?"

"I want to annoy my sister-in-law. Don't worry, it won't last."

Toyin glanced down dismayed. "But I can't go dressed like this. We look completely different. I—"

He pressed his lips against hers in a feather light kiss. "Look perfectly beautiful."

The way he said it she almost believed him. "I can still change." She heard a loud cough. "Oh," she said turning. "This is my older sister, Maryam. The cause of all this mayhem and—"

"Nice to finally meet you," Maryam interrupted, holding out her hand. "You look better in person."

Toyin grabbed her purse and coat not trusting the look in her sister's eyes. "We're leaving now. No, first I have to change."

"No," Jackson and Maryam said in unison.

"Listen to your sister," he said.

"Listen to your husband," she said.

Toyin glared at them both then pointed at her sister. "I will get you back for this one day." She pointed at Jackson. "And you—" She looked him up and down at a loss for words. "Never mind. Let's go."

"Have fun," Maryam called out in a singsong voice as Toyin closed the door.

"What should I expect?" Toyin asked as they walked to Jackson's red Porsche. "What's your sister-in-law like?"

"Depends on who you ask. To my brother, she's a dream. To me a nightmare."

Jackson never knew shock could be such a beautiful expression. He enjoyed the look on both James and Ava's faces when he walked into the great room of the family home.

"Toyin," Jackson said. "You've already met my brother, James and the frozen witch, I mean wife, by his side is Ava."

"A pleasure," Toyin said.

"What game are you playing?" Ava asked him.

He shot her a look. "One I plan to win." He looked at James. "Where's Dad?"

"He'll be down soon."

"I'm here right now," Edgar said, displaying no sign of illness. He was a man of average height with a thick, muscular build and skin the color of roasted almonds and looked ready to take on the world. He patted Jackson on the back. "I looked over the report thanks, James."

"You're welcome," James said from across the room.

Edgar frowned and looked up at Jackson then looked at

James. "Wait," he stumbled over to a chair and sat down. "I think I may be suffering a stroke."

"It's not you, Edgar," Ava said. "It's one of Jackson's childish pranks."

Jackson grinned. "Speaking of pranks...kidnapped anyone lately?"

"I said I was sorry."

"I thought you meant it until you tried to get me fired."

"I never said that. I only—"

"Why don't we all sit down to dinner?" James said.

"Where's Rudy?" Jackson asked, referring to his younger brother Rudolph. "I'd hoped Toyin would get a chance to meet him."

"At a friend's house," Edgar said. "He'll meet Toyin at the wedding."

"We wouldn't want him getting too attached to someone who may not be around long," Ava said under her breath.

IN THE DINING room Edgar took his place at the head of the table briefly looking over the couscous-stuffed green and yellow peppers in the center of the table before he looked at his two stepsons. He frowned. "One of you take off your jacket or something. It's disturbing to see you two looking so similar."

"Oh, give it time Edgar," Ava said. "You'll soon notice the difference. Jackson could never replace his brother."

"No," Toyin said, sensing Jackson stiffen beside her. She covered his hand. "I'm not in love with James."

"True," Ava allowed, "but some may wonder if you're really in love with Jackson."

Jackson shoved his chair back ready to stand.

Toyin squeezed his hand, stopping him. "No, it's okay. I expected your family to be suspicious of me. You haven't had the cleanest record with women after all. She's only looking out for you."

Ava nodded. "I'm glad you understand."

"Completely." She patted Jackson's hand. "And I'm not going anywhere soon. So we'll get a chance to get to know each other."

"I'd like that."

"We're not the easiest bunch to know," Edgar said. "What do you do Tonya?"

"It's Toyin."

He nodded. "What do you do?"

James cleared his throat. "I told you she—"

"I know what you told me," Edgar cut in with a hard look. "I want to hear her say it."

"I own a store called New Worlds and another business called TJ Studios," Toyin said.

"Profitable?"

"One more than the other."

"That will have to change. You're a Fortune now. If one of us fail we all fail. We'll have someone look over your financials."

Toyin shifted in her seat, uncomfortable. "That's not necessary."

"Of course it's necessary."

"Jackson is already helping me with my legal fees."

"Legal? Are you being sued?"

"No," Jackson said. "One of her employees stole from her. She's working with Moore's firm."

Edgar grinned. "Excellent. She'll crush this person like a maggot." He rubbed his hands together. "You'll soon learn not to turn your back on your business. You can't be too nice or too careful." He looked at Jackson. "I'm glad you've decided to settle down. I was getting worried about you and you know I hate worrying about anything."

"We have a new campaign rolling out soon."

"Hope it won't cost me as much as the costly new logo launch."

"It won't."

Edgar shifted his gaze between Toyin and Jackson. "She even dresses like you when you're not trying to confuse me. She's as colorful as a piñata," he said with a laugh. "A shame your mother couldn't see this."

"I think Flo would see right through it," Ava mumbled.

Jackson glared at her.

She winced when her husband kicked her. "What? We're all thinking it."

"Thinking what?" Edgar said.

"Nothing," Jackson said.

Ava looked at Toyin then glanced at her hand covering Jackson's. "You don't have to try so hard. No matter what this really is we're all willing to accept it."

Toyin looked around the table not knowing what to say. She felt exposed as a fraud. Like a big red tomato in a barrel of peanuts. But then she remembered him sharing what Ava had done to him, how this marriage would protect his position at the company. So for his sake she wanted to stand strong. She would show Ava that she wasn't a pushover and that Jackson wasn't the man she believed him to be.

Toyin took a deep breath and thought of a moment when

she was ten and had handed in a book report using only pictures. She'd been proud of it, but her teacher had given her an F for not following instructions. She recalled that pain now and let her eyes fill with tears.

She stared at Ava, making her voice shake. "Yes, you're right. You all know that I'm fooling myself." She brushed away a tear. "This is all too wonderful to believe and I know that Jackson could never love me as I love him. Even though he's loved many other women, including you. Excuse me." She jumped to her feet and raced out of the room.

She left them all in silence.

"What the hell just happened?" Edgar finally asked.

James turned to Ava. "Why did you have to push it?"

"I didn't think I'd make her cry." She glared at Jackson. "What did you tell her about me?"

"Enough," Jackson said. "Although I never told her I loved you."

James rested his napkin on the table. "Aren't you going to go after her?"

"I'm sure she went to the powder room."

"Assuming she knows where it is." James stood. "I'll go find her."

"No," Jackson said standing. "I will." He glared at Ava. "And when I get back you'll apologize."

SHE DIDN'T WANT to go back.

Toyin rested her head against the wall in the hallway and closed her eyes. It was too much. Edgar talking about killer lawyers. Ava wearing a black suit that could easily cost several thousand dollars. They lived in a mansion. What was she doing? She felt like an actress lost in a melodrama. *I'm fooling myself that he'll ever love me?* Who says that in real life? They'll know she's a fraud. Especially Ava. Beautiful, smart Ava. She shouldn't have tried to pretend she could defeat her.

"Hey!" Jackson said in a loud whisper. "What are you doing?"

"Hiding. That woman scares me."

He held her shoulders then cupped her face, his eyes searching hers. "Did she really make you cry?"

"No." She sniffed in derision. "I just remembered a bad memory."

"You're doing great."

"Nobody believes a word I'm saying."

"Yes, they do. James is really upset Ava made you cry. I think she'll leave you alone from now on."

"I hope so." Toyin shivered. "Sitting in front of those two is creepy. She has eyes like laser beams and his are no better. I feel like I've been abducted and being analyzed by aliens who have taken human form."

Jackson laughed. "I understand the feeling but they're really not that bad, at least James isn't and...Ava has her moments."

"She reminds me of someone. Is she *really* the one you nearly married?"

"Trust me. She wasn't like this when we were dating. It was later that I started to get suspicious."

"She's really beautiful."

"Brilliant too, but I never slept with her."

"I didn't ask."

"But you were wondering."

She looked down.

He rested his hand against the wall behind her head. "You're making this look easy."

She lifted her gaze to his, startled. "What?"

"Being in love with me."

"If—" Toyin stopped when she heard footsteps, but she lost her breath completely when Jackson pulled her close and covered her mouth with his in a wild, hot kiss.

James stopped short. "Oh, I wondered what was taking you two so long."

Jackson waved him away. "We'll be there in a minute."

James laughed. "Take your time."

Once he was out of hearing, Toyin pulled away, breathless. Her body felt heavy and warm. "Why did you—?"

"You know why," Jackson said in a deep, husky voice before he pressed his open lips to hers once more.

After a few more seconds of shimmering, burning pleasure, Toyin reluctantly drew back. "Nobody is watching now. We have to go back."

A sly grin touched his lips. "You heard my brother. We can take our time."

"That's just a saying. He didn't mean it."

He kissed her neck, letting his hand slide down her side. "I do."

She ducked away and headed down the hall. She didn't want to go back, but being alone with him was far more dangerous. "Come on. If you're right, the rest of dinner should be a breeze."

"I know her from somewhere," Ava said as she sat beside her husband in the great room after their guests had left. Edgar had retired to his room.

"Probably because you saw her picture," James said.

Ava shook her head. "No, it's not that."

"I'm relieved that he finally found someone who loves him more than he loves her."

"You really think she loves him?"

James threw his head back amazed. "Why are you being so suspicious? You met her. You made her cry."

"I know, but I have this feeling that I'm missing something important."

He kissed her forehead. "Put away your knives. You did enough damage today."

Ava sighed with remorse. "I didn't mean to hurt her feelings. She really was a shock. She's not at all what I expected." Ava hit him in the stomach. "You should have warned me."

James rubbed where she'd hit him and said in a wounded

voice. "She shocked me too. She didn't look like that when I first met her. Her hair was longer and her eyes seemed bigger somehow and the clothes were more...uh...different."

"Not his type at all."

"She draws and likes comics. They probably fell in love over manga."

Ava sat up and clapped her hands. "That's it! Why didn't I think of it before? The comic shop! New Worlds...of course. It was staring me right in the face. It's her! That's where I've seen her. I haven't gone there in awhile, but when I was seeing Jackson I once took him there." Ava sat back pleased by the connection and remembered that spring day and how he'd behaved.

He'd been mildly impressed by the décor when she'd told him about the popular store that catered to women. She had left him to wander around so that she could look at a selection of graphic novels when she heard the sound of a display crashing to the ground. She turned and saw Jackson quickly trying to right it as well as the magazines that had been scattered on the floor. "I'm sorry," he said in a frazzled manner she'd never seen before. "I...I didn't see it."

"What happened?" Ava asked staring at the mess.

Jackson didn't reply as he fell on his knees and quickly gathered the magazines. A pretty woman in a silver wig, dark framed glasses, wearing a yellow shirt with the store logo on it, came up to them. Before she could speak, Ava said, "I apologize on my boyfriend's behalf. Maybe you should ban men entirely."

"No," the woman said with a laugh. "It's okay. At least it wasn't the collectible display case. I'll take care of it. Is there anything you were looking for? I could—?"

Jackson jumped to his feet, keeping his gaze lowered. "No, I'm fine. Thanks." He turned to Ava. "I'll meet you outside." He held out his hand. "Give me the keys, I'll wait in the car."

Ava gave him the keys. "I'll just—"

He snatched the keys and turned. "No rush. Take your time."

Ava watched him hurry out of the store confused. "He's not usually like that."

"He looked really embarrassed," the woman said as they both watched him jump into Ava's car like a storm was chasing him.

Ava agreed. That wasn't like Jackson either. Few things embarrassed him. He usually had a smile, laugh or joke to cover any awkward occasion. She didn't think too much about it as she had her items rung up.

She returned to the car where she found Jackson with his head on the dashboard. She handed him a magazine. "The woman you met was the owner and she says no hard feelings. She hopes you feel comfortable coming back. She thought you might like this. It's a comic she published."

Jackson barely glanced at the magazine before he tossed it in the backseat. "Thanks."

Ava turned to reach for the discarded item, offended. "If you don't want it—"

He stopped her, grabbing her arm. "I do...I just..." He took the magazine, rolled it up and tucked it inside his jacket. "I'll look at it later."

Ava chewed her lip as she thought about that forgotten incident. She'd figured that Jackson had been so overwhelmed by the décor that he hadn't paid attention, he did things like that, but now she wondered if it had been Toyin instead. "I think he knows her."

"Maybe. Jackson knows a lot of people."

"Yes, and I think there's more to this story than he's telling us. But I'll offer Toyin one little test, just to make sure."

"What?" James frowned. "I warned you about going behind my back."

Ava smiled in return. "If it works, you'll thank me."

CHAPTER 20

"I don't feel like taking you home yet," Jackson said, as he navigated his Porsche on the city streets. The dark sky made the evening feel closer to midnight than nine o'clock. "Do you mind?"

"No. Actually, I sort of come alive at night."

He grinned. "Me too."

"Why did you dress up like your brother?"

His smile disappeared. "Because that's who they want me to be."

"You're so lucky you haven't had to meet any of my family yet."

Jackson tapped his finger against the steering wheel. "Hmm."

"Where are we going?"

"Shopping."

"Shopping? I've done enough shopping for a lifetime."

He sent her a curious glance. "You can never do too much shopping."

She decided not to argue. "What are we shopping for?"

"Clothes. I want to dress you up."

"Why?"

"I'm bored. I like to shop."

TOYIN STOOD in a private room surrounded by mirrors dressed in an embroidered mesh lace mermaid dress in gunmetal gray. Before that she'd tried on a gold colored off the shoulder silk tunic dress and champagne colored v-neck beaded gown.

"Do you like it?" Jackson asked while he watched her from a white chaise lounge.

"What's not to like?"

He stood and walked towards her. "How does it feel?"

"Great."

Jackson touched the fabric, his knuckles brushing her skin causing her to tremble, before he looked at the assistant. "Cotton voile?"

"Yes, sir."

He looked at Toyin. "How are you with velvet?"

"I've never worn velvet."

"That's about to change."

They left the store with three large shopping and garment bags and Toyin wearing a crushed red-violet velvet dress while Jackson bought and wore a suit to match. She knew they both looked outrageous when they walked into a late night specialty bakery with an assortment of gourmet cookies, but she liked the feeling.

They ordered soft, moist chocolate chip cookies. Toyin never thought such a simple treat could taste so good.

"If you like this," Jackson said. "I also know an ice cream shop we can go to next time."

Next time. There would be a next time. This wonderful feeling could continue. Until this moment she hadn't realized how much she enjoyed his company. Being with him... She had missed this feeling the past several months. She'd thought fighting to save TJ Studios had been the true reason for her depression, but she'd missed him.

When she was in Vegas all her senses felt more heightened. The smells, the taste of the food, the bright lights. All this time she'd given credit to the city, but not the man. She felt that same way now. With Jackson, everything felt like a brand new adventure. Her eyes seeing the world in a new way. She'd looked but never really seen before. What others may deem unimportant, like the feel of fabric against the skin; the dash of pepper added to a meal; the taste of semi-sweet chocolate in a cookie, he made almost epic. She felt alive, vibrant in his presence. She now knew he hadn't been teasing her when he had called her beautiful. She was beautiful because he saw her that way. And that was how he made her feel. She never felt awkward, she felt interesting, witty. He was a magician.

Then why hadn't any other woman seen it too? Why had he had such bad luck in the past?

In two days she'd be marrying him again.

She licked chocolate from her lip then looked at him, making a decision. "You don't have to take me home tonight."

His eyes darkened. "Are you sure?"

"Do you care?"

His slow smile told her all she needed to know.

It had been one long night of foreplay.

That's what Toyin realized as she lay naked in his arms.

Every move, gesture or glance since the seemingly simple kiss in the hallway had been a careful, calculated seduction. From how he dressed her in silk and velvet, touching the fabric while also touching her skin; to the soft, moist cookies, the semi-sweet chocolate dissolving on her tongue. She remembered being mesmerized watching him lick a stray crumb from his mouth, the bright pink tip of his tongue sweeping slowly over his full bottom lip; she bit her own lip as she noticed him suck smothered chocolate from his thumb.

It had all been a subtle, decadent invitation.

And now she was at the ball. She glanced up at the soft recess lighting in his bedroom, the fine cotton sheets against her back. She'd expected him to be a bold, flamboyant lover, but instead he was a masterful one. As his warm hard body covered hers he smelled like brown sugar and vanilla just like the cookie, reminding her of when she was a child and had discovered finger painting, the wild thrill of pressing her hands in the wet colorful mixtures and splaying them on paper.

He was her canvas now and she let her hands run free along the front of his chest, down his back and along the hard, swollen length of him.

Jackson rolled on a condom then turned off the lights.

Toyin gasped before she started to laugh.

Jackson paused halfway on top of her. "What?"

"You have glow-in-the-dark condoms?"

She could hear the smile in his voice. "You like it?"

Toyin stroked it with her forefinger. "It's like getting intimate with a light saber."

"You'll be the first."

"To get intimate with a—"

"No," Jackson said with a chuckle, covering her body with his, "you'll be the first I've used them with. I know I'm taking a risk."

Toyin closed her legs around him, wanting him even closer. "I'm glad you did. Next time I'll wear my silver wig and an outfit you might find interesting."

"What?"

"It will be a surprise," she said then neither needed to say much else. Passion and desire consuming them.

Why had she denied herself this pleasure for so long? Since the moment he'd fallen on his knees and asked her to marry him she'd been tempted. Tempted to lose all inhibitions and forget her worries, if only for a moment. The magician in him made Lance disappear from her thoughts; Shanna became a whisper; Mama Bisi's disapproval a vague notion.

She wasn't a loser. A failure. A disappointment. She was a

free, powerful woman claiming her desire. She didn't care about his past, the many women before her. Her passion left no room for fear.

He was hers tonight, feeding a burning sweet hunger. He'd married her and no other. No matter how long this lasted, she'd enjoy the moment. She would prove Ava wrong. She would prove them all wrong. Nobody knew them really.

But tonight they knew each other.

CHAPTER 22

His bride.

Jackson watched his future walk towards him wearing an A-line wedding dress, the beaded sequins seeming to sparkling under the chapel lights as her ivory train softly flowed behind her. She looked beautiful. He knew the taste of her lips, the sexy swell of her hips, the liquid heat between her legs, but he wanted more. Much more. He wanted to remove every inch of that ivory organza lace with steady, slow hands. See her eyes darken with desire. Hear her breath catch as he entered her. Feel her tighten around him all over again.

Dominion. He wanted every inch of her to be his and no one else's. Las Vegas hadn't been a coincidence or a mistake, but part of a careful plan. She still hadn't made the connection. He'd give her more time. It may not make a difference if she did.

But this moment meant more than he'd expected it to. He looked at her and she flashed him a soft nervous grin, as if in apology for everything. But she had nothing to feel sorry for. If he had to marry anyone, even briefly, he was glad it was her. With her, his life made sense. She didn't demand, she didn't cajole. He felt safe.

No, it was deeper than that. He knew he'd been in danger of losing his heart since the first moment, when she listened to him in Vegas and didn't judge. She came to warn him about the online story spreading. She came to get him from the club when he asked her. She was there when he needed her most. As he stood in front of the crowd and took her hand in his, Jackson felt his heart sliding into a dangerous abyss that he couldn't stop.

He knew he was in trouble. He knew his friends would laugh, his brother wouldn't believe him. But none of that mattered. He was in love.

WAS it normal for a bride to want to cry on her wedding day? Toyin watched the pastor's mouth move wanting the day to be over. The night she'd spent with Jackson had been amazing. Everything had felt true, but this was a spectacle. Her cousin beamed at her and giggled at the most inopportune times. Soon

Jackson would slide a ring on her finger and repeat words he didn't mean. She felt like bursting into tears her heart heavy with regret. Poor Jackson. He deserved better than this showcase. She did too.

Her mother looked so proud, her father pleased and Mama Bisi...

She knew she would still have to pay for her deception. Her grandmother wouldn't let this slide.

Toyin briefly looked over at Ava, remembering the strange request she'd given her when they'd had a moment alone after dinner.

"I didn't mean to upset you," Ava had said as they sat in the great room, the men had gone to talk in the library.

"It's okay," Toyin said. Ava sounded sincere.

"So I hope you won't take what I have to say the wrong way."

"What?"

"I'll pay you five thousand dollars not to sleep with him for a month."

"What?"

Ava held out a piece of paper. "It's for your own good and his."

Toyin stared at the contract stunned. What was it with this family and contracts? "What if we've already been intimate?"

Ava folded her arms.

"You don't think we have?" Toyin guessed.

"No, I don't."

"And you don't think our relationship is real?"

"Correct."

Toyin felt her heart hammering in her ears. Ava was clever and savvy. She didn't want to ruin this for Jackson. He said his job depended on Ava believing their relationship was real. "You're right. Jackson isn't interested in me that way, but I'm hoping—"

"I'll pay you to stop hoping. He's not worth it."

Toyin paused surprised by her words. "I thought you liked him."

"I do."

"And I love him."

Ava flashed a tight grin. "Let's see how much."

Toyin had signed the contract knowing she wouldn't comply. It was one of the reasons she'd slept with Jackson that same night.

Ava's presumption and challenge didn't sit well with her. The dare in her eyes had galled her. She didn't like that Ava thought she was using him. Ava should have better faith in him. He may come off showy and a little shallow, but there was much more to Jackson. He was more than just style, he also had substance and that's what made him memorable.

And why would sleeping with him be so terrible? What business was it of hers? Did Ava fear she'd try to get pregnant or something?

Considering the women he'd been with in the past she could understand Ava's concern, but it still didn't feel right.

That didn't stop her from trying to see it from another woman's perspective. Jackson had been drunk in Vegas, sober he'd never look at someone like her. If her sister and his brother hadn't come into the picture they would have gotten a quick annulment and she'd never see him again. They did make a strange pair. Who in their right mind could believe it was real? It was as likely as a stallion falling in love with a pug.

There were few men like her father who'd taken one look at her mother and said that she was the only one for him. That kind of fairy tale was not in the cards for her. This was purely business.

And common sense would keep her from even once imagining that any of this could be real. No matter how much she might wish it to.

Toyin turned sharply when she heard something move

behind her. She saw Mama Bisi standing tall, her finger pointing at her in accusation.

"Stop the wedding! This marriage is doomed!"

The crowd gasped and a wave of uneasy murmurs swept through the chapel.

"Mummy please," Toyin's mother said.

"Why is that woman shouting?" Rudy asked his brother James.

"I will not keep quiet," Mama Bisi declared. She motioned towards the two couples. "There is only one pair that should be at that altar." She pointed to Toyin again. "This must not continue. Walk away now before this farce becomes real." She narrowed her eyes. "I was right about Lance."

Toyin's cheek burned in remembrance.

"I am right about this. I am always right."

"I'm sorry," Toyin stuttered feeling weighted by the crowd's gaze on her. "I know I didn't consult with you first, but I care—"

"Don't lie so blatantly in a church. I know what I know and I see what I see. She doesn't deserve him."

Jackson frowned. "Madam—"

Mama Bisi rested a hand over her heart. "I love my granddaughter, she is my flesh, but I also know a poor match when I see one. Especially for you. I will not sit here and be silent."

Aunt Gretchen stood to her feet and pressed her hands together, pleading. "Mummy, please it's already done. This man is Toyin's choice and—"

Mama Bisi folded her arms and pinned Jackson with a stare. "His heart is too big." She shifted her gaze to Toyin. "Her heart is too small. They do not suit each other. There is no balance here. How can grass grow in a desert? Heed my words. Continue at your peril. You won't—"

Edgar stood. "He will do what he damn well wants to!"

The crowd turned to him.

"I do not know you," he said. "But I know Jackson. He is a Fortune and we Fortune men know our own minds. If my stepson wants to marry your granddaughter a hundred times he will do so. She's one of us now. Do not interfere."

Mama Bisi sent him an ugly look. "You use people as pawns. You have no idea what I'm saying."

"You can—"

"Enough!" Jackson said in a voice that left everyone quiet. He turned back to the pastor and said in a soft voice, "Continue."

The pastor hesitated then did so as the sound of Mama Bisi's heels pounded the ground as she stormed out of the church.

Toyin began to look back, but Jackson grabbed her hand, stopping her.

The rest of the wedding ceremony continued under a more somber air, but they both made it through. Tansy sniffed instead of giggled and before they parted she gave Toyin a watery kiss on the cheek.

In the limo on the way to the reception, Toyin held her head in her hands.

"She's wrong," Jackson said in a fierce tone. "I deserve you. I want you and no one else."

"She should have punished *me*, not you. I should have just left. Now everyone knows."

"They don't know anything."

"They'll suspect this isn't real. Now they'll—"

"I don't care."

Toyin lifted her head. "Yes, you do. She's right. I don't deserve you and now everybody knows it. How humiliating."

"She's wrong."

"She's never wrong."

Jackson's tone hardened. "She's wrong about us."

"Is she? What are we doing and who are we doing it for? For money and a job position? Does that even make sense? She probably won't speak to me again."

Toyin could understand her grandmother's words. Jackson was just a man who loved being in love. He could fall in love with anyone and be happy. However, she had never been in love. She liked people. Cared. But love...she'd never felt that way or maybe she'd never tried. Whatever the reason they were two very different people and that wasn't going to change.

"Is there a way to change your grandmother's mind?"

"Why would we want to do that? She knows this isn't real. It's all make believe."

"Is there a way?" he insisted.

"You're not making sense."

"Answer the question."

"I suppose nothing is set in stone. But I'd have to ask my mum—"

"Ask her."

"You don't see how lucky we are. We dodged a bullet. We can shorten this farce and—"

"I need this to work. Even if it's just for a year. I need the world to see that someone's willing to marry me because she wants me. Not because of a business deal or some other reason, just me."

"Jackson—"

"These last few days have been the best I've had in a long time. And it's because of you. I'm not asking you to love me for real. I didn't realize how much I needed this wedding until now."

"You heard my grandmother. I don't deserve you." She shook her head. "And stop saying she's wrong. She rarely is. I don't want to hurt you." Toyin called out to the driver. "Stop the limo."

"No," Jackson countered. He took her hands in his. "I know you're nervous about the reception. I know this has been a lot to take, but you're doing great. Don't worry."

"That doesn't help."

"What?"

She pulled her hands away. "Telling a person who's worried not to worry. It doesn't help."

"Okay, then relax. Take deep breaths. You don't have to do anything but smile."

"I'm not looking forward to an encore of humiliation. I was crazy to do this. I should have known Mama Bisi would make me pay." She hung her head. "I'll do everything else, please don't make me do this."

"I need you to. It's important that Ava and Edgar—"

"I wish I could." She held his gaze, pain squeezing her heart. "When we're alone it's like magic. I feel completely myself. It's wonderful but when others see us together something in me just...dies. And now Mama Bisi's words keep echoing in my head. I can't face another crowd. Tell them I'm sick. Tell them an emergency came up."

He grabbed her shoulders, desperate to convince her. "Everyone will be waiting for us."

"I can't go." Her voice cracked in misery. "I can't...I can't." Her mind raced but she couldn't find the words. She hated disappointing everyone. Why did she always have to be a disappointment?

Toyin rubbed her hands feeling as if she were being torn apart inside. She wasn't good with words. She wasn't good with people. She pulled out her cell phone and began to draw the image of a woman underneath an anvil about to fall. She showed it to him.

"I won't let that happen to you," Jackson said.

She drew another sketch showing the same woman and people pointing and laughing.

"I won't let that happen either."

She felt his chin as he rested it on her shoulder. It had a calming effect on her. She drew a woman melting into the floor.

"Not that either," he said in a quiet voice. He pointed to the screen. "Now draw me."

She looked at him in question.

"What?"

"The way you said that reminded me of—"

His gaze held hers, intense. "Who?"

She shook her head. "Just a boy I once knew. It was a long time ago."

"I acted like him?"

"It's was just a memory and you're not him so it doesn't matter."

"Are you sure?"

"That it doesn't matter?"

"No, that I'm not him."

She frowned. It was a strange question. "Of course you're not him. He had a different last name and—"

Jackson nudged her with his elbow. "Go on and draw me."

She began to sketch him in his tux.

"Now add a sword. Go on," he urged when she sent him a skeptical look.

She rolled her eyes. "Do you want a cape too?"

"Next time. Better yet, draw me with my shirt off."

"No."

"Naked?"

"No."

"I'll pose if that helps."

The memory of Jacky came back to her again. *Draw me. Draw me. I'm strong.*

She remembered standing outside of school and seeing Jacky show the picture she'd drawn for him to his mother and brother.

His brother...

His *twin* brother.

Jacky had a twin brother.

But that was impossible.

She remembered he was sad towards the end of the year. She heard from another student that he had to move. She remembered giving him another drawing and her address but he never wrote back. She always imagined him having three more girlfriends at whatever new school he would go to. She didn't cry like the others, but she did miss him. She wondered what he would be like now.

"Figured it out yet?" Jackson said.

She turned to him. "How can you be Jacky Brownson?"

He nodded and grinned. "In the flesh."

"I don't understand. Your name—"

"When my mother remarried my stepfather adopted us and gave us his surname. I started to go by 'Jackson' in the fourth grade."

"I don't know what to say."

"How about 'Long time no see'?"

"When did you know who I was?"

"The moment I heard someone say your name then I saw you in the New Worlds store. I was so shocked I toppled the display."

"Oh, right...that was you. I thought I remembered Ava..." She paused. "And now that I come to think of it—"

"Don't think of it," Jackson said with a groan. "It wasn't a good day.

"Why didn't you say anything before?"

"Pride, I was hoping that you'd finally recognize me. But then I got tired of waiting."

"You look..."

He lifted his chin in a haughty manner. "Amazing I know."

She rolled her eyes. "I should have known it was you. It was the lack of three girlfriends that threw me off. But then again you did have Ava, Enomwoyi and Sylvia." She shook her head. "I was so silly. I even gave you my address to write me so that we could be friends."

"I know."

"You never wrote me."

He nodded. "I know. Don't ask why. I was six. But I did make up for it." All humor left his voice and eyes. His gaze darkened and his voice deepened. "Toyin, I love you."

She smiled, sad. "You love sex."

"No, I *like* sex. Actually I like sex a lot but I *love* you."

She didn't know how to respond. Why was he saying this to her? Had he really married her on purpose because of some faint connection years ago? That didn't make any sense.

Finding out who he really was had come too late to save her. She shouldn't have fallen for him. Despite all his female woes he would keep having them. She now knew why he always got his heart broken. Her grandmother was right, his heart *was* too big. He was a man who loved being in love. The woman didn't matter, only the feeling. He was a man who could find pleasure anywhere. Once she was out of his life, he'd fall in love with someone else all over again.

Women would always be part of his life just as he'd been surrounded by girls as a child, as an adult it hadn't changed. There would be adoring women outside a club, in a bar, at the office. Everywhere.

And she'd fallen in love with him. But she would not continue down the doomed path Mama Bisi had predicted. Her tiny heart could not weather the pain he could inflict.

Toyin looked up at the driver. "Stop the limo."

"Toyin."

"I'm not going. I've already ruined my poor cousin's

wedding day I won't ruin her reception as well. Don't worry, I'll fulfill my contract."

Jackson looked at her both hurt and surprised. "Contract? Did you hear what I said? I love you. I want to be with you. I want to spend my life with you."

When the limo pulled up to the curve, Toyin reached for the door. "Tell everyone I'm sorry."

He stopped her, his tone pleading. "Stay with me. I'll do whatever it takes to make you happy. I don't care if you don't love me."

Toyin looked at him for a long moment, her heart breaking. She opened the door and got out afraid she might stay, the cool autumn air chilling her skin spite the bright sunshine. She turned to him, blinking back tears. "That's the problem, Jackson. You should."

"Sorry about your wedding," Ava said, entering Jackson's office at BioMed Solutions that Monday.

"Are you?" he said, doubtful.

"It was interesting. Has Toyin recovered?"

He hadn't seen her since she left the limo. But Ava didn't need to know that. He'd arrived at the reception alone and made excuses that everyone understood. But he hadn't been able to fool his brother James for long. While people were dancing he called him aside and said, "What's going on?"

"I told her who I really am," Jackson said, staring down at the champagne glass in his hand.

"That doesn't make sense."

He took a sip. "I mean who I was."

"And who were you?"

He lifted his gaze. "Jacky Brownson."

James looked at him sharply. "She knew you from before? Who is she?"

"A girl I knew from elementary school. The one I told you about. She drew me on the elephant."

James's brows shot up. "The girl who barely spoke? The girl who had you drawing hearts for days?"

"Shut up."

James looked at him for a long moment. "You fell in love with her, didn't you?"

Jackson looked down at his drink. "I didn't plan to. At first I only wanted to..." He let his words fall away.

James patted his brother on the back. "Once the shock wears off, I'm sure she'll understand."

But Jackson knew there was more to the story than his brother could fathom. He'd told her he loved her and she'd run away. How come his love was never enough?

He looked up at Ava now, dressed in her classic dark suit, in no mood for sarcasm or pity. "What do you want?"

"I want to talk to you and there's no point in saying no." She closed the door before she took a seat.

He reluctantly sat back in his chair and waited.

"Her grandmother's words hit a nerve and made me wonder. How long are you going to keep this up?"

"I'll keep it up for as long as it takes."

"What takes?"

He shrugged and came from behind his desk. "What do you want?"

Ava crossed her legs and sighed. "I'm sorry about thinking of suspending you. I was out of line."

Jackson folded his arms, wishing she'd get to the point. He glanced out his window at the clear blue autumn sky. "Is it summer already?"

"Alright, I'll get to the point. I don't like coincidences. I have a devious mind."

Jackson sat down beside her and rested his chin in his hand, bored.

"Toyin surprised me. By some stroke of luck you found someone who genuinely cares for you."

He slowly blinked. "Miracles do happen."

"Since I no longer thought that Toyin sought you out to use you in some way, I started to think about something else. You."

He straightened. "Me? I'm flattered."

"Don't be. What were you doing in Vegas? How did you happen to bump into someone whose comic store you've visited before? I find that very odd. You targeted her for a reason and it's not the reason everyone thinks, is it? I wonder what Toyin would say if I told her my suspicions?"

Jackson lightly rested his hand around her throat. "There are times when the thought of squeezing your neck is so tempting."

Ava grinned. "I'm right, aren't I? Who is she to you?"

"None of your business."

"Try again."

He tightened his hold a fraction, his gaze darkening. "So tempting."

"I like a little pain. Be careful or you'll make your brother jealous."

"What?"

She pushed his hand away. "Never mind. Now confess."

"No."

"I will find out."

"Maybe."

Ava swung her foot. "Should I tell her that you're her new landlord?"

Jackson swore. "How did you find out about that?"

Ava clicked her tongue. "Because I know you too well. I remember how you reacted when we first entered New Worlds. I also went to the store and heard about their current plight with the landlord and then miraculously the landlord said that all was well. That got me thinking. So I tracked down said landlord and he was very cagey at first, until I treated him to a drink or two, then he because a little more chatty."

"What do you want?"

"I just told you."

"Toyin has nothing to do with you or this company. I'm good at my job."

"I know that—"

"But you still want me out of the company."

"No," Ava said shocked. "I never said that."

"You wanted me suspended."

"For your own good."

"I know you love my brother, but don't pretend that you ever loved me."

"I thought you'd forgiven me for that."

"I did too, until you went behind my back and tried to turn my family against me. This is all I have. I don't mind sharing, but I won't have it taken away."

"I wasn't trying to do that. Okay, I should have talked to you first, but I was worried about you. We all were. Really. I—" Ava suddenly stopped and swore. She jumped to her feet and stared at him reluctantly impressed. "You clever bastard. You put me on the defensive so you could distract me. That maneuver almost worked."

Jackson leaned back and held out his hands in surrender, a sly grin dancing on his lips. "A man can try."

"Actually, I may be helping you."

"How?"

"We both know you're terrible at judging women so the same night she came to dinner I had Toyin sign a contract—"

Jackson surged out his chair. "You did what!"

Ava calmly continued despite his outrage, "—to prove how much she loves you. I offered her five thousand dollars not to sleep with you for a month."

"What?!"

"If she holds out then the money is hers."

Jackson stared at her in shock.

"I know it sounds crazy, but it's for your own good. Money or you. It will be easy to see what she decides. She signed it right away." Ava paused, watching his expression change. "I can tell by that look that I did something right." She turned to the door. "You can thank me later."

Jackson heard the door close, but didn't move. She had given up five thousand dollars?

Toyin's words came rushing back to him. *That's the problem, Jackson. You should...* She was right, her loving him should matter. It should be what he wanted. What he craved. What he treasured. Claiming her heart should be as big a victory as convincing her to stay by his side. He'd been selfish. He'd only thought about how she made him feel, how much he wanted her. What he could do for her. He'd even made love a game, paying her to say the words. But just as he'd been blinded by data in the past, he'd been blinded by his own ego now.

Mama Bisi was right, I don't deserve you. There had been tears in her voice when she'd said that but he hadn't heard her pain. True pain. Her silent question. *If I loved you back, would you even care?*

He had to find her and tell her the answer was "I do."

Toyin sat in the back office of New Worlds and stared down at her unfinished comic. She knew she would never finish it now. Every time she started, she thought of Jackson and it hurt too much.

She would not cry.

She would not regret loving him. She'd get over her feelings one day. Right now she had to focus on working with her lawyers to fight Shanna, try to save TJ Studios by drumming up new projects and clients and continue to run New Worlds. If pretending to be Jackson Fortune's wife helped her, she would treat it as the job it was and fulfill her contract. As part of their agreement, she was supposed to move to his place, but she didn't have the heart yet. Perhaps next week. Perhaps next month. She had to think about the money.

Her lawyers had overwhelmed Shanna's enough that they were thinking of settling. The money from the Fortunes was worth it. After a few months she'd never have to see Jackson again and he'd shower someone else with his affection.

Toyin looked up at the framed photos on her walls. She hadn't expected her world to feel grey without him. She'd expected to leave the limo feeling liberated. She'd walked away. She'd had the courage to admit she was wrong. She would let Mama Bisi choose her next match. She didn't care if she loved him or not. Love was for losers. She no longer wanted to be that.

Toyin tasted her tears before she felt them.

Jackson never made her feel like a loser. Even as a child when Mrs. Lorquette made her feel stupid, he made her feel smart. When Lance made her feel discarded, Jackson made her feel wanted. When her family made her feel like a disappointment, Jackson made her feel like a success.

Something clicked in her brain. She loved him. And that love didn't make her feel low or worthless. It didn't make her feel like a loser. It made her feel strong and alive.

And angry.

Toyin pushed the comic aside and grabbed her keys.

Nearly an hour later Toyin faced Mama Bisi in the living room of her parents' house. A Fela Kuti protest song played softly in the background, while the smell of baked plantain scented the air.

"You were missed at the reception," her father said. He sat on the sofa next to her mother. He cast a nervous glance at Mama Bisi before returning his gaze to Toyin's angry features.

"We managed a nice chat with Jackson," her mother said, trying to fill the silence.

"Seems a nice chap."

"Very nice. He—"

"I came to speak to Mama Bisi," Toyin said in a low voice. "In private, if I may."

Her parents nodded then left the room.

Mama Bisi folded her hands in her lap and fixed her with a cool look. "What do you have to say to me?"

Tears gathered in her eyes, but she felt no shame in them. "You say you are never wrong. But you were wrong Saturday. My heart isn't small. My love isn't worthless. It's as deep and true as anyone's. And I am able to love many things. My heart is big enough to hold them all—my family, my friends, my art, my business and...and yes a man. A man you don't think deserves me." She took a steadying breath. "But he does, because I can love him like no one else can. He may not see it. He may not care, because it's not flashy and showy like his. I may not express myself the way he does or the way others think I should, but I still have a heart." She pounded her chest. "A big heart that beats and bleeds and longs and dreams and loves just like any other heart does."

Toyin briefly covered her eyes, her voice shaking. "It wasn't fair what you did to me on my wedding day." She wiped her tears and met her grandmother's gaze. "No matter how right you felt you are, you hurt me, wounded me to the core because you shamed me in front of the man I love."

Mama Bisi lifted her chin. "And does he know this?"

Toyin wiped away a tear confused. "What?"

"Does this man you tell me you love, know that you love him?"

"I...no but—"

"You don't think it matters. You don't have the courage to make it matter."

Toyin frowned. "I don't understand."

A tiny smile touched her lips. "I lied. The moment I met him I knew."

"You met him?"

She nodded, but didn't explain how. "I could not scare him away. I knew he was a good match for you, but I knew that I could never convince that rebellious heart of yours to accept him. You would be contrary just for the sake of it. I pushed you on your special day so that you could see what was staring you in the face. What you thought was false has always been real."

"But how did you—?"

"Your sister explained the true facts to me. That she forced you to reveal your secret marriage. Don't blame her; you know I have my ways."

Toyin stared at her stunned. "Are you saying that Jackson and I are meant to be?"

Mama Bisi nodded. "Yes. On your own you managed to find the right man to love who will love you back."

Toyin thanked her grandmother then left her parents' house in a daze. Mama Bisi approved? She saw Jackson and her together?

She didn't know what to do. Should she call him? Go by his place? No, she couldn't risk that. What if he was with someone else? She loved him but what if he didn't care?

Toyin drove home.

She found Jackson outside her apartment door. Before she could ask him what he was doing there, he held out a booklet.

"I did a 24-hour comic I want you to read," he said.

Her hands trembled but she took it from him and unlocked the door. She nervously dropped the keys on the floor and quickly picked them up not knowing how to feel. She felt thrilled that he'd come to see her, but also fearful that she'd broken whatever bond they'd had. She'd never felt this awkward with him before.

"Do you want something to drink?"

Jackson looked around her apartment briefly smiling at the picture of Storm. "No."

Toyin sat down and looked at the stick figure drawings he'd given her. She pointed. "What is this supposed to be?"

Jackson sat down beside her. Close enough to touch. "It's a man on a horse."

She swallowed, aware of his nearness. He smelled like mint. "It looks like a twig."

"I'll narrate it for you. Just listen." He motioned to the first page. "It starts on this panel."

"Okay."

He tapped the stick figure. "It's a story about this man."

"Does the man have a name?"

"No, he's just a man who likes to be a hero. We'll call him The Hero. Because of this trait he always falls for women who trick him."

"Is this why he's standing next to a heart with an arrow in it?"

"Yes. Now be quiet." Jackson pointed to another panel. "One day The Hero sees someone from his past, someone who he'd rescued before. A girl who scared him a little."

"Scared him?"

"Yes, don't interrupt. She scared him because she was different. She barely spoke, but he knew she was smart. Smarter than he was. So when he saw her again he wanted to rescue her once more. He would come by the market and spy on her and learn more about her and wondered what he could do because she didn't seem to need anything. Until one day he heard something that finally gave him that chance.

"It was one of those moments of fate people talk about. Now This Woman that The Hero wanted to rescue was seeing someone else. Let's just call him 'The Bastard.'"

Toyin couldn't help a giggle. "I could call him something else."

"So could I, but this is my story and I want to keep it clean. Anyway, The Hero went to the bank one day and overheard The Bastard talking to a woman we'll call...hmm...The Bitch."

Toyin started to laugh.

Jackson continued. "The Hero heard The Bastard talking to The Bitch about a conference in Las Vegas and how he planned to propose to This Woman and how they could cover their misdeeds. So—"

"Wait, you can't keep calling her 'This Woman'."

"Yes, I can."

"Call her 'The Heroine'."

He shook his head. "No, it's my story."

"Please."

He sighed. "The Hero knew...The Heroine—"

"Thank you."

"—would need his help so he flew to Nevada to find a way to stop her, but he caught her finding out the truth on her own. So—"

"So he followed her to the hotel bar."

He turned a page. "You're interrupting."

"Sorry."

"He stayed away wondering what he should do. Then he gathered the courage to approach her at the bar."

"Don't you think The Heroine would have preferred that The Hero told her what he knew before she left for Vegas?"

"Would she have believed him?"

Toyin paused. "Probably not."

"Any more questions?"

"No. Go on."

"The Hero persuaded This Woman—excuse me—The *Heroine* to marry him because he thought it would be fun and it would make her happy. And he felt he had won when she needed money, which he had plenty of and he convinced her to stay by his side. The Hero didn't expect to fall in love with The Heroine, but he did. Then he got cocky. Because he forgot one thing. He hadn't won the true prize."

"This is a very long story."

"Do you want me to finish?"

She bit her lip and nodded.

"He hadn't won her heart. So he took his sword and killed himself."

Toyin looked with dismay at the last panel of the stick figure with a sword through his chest, bleeding. She looked up at him outraged. "That's an awful story."

Jackson's eyes searched hers, his voice thick and unsteady. "How would you end it?"

She chose her words carefully. "The Hero would find out how much The Heroine loved him and he would realize that he didn't have to do anything to be loved."

His eyes brightened with joy then darkened with passion. "I like your ending better," he said, gathering her in his arms.

"Me too." She wrapped her arms around his neck, her fears wiped away in the glow of love. "Mama Bisi told me we're a perfect match."

Jackson pressed his lips against hers then whispered, "I always knew that."

"Think we should get married?" she teased him.

Jackson laughed. He held her tighter, letting her know he had no plans to ever let her go. "No, I think we deserve a honeymoon."

Toyin nodded, seeing their lives bound together forever. "Me too."

ABOUT THE AUTHOR

Dara Girard, an award-winning, national bestselling author of more than forty books continues to gain readers with titles such as *Private Lessons, Always and Forever, Sweet Temptation,* and *Midnight Promise.* Dara loves to travel and hear from readers.

Visit her website to sign up for her newsletter and get sneak peeks, monthly updates on new releases, and special offers.

For more information visit
www.daragirard.com